Who was she kidding?

Here, at least, Blue was a vice president, even if the Grizelle Gadget and Toy company wasn't a Fortune 500 company....

"Can you believe this?" Tad's voice stopped her. His hand cupped a large yellow rosebud. "Look, Blue. It's perfect." The expression in his eyes coaxed her toward him.

She didn't have time to look at a flower...no matter how perfect it might be. She needed a plan. She glanced and started to walk on.

Tad put both hands on her shoulders and positioned her in front of the rosebush. "You need to learn how to look at a rose, Blue. Do you know how much work is involved in coaxing this one rosebush to produce this one rosebud? There's still an element of miracle in it."

Blue looked, even though she felt silly. It was just a flower. An ambience of intimacy suddenly pervaded the evening air. If Tad hadn't been standing so close to her... The truth was, he was a little too close for comfort.

ABOUT THE AUTHOR

Karen Toller Whittenburg claims her love of reading inspired her writing career. She has always enjoyed all kinds of fiction, but writing and reading romances holds a special place in her heart and in her life. Karen lives in Oklahoma and divides her time between writing and running a household, both full-time and fulfilling careers.

Books by Karen Toller Whittenburg

HARLEQUIN AMERICAN ROMANCE

HARLEQUIN TEMPTATION

Don't miss any of our special offers. Write to us at the following address for information on our newest releases.

Harlequin Reader Service
P.O. Box 1397, Buffalo, NY 14240
Canadian address: P.O. Box 603,
Fort Erie, Ont. L2A 5X3

KAREN TOLLER WHITTENBURG

FOR THE FUN OF IT

Harlequin Books

TORONTO • NEW YORK • LONDON
AMSTERDAM • PARIS • SYDNEY • HAMBURG
STOCKHOLM • ATHENS • TOKYO • MILAN

For Brenda, Crystal, Debbi, Kathie, and Maureen.
Thanks for sharing your talent, time and
enthusiasm. Writer friends are the best.

Published January 1992

ISBN 0-373-16424-6

FOR THE FUN OF IT

Chapter One

A remote-controlled car careened around the corner, fish-tailing as it came out of the curve. Blue Garrison stepped from the elevator and watched in fascination as the toy raced, hell-bent for leather, straight toward her. She barely had time to wonder if she should get out of the way before the high-pitched whine of finely tuned electronics stopped, along with the vehicle, two feet in front of her.

It sat there, quivering from the sudden stop, and Blue could almost imagine it was waiting for her to make the next move. She stepped forward. The car inched back. She tried again with the same results. Hitching the slender strap of her Gucci bag on her shoulder, Blue sidestepped, bent down and in one swift move picked up the toy car. The wire antenna slapped her arm in protest, the tires spun, seeking vainly for traction, and Blue walked down the hall expecting to confront at any moment the boy who owned the toy.

He came around the corner just as she reached it, but he was hardly a boy. He was tall and on the lanky side, and he greeted her with a lazy grin. His faded blue jeans and the pullover knit shirt he wore challenged his pair of well-worn basketball shoes for first place in the "fashion risk" category. A wave of sandy-brown hair dipped slightly over his high, wide forehead. His eyes were brown and sparked with laughter. He didn't look polished enough to be in management or official enough to be security. Blue decided he must be one of the cleaning crew.

"Hi," he said. "I see you found my car." His voice was deep, with the confident undertones she'd expect of a much older man.

Blue decided she could afford to be generous. She offered a tentative smile. "Actually, it found me."

"And they say you can't program toys to be intelligent." His smile held steady as he offered his hand in greeting. "I'm Tad Denton. I work here."

Blue nodded as she forfeited the handshake to put the remote-controlled car into his open hand. "What a coincidence," she said. "So do I."

That caught him by surprise, she noted as she stepped past him and continued down the hallway. Of course, she was a bit surprised about being here herself. The Grizelle Gadget and Toy Company had never been on her list of dream jobs.

"Wait." Tad caught up with her in a matter of seconds. "I've never seen you before. How did that happen?"

"One of us is lucky, I guess." She smiled and kept walking.

So did he. "When did you start working here?"

"Today."

"Today? Who hired you?" he asked.

He was awfully nosy—and noisy—for a janitor. "Horace Garrison," she said.

"Horace?" He sounded surprised. *"Horace?"* he repeated more loudly.

Blue stopped in front of the frosted-glass door at the end of the hall. Grizelle Gadget and Toy Company was painted in bold, black letters on the glass, with Executive Offices printed in smaller letters below. Below that, in even smaller letters, were the words, Trick Or Treat, Horace Garrison's ambiguous way of saying, "Enter at your own risk." Blue reached for the door handle, but Tad was quicker.

"Are you telling me that Uncle Horse hired you?" Tad pulled open the door and gestured her into a large reception area. A secretarial desk sat square in the middle of the room, and several upholstered chairs were scattered around a cluttered coffee table. Four offices opened off the main area. Blue took it all in in a glance and was unimpressed.

She turned and met Tad Denton's curious regard. He still held the remote-controlled car, but the unabashed laughter in his eyes had faded to a more speculative wariness. For some reason Blue found the change—and him—appealing. Appealing and...sexy. That was silly. He couldn't be more than twenty-five. Twenty-eight at the outside. But regardless of his age, she wasn't—couldn't afford to be—interested. "Horace Garrison, presumably known to you as Uncle Horse, hired me. Would you mind telling me which office is his?"

With a frown Tad indicated the farthest door on the right. "That one."

His clipped answer made Blue regret her own abruptness. It wouldn't have hurt her to have been nicer. She'd be staying awhile and she was going to need friends here at Grizelle Gadget and Toy Company.

The thought tightened in her throat. The last thing she needed at work was friends. *Friendship* was the reason she'd come to this sorry pass in her life in the first place. She walked past the vacant secretary's station and glanced into Horace Garrison's office. It, too, was empty.

"He's not here yet," Tad said.

Blue glanced at her watch. Eight o'clock on the dot. Weren't employees supposed to be on the job by now? "I guess I'll wait," she said with a resigned glance at the stack of magazines on the coffee table.

"You can wait in my office, if you'd like." Tad didn't know why he made the offer. This woman was as cool as a cucumber, and the only way he liked cucumbers was pickled. But, well, he was a forgiving kind of guy and she was easy on the eyes. He could think of worse ways to start a Monday than talking with her. "I'll even make you a cup of coffee."

She looked startled. "You have an office?"

Tad considered her surprise for a moment. "I have a desk, too. And a chair. And a wastebasket." He tipped his head slightly to one side. He was beginning to get a bad feeling about this. A very bad feeling.

"You're not the janitor?"

"Right. Each night after everyone has left, I vanish into the broom closet and emerge a second later as Janitor Man. Then at 8:00 a.m., shazam...I turn back into a normal, everyday guy. If you'd been here a couple of minutes earlier this morning, you'd have seen me whizzing past in my blue-and-red cape. You'd have recognized me by the big red *J* on my chest."

She looked a little distressed. "I'm sorry. That was tactless of me."

He shrugged. "How could you know you'd stumble on to my secret identity your first day on the job? Now you'll have to swear not to tell anyone else. It would never do for the rest of the world to find out that mild-mannered Tad Denton is really the infamous Janitor Man."

"I swear I'll never tell another soul."

She sounded more chagrined than teasing, but Tad was glad she had at least enough humor in her to find a comeback. He'd been almost afraid she'd take him seriously and tell him to get out his broom and sweep the floor. "In that case the offer for coffee is still open," he said, "providing you tell me who you are."

She debated that, standing there in her Christian Dior suit. "Blue Garrison," she said after a moment. "I'm Horace Garrison's niece."

"You mean Uncle Horse is really your uncle?"

The first sign of a genuine warming trend tipped the corners of her mouth and crinkled around her pretty green eyes. "And Aunt Grizelle is really my aunt. Small world, isn't it?"

Tad shook his head and turned toward his office.

A new employee. Starting work today. Uncle Horse had a real, live niece.

Tad did not like the way this was adding up. "Come on in," he called to her. Blue, he thought. What kind of a name was Blue? "I'll clear off this chair so you can sit down."

Blue paused in the doorway. "Are there booby traps between here and the chair?"

Tad glanced up, knowing his office looked cluttered to the untrained eye. Hell, it would look cluttered to any eye. "Perfectly safe, I assure you, though my filing system is something of a mystery to the uninitiated."

"Yes," she said. "I can see where it would be."

He scooped the magazines and mail from the chair cushion and settled them in a pile on the floor, wondering the whole time how a man like Uncle Horse had wound up with a niece who looked like Blue. "There," he said with a sweeping gesture. "Have a seat. Would you like coffee?"

"If it isn't too much trouble." She sat gingerly, as if she thought his chair might turn into a man-eating plant or something.

Tad moved to the coffee maker and wished that he'd remembered to rinse the pot out Friday before he'd left the office. Not that he wanted to impress Blue or anything. But, well, she did have really pretty eyes and she was his favorite person's real live niece. "I'll be back in a minute." He headed for the door, holding the glass carafe at an angle so she wouldn't see the dried coffee stains in the bottom. "Just have to get some water."

She nodded and smoothed the wrinkles from her linen suit. As he stepped over a box of toy parts, she crossed her legs. He couldn't help but notice that hemlines were worn shorter wherever she was from. If he were guessing, he'd say California. She didn't talk like a Texan, that was for sure.

He cleaned the glass pot and filled it with fresh water before returning to his office. Blue was still sitting where he'd left her, her dark hair sleek and curving just above her shoulders. She held his acrylic nameplate in one hand while she traced the outline of his name with a fingertip.

"Here we go," he said. "You'll have coffee in no time."

"T. A. Denton." She looked up. "What does the T. A. stand for?"

"Thadeus Andrew," he answered. "Since Tad is short for both Thadeus and my initials, I never had much chance for any other nickname. What does Blue stand for?"

"My father's favorite color."

"Good thing his favorite color wasn't puce." Tad wiped his hands on the back of his jeans and then switched on the coffee maker. "Or orange. Imagine going through life as Orange. Or Green. The possibilities are mind-boggling."

She set the nameplate on the desk. "Yes, well, my father is an unusual man."

"So is Uncle Horse. He and your father are brothers, right?"

"My father says the resemblance ends right there."

Tad, satisfied that the coffee maker was going to work, turned to look at Blue. "Do you think there's a family resemblance?"

"I wouldn't know. I haven't seen my uncle since I was very young."

Tad frowned at that and leaned against the wall, bracing one shoulder and crossing his arms at his chest. "You haven't seen your uncle in years, but you're coming to work for him?"

Blue glanced up, a hint—just a hint—of distress in her eyes, before the poised facade slipped back into place. "So it seems," she said noncommittally. "Is that a problem for you?"

"For me? No. No way." He tried to look suitably unconcerned, even though he had a gut feeling that she was going to be a big problem for him. "The more the merrier, that's what I always say."

With a dismissive shrug, Blue settled back in the chair and smoothed her black hair away from her temple with a gesture as simple as it was provocative. She adjusted the sleeves of her jacket and needlessly smoothed the lapels. She dusted her hands, checked her fingernails and glanced idly around the room. She obviously found nothing in it of interest, including him.

A knot of tension coiled in Tad's stomach. Blue Garrison was a beautiful woman, and she was acting as if he were beneath her notice. And Tad did not like being ignored. "Would you go out with me if I were the janitor?" he asked.

That got her attention. "What?"

Tad knew she'd heard him perfectly well the first time, but he got a kick out of repeating the question slowly and clearly. "Would - you - go - out - with - me - if - I - were - the -janitor?"

She sat much straighter in the chair all of a sudden. "No!"

"Do you have something against blue-collar workers?"

"I don't believe this." Her color was high and she looked anything but indifferent. "Did you really just ask me for a *date?*"

Tad's lips curved with satisfaction. "Nope. I asked if you'd go out with me *if* I were the janitor. Big difference."

Obviously Blue didn't see the logic in that, and Tad congratulated himself for having managed to ruffle her professional feathers. Her holier-than-thou act might impress folks in California, but it would just get in the way here at Grizelle Gadget and Toy Company, whether she was Uncle Horse's niece or not. "See," he said. "If I *were* the janitor, I wouldn't ask you out because I'd be afraid you'd say no, which obviously you would since you just said you wouldn't go out with me if I were a janitor. But since I'm *not* the janitor, I was simply asking if you would go out with me *if* I were. So, now we know."

Blue looked confused...and just a bit alarmed. But, no doubt about it, she was no longer ignoring him. "Is...the coffee ready?"

Tad glanced over his shoulder to check. "As a matter of fact, it is. Do you want a cup?"

"Yes." She sounded definite about it.

Tad poured coffee into two paper cups and handed one to her. "Instant gratification," he said with a smile. "There's a lot of that around here. This coffee maker, for instance. I tinkered around with it, modified the heating element and came up with this ninety-second wonder."

Blue tried not to look as unsettled as she felt. If her success in handling Tad Denton was any indication, her employment history at Grizelle Gadget and Toy was going to be short and not very sweet. She'd been here less than ten minutes, and he'd already asked her for a date. At least she thought he had. Not that it mattered. She'd heard more objectionable proposals on shorter acquaintance. What bothered her was the idea that he was playing with her, much as he'd played with the remote-controlled car.

"What exactly," she asked carefully, "is your job here, Mr. Denton?"

"We're informal around here, Blue. Call me Tad."

Blue lifted her coffee cup and frowned at the tiny specks of paper floating on the surface of her coffee. The lavish offices of McKinley Enterprises, where she'd had a real coffee cup with the company logo on it, seemed far away now. "So, *Tad,* what do you do here...besides tinker?"

His pause was hardly long enough to notice, but Blue knew she'd irritated him. Touché, she thought.

"That's all I do," he said as he stepped over a box and a stack of papers to reach his desk. "Tinker around. I fix things, play with the toys, flirt with the women, and that just about takes up all my time." He gave her a smooth smile as he settled into his chair and lifted his coffee cup to his lips.

She knew she should probably apologize for her tactless assumptions. It was entirely possible she would have to work with this man. And it wasn't his fault that she didn't want to be here. She sipped her coffee and composed a peace offering. "Actually I'm a little nerv—"

"Tad! You're not going to believe this. Tad? Are you in there?" The voice yelling from the reception room was female, the drawl was pure deep Texas.

"In here, Ellie," Tad called, and Blue turned to look over her shoulder.

There was the sound of a bag hitting the floor outside, then a thump as if someone had set something on the desk, and then Ellie came to stand in the doorway of Tad's office. She was tall, but well filled out. Young. Blue thought she might be still in her teens. Her face was heart-shaped and cute... at least it might have been if her hair hadn't been a wild, henna-red mane. "You are not going to believe this," Ellie said with a snap of her chewing gum. "I just about died— Oh... hi there. Who are you?"

"This is Blue Garrison, Ellie." Tad made the introductions from his chair, not bothering to stand. "Blue, Ellie Compton. She works here, too."

Ellie moved across the room like a Texas wind, offering her hand and her brightest smile. "I'm awful glad to meet you. Blue? Now, who would name somebody that? It must be a nickname, huh?" Vivid red, super-strong nails jabbed Blue's palm as Ellie shook her hand. "Just like me. My name's really Elinor, but everyone calls me Ellie. Oh, wait, Blue *Garrison?* Does that mean...?"

"Back off, Ellie. Give her time to catch her breath."

Ellie laughed, a pleasant combination of a woman's laughter and a girl's giggle. "Sorry. I come from a family of talkers. It just plain carries me away at times."

Blue unobtrusively rubbed the palm of her hand. "It's nice to meet you, Ellie."

Ellie blinked, revealing heavily made up, blue-shadowed eyelids. "Are you kin to the Garrisons?" she asked. "Uncle Horse and Aunt Grizelle?"

"Horace Garrison is my uncle," Blue explained.

"Whoo-ee! Won't he be excited to see you. Uncle Horse is always talking about his niece, isn't he, Tad? He'll be so happy you came for a visit."

By the look on Tad's face, Blue suspected it was the first he'd heard of Uncle Horse's fond reminiscing, but she supposed Ellie was simply trying to make her feel welcome. "I'm looking forward to seeing him, too."

"You couldn't have picked a better day to come." Ellie fluffed her rooster-comb bangs with a few swipes of her long fingernails. "This is a real important day for us. Tad is going to be—"

"Ellie." Tad tried to cut her off with a stern word to the wise.

"Oh, Tad. Everybody knows you're going to get the job. Who else around here could be vice president?" Ellie snapped her fingers. "That's what I was going to tell you. I saw Cynthia Mears at the store. You remember, she works at Mrs. Judy's Flower Shop? She says you're getting flowers today. Con-grat-u-la-tor-y boo-kays, she called them. You'll never guess from who, either, but go ahead— guess."

"Ellie, nothing is definite about it. You know that." Tad looked a little embarrassed.

"It's Lynette Wilson." Ellie reported with glee. "You remember, the blonde you got stuck at the top of the ferris wheel with last year at the fair? She's still got a crush on you, Tad. Didn't I tell you she did?"

Tad pursed his lips. "Yes, Ellie, you told me. But there shouldn't be any flowers. The job hasn't even been offered to me yet. A lot of things—" he couldn't keep his gaze from straying to Blue "—can happen."

"Oh, pshaw!" Ellie said with a snort. "You're too modest." She turned toward Blue. "He's too modest for his own good."

Blue nodded politely and wondered about Tad and the new job. Was he about to become vice president of Grizelle Gadget and Toy Company? And would that mean she would be working for him? The thought started a ripple of panic inside her. All the more reason not to be friendly. She was suddenly thankful her apology had been interrupted. "What is your position with the company, Ellie?"

"I'm the executive secretary," Ellie said with another snap of chewing gum.

Blue smiled to conceal a sigh. She'd been afraid of that. "How nice." Blue stood and tucked her purse under her arm. "Since my uncle isn't here yet, maybe I'll find the ladies' room and freshen up before he arrives."

"Good idea," Tad said. "Ellie can show you where it is."

Blue felt a bit pushed, but she followed Ellie into the reception area and out into the hallway beyond.

"It's right over here." Ellie indicated a door with a plastic cowgirl on it. "See, if you pull this chain—" Ellie demonstrated and the cowgirl let out a tinny "Yippee-ki-yay."

Blue almost strangled at the tackiness of it all and hurriedly pushed inside the room. To her dismay, Ellie followed. "I can't believe it. Who would have thought Uncle Horse could have a niece who looks as good as you? All the girls will be crazy, thinking you'll move right in on Tad. *Everybody* wants to go out with him. Don't you think he's cute?"

"He's cute," Blue agreed as she stepped to the mirror. "But the *girls* can rest easy. Tad is safe from me."

Ellie chewed her gum and appraised Blue openly. "Yeah. I guess you are a little old for him. It's not that he has a thing for *younger* women, you understand. I mean, he doesn't date teenagers or anything like that. It's just that his dates are usually about his age, and he's twenty-seven.'' Ellie leaned against the door, obviously prepared to stay for a while. "Now, me, I'm almost twenty and Tad still treats me like his kid sister. 'Course, I'm not available. I'm getting married next year. Soon as Jim Bill gets out of the Navy. Have you ever been married?''

"No.'' Blue suddenly felt ancient and careworn... and eager for a moment alone. "Oh, Ellie, I left my coffee in Tad's office. Would you mind getting it for me?''

Ellie straightened with a smile. "Sure. No prob. I'll be back before you know I'm gone.''

Blue hoped not. So far Ellie had made her feel about as useful and attractive as a three-day-old dishrag. Blue leaned close to the mirror and looked for wrinkles. With the flat of one hand, she patted the skin under her chin. Thirty-three is *not* old, she told herself. And a lot of women didn't get married until late in life, if at all. It wasn't as if she'd never had opportunities. It wasn't as if she was *dying* to marry some man and live like Donna Reed. She'd made her choices, and in general she was pretty darn pleased with them, too.

The mirror gave back an accurate reflection, and Blue admitted that her choices of late had been neither pleasant nor wide-ranging. In fact, her problems at McKinley Enterprises had quickly and firmly narrowed her options to one... this job at Grizelle Gadget and Toy Company. How had she let herself get caught in such a predicament in the first place? How could she have allowed the situation with Rob McKinley to get out of hand? Or, as she would prefer to believe, had it been out of her control all along?

She broke the visual argument with her mirror image and ran cold water into the sink. Ellie would be back any moment and Blue wanted her composure firmly back in place. To be sure, she hadn't had great expectations when she'd accepted her uncle's invitation to come and work for him. But she certainly hadn't expected a gum-chewing, Chatty-Cathy receptionist or a potential vice president who dressed like a janitor, ran remote-controlled vehicles up and down the halls and had the strangest come-on Blue had ever heard. She wasn't even sure anymore that it *had* been a come-on. Maybe he really had just wanted to know if she would date someone who was a janitor.

Maybe he really was the janitor and was just pretending.... No. Ellie had cleared that up. Tad Denton was twenty-seven . . . and about to be named a top executive in the company.

Blue was thirty-three, a disillusioned, vulnerable thirty-three. She could no longer tell a come-on from a joke . . . and she was about to be named general flunkie at a company with less professional ambience than pro wrestling.

Blue splashed water over her hands and patted the cold into her cheeks to dispel the negative thoughts. She was here now. And whatever job her uncle found for her to do, she'd do it to the best of her ability. She'd keep to herself, avoid T. A. Denton and his off-the-wall remarks, and if she were lucky she'd get her life back on track and be out of this place in a few months. Some other job was bound to come open. Somewhere. Soon.

"Here you go." Ellie pushed into the room and handed Blue the paper cup. "Uncle Horse is here. He can't wait to see you. He told me to hurry you up."

Blue tried for a smile, knew it was a poor attempt. "Let me put on a bit of lipstick and comb my hair. Okay?"

"I'll tell him you'll be out in just a sec," Ellie said, giving her a conspiratorial wink and backing out the door.

Moments later, with lips faintly tinted and every hair in place, Blue followed Ellie into her uncle's office. Tad was there, standing by the only window and looking quite at home. He might as well have worn a neon sign that said This is My Territory. Keep Out. He acknowledged Blue's presence with a cursory glance. But Horace Garrison more than made up for Tad's lack of enthusiasm.

"Miranda Blue!" The wild man, who had been the central figure of many a family story during her lifetime, grabbed her in a hug that would have made any grizzly bear proud. He was a tall, thin man and his embrace pressed Blue's nose squarely against the sharp edge of his collarbone. He squeezed tightly once more and then, shifting his hands to her shoulders, he pushed her back so he could look at her. "Look at you. Why, you're all grown up and as pretty as your mama ever was. Prettier, even. I always did pray you wouldn't take after your pa. Henry's uglier than I am."

Blue had a moment to take in her uncle's unruly shock of ghost-white hair, his bright brown eyes, and a glimpse of his toothy grin, before she was caught close in another hug. She knew, suddenly, why everyone called him Uncle Horse. Everyone, that is, except her father...who referred to his only brother simply as "that lunatic."

Pulling out of the avuncular embrace, Blue gave a shaky smile and smoothed down her suit jacket. "It's good to see you, Uncle Horace. I've looked forward to this meeting for a long time."

"You and me both." Uncle Horse ran a hand through his hair, making it stand on end all the more, then gestured toward a chair. "Sit down. Sit down. You, too, Tad." He waved at Ellie, who stood in the doorway, snapping her gum. "Ellie? You want to hold my calls for a while? Tell 'em I'm visiting with my niece, and take messages. Go get us some breakfast muffins, too. A couple of blueberry and a couple of those pineapple-bran ones. You know my favorites.''

Ellie giggled for some reason and left the room, closing the door behind herself. Blue took the seat her uncle had offered and shot a questioning look at Tad. He returned it calmly and remained standing by the window.

''My two favorite people,'' Uncle Horse announced as he moved around the office, picking up an electric train engine, then putting it down to pick up a wooden paddle. ''Tad and Miranda. This is going to be great.''

Blue frowned as her uncle began to hit the rubber ball that was attached to the paddle with an elastic string.

''Your Aunt Grizelle and I want you to stay with us, Miranda. We have a guest cottage where you can have all the privacy you want and—''

Tad let out a strangled sound, but Horace Garrison didn't seem to hear.

''—you can take all your meals with us. Of course, your aunt doesn't care for breakfast. She has to get out to her garden before the sun gets ahead of her. But you can always get muffins here at the office. We have a canteen downstairs. The blueberry are the best. But I like the pineapple ones, too. Which do you like best, Tad?''

''Uncle Horse—'' Tad tried to interrupt, but the bouncing ball and the discourse went on without a break.

''You can have the office next to Tad's, Miranda. It hasn't been used for quite a while, but you decorate it however you want. Colors don't have to match. We're not particular about stuff like that. You can wallpaper it in wrapping paper, if you want. Just make yourself at home. Isn't that right, Tad?''

Blue felt a tightening across her chest. She didn't want the office next to Tad's. She wanted an office on the other side of the building somewhere. Maybe on the other side of Dallas. "Uncle Horace?"

"Who the *hell* is *Horace?*" Her uncle gave a huge, hearty laugh. "I'm your Uncle Horse and don't try to pretend Henry hasn't told you it's because I look like a horse, either. I know my brother. He looks like a horse, too. But he always considered himself the Thoroughbred and me the mustang." Uncle Horse laughed again. "So, let's see. We've covered breakfast, a place to sleep and an office. What else do you need to know?"

"How about position?" Tad's voice was thick with tension, and Blue knew, all of a sudden, what was coming. "What is your niece going to do here?"

Uncle Horse's long face took on a perplexed look, and the rubber ball missed the wooden paddle. "Well, I hadn't really thought a lot about it, but I guess she can be a vice president." He nodded as he tapped the paddle on the desk top. "That's it. You can both be the vice president."

"What?"

"What!"

Tad stepped away from the window.

Blue straightened in her chair.

Uncle Horse began bouncing the ball against the paddle again.

Blue was amazed her uncle's company was still solvent. "Vice president in charge of what, Uncle Horse? Each vice president needs a designated area."

"Okay," Uncle Horse agreed. "You two can work that out between yourselves. This is going to be great. Just spit-and-polish great."

And all these years Blue had thought her father was exaggerating. She was beginning to see that *eccentric* was a totally inadequate way to describe her uncle. How on earth had he run this company for almost forty years? And what was she going to do now? Be a vice president?

One glance at Tad told her that if she managed it, it would be over his dead body.

He looked...outraged. She could understand that. She'd have been madder than a wet hornet if he'd walked into McKinley Enterprises and been handed a vice presidency over her head. But it wasn't her fault she had a lunatic for an uncle and Tad had a lunatic for a boss, and it was more than obvious that this company desperately needed someone in authority making rational decisions. It seemed, as fate would have it, she was it.

"Uncle Horse," Tad said. "Could I talk to you for a minute? Alone?"

"Later, son. I'm really busy right now." The ball slapped the paddle and bounced back into the air. Uncle Horse watched the movements with complete fascination. "You go on and settle Blue in. Show her around. Explain the setup to her. Show her where the canteen is. And the playroom."

Tad turned on his heel and headed out the door. Blue paused, wondering if she would have any better luck than Tad had had in getting her uncle to listen to reason. The expression on his face as he watched the bouncing ball was rapt. Obviously this wasn't the time to try. With a sigh she stood and walked to the door.

Just as she stepped into the reception area, there was a burst of laughter and clapping. A small group of people had gathered in front of Ellie's desk, in front of three very large, very floral bouquets. And in the midst of this celebration was T. A. Denton, who looked ready to chew nails.

Chapter Two

"Ellie? Would you ask one of the stock boys to move these boxes out of my office?"

Blue's voice carried clearly from her office into Tad's. He drew a bead on the dart board and threw. Dead center. He was on a roll.

"We don't have any stock boys," Ellie yelled from her desk in the reception area.

"What about a maintenance man?" Blue called back. "Do we have one of those?"

"That'd be Bobby, but he doesn't show up every day." Ellie's voice went up a decibel. "You want me to ask Tad to help?"

"Never mind, Ellie. I'll ask him myself."

Tad picked up another dart. Two hours. She'd been here for two hours and already she was a nuisance. She was in there, right next door, cleaning out the office with missionary zeal. And he'd hit dead center on the dart board eight out of ten throws.

"Tad?" Blue hesitated in the doorway. "Could you give me a hand?"

Uncle Horse would have given her just that. A hand. Tad wished he'd had the foresight to keep a trick like that in his desk drawer. "That's my reason for living," he said as he took careful aim at the dart board. "What do you need?"

"More room in my office." Her voice sounded tight, as if her patience was stretched to the limit. "Could you help me move a couple of boxes?"

He let the dart fly, but it glanced off the rim and dropped to the floor. His lucky streak was over. With a shrug Tad slid his feet from the edge of the desk to the floor and straightened in his chair. "Anything for you, Ms. Vice President."

Blue's lips tightened. "It won't take long. There are only three boxes, but they are rather heavy."

"Tater Tossers."

"What?" Blue took a tentative step into the room.

She'd taken off her jacket, Tad noticed. And she'd pushed up the silky sleeves of her cream-colored blouse. Her hair was tousled, as if she'd been combing it with her fingers. There was a smudge of mascara, like a sooty thumbprint, just below her right eyelid. Disheveled, she looked even more attractive and appealing. Abruptly Tad stood up. "Don't tell me you've never heard of a Tater Tosser."

"You mean those whirligigs for mashing potatoes?"

"Exact-a-mundo. Your uncle invented that little gadget some thirty years ago and it's still supporting us all. There's always a box or two sitting around here someplace, even though Uncle Horse leases the patent to another manufacturer."

"Why doesn't he produce them? They can't be that complicated."

Tad gave her a patient smile. "Genius is deceptively simple, isn't it? The truth is, Uncle Horse got bored making Tater Tossers so he moved on to other things like jump ropes, robots, vegetable dicers, fruit juicers, remote-

controlled vehicles, dolls, exercisers. . . . The list is end-
less.''

''He can't possibly make all those different things.''

''I wouldn't mention that to him, if I were you.''

''But it would require a huge manufacturing conglom-
erate to produce all those items in a quantity sufficient to
reach even a break-even market. Unless this place is a lot
bigger than it looks—''

''Blue, Blue,'' Tad interrupted, stepping over a toy airplane and shaking his head at her skeptical tone. As he
drew closer to her, he caught the faint, enticing scent of
gardenias. ''You should have done your homework, dar-
lin','' he said. ''This 'place,' as you call it, manufactures
ideas. Sure, we make some prototypes and we have, on
occasion, done a better-than-break-even production run.
But by and large we create ideas. Simple, huh?''

Her frown deepened and Tad knew that though she
couldn't deny he was right, she was not immune to his
sarcasm. He didn't mean to hurt her, but right now he was
too annoyed to be polite. He knew he didn't have any
choice in the long run. But if Blue was going to be here,
she'd better have more than criticism to contribute. ''Any
other questions, *Ms*. Vice President?'' he asked abruptly.

''Yes.'' Blue grasped the edge of his office door and
closed it with a sharp push to relieve her frustration. ''I
want to know where to put those blasted boxes. I want to
know who the hell is in charge of this company. And I
want to know why you've developed this sudden massive
attack of antagonism.''

Tad recognized the spark of irritation in her green eyes.
And he found he rather liked her forthright way of getting
to the point. A few hours from now he might even be ready
to like her. But right at this moment friendly feelings were
still a little out of his reach. He ticked off the answers to

her questions. "The boxes go to the basement on the bottom level. Your Uncle Horse is in charge of the company, even though there are days when it seems obvious he doesn't know what he's doing. And I didn't just develop my case of antagonism. I've had it for about two hours."

She ran her fingers through the wavy strands of her hair with burning frustration. "You're not going to make this easy for me, are you?"

"Nope."

She brought her gaze up to meet his, and for a moment he thought he saw pain flicker in her green eyes. He was certain he felt sympathy stir in his belly.

She turned to the door, put her hand on the knob, and some idiotic impulse made Tad want to move to keep her from leaving. "You can't go out there," he said, slipping between her and the door.

"Why?"

"Ellie's out there." His voice dropped to a throaty whisper.

"That's where she's supposed to be. Her desk is there."

He jerked his head in the direction of the door. "If you open this now, she'll fall in."

Blue dropped her gaze to the floor. "You mean she eavesdrops?"

He reached for the doorknob. "Here, I'll show you."

"No," Blue insisted in a whisper as she covered his hand with hers in protest. "You'll embarrass her."

Tad was relieved that Blue was being so considerate of Ellie's feelings, especially since he had no idea if Ellie eavesdropped or not, and it might very possibly be himself who was embarrassed. What was wrong with him, anyway, that he saw one little flicker of emotion in her eyes and his too-soft heart lost its tough veneer? What was wrong with him that he could never hold a grudge for more than a couple of hours? Even if it wasn't entirely her fault, Blue *was* trespassing on his territory. He'd worked hard to prove to Uncle Horse that he was ready for the position of vice president. And then Miranda Blue had walked in and all she had to recommend her was . . .

Tad decided she had much to recommend her and, damn it, it wasn't just her appearance, either. She looked, talked, even walked like a high-powered executive. He'd bet she even dreamed about business.

She made him feel like a kid who was unprepared for a test. And he was an idiot to stand here and stare into her incredibly green eyes while his palms started to sweat.

"So what are we going to do?" she whispered, pointing to the door.

"You're the new vice president, you tell me." Tad tried to regain that taut, sarcastic tone in his voice. It had come so easily a few minutes ago. "Why don't you just go out there and tell Ellie to quit goofing off and get back to work?"

"Shh." Blue pointed to the door. "She's listening."

Tad leaned a shoulder against the doorjamb. "Maybe she is. Maybe she isn't."

Blue looked at him for a minute before her eyes narrowed in understanding. "I see. This is another one of your little games. You're trying to get me to create an unpleasant situation with Ellie so she won't help me, either. Is that it, Tad?"

"Gee," he said slowly. "I thought I was just trying to get you to leave town."

Her chin came up. "It's not that easy. I need this job."

"Sure you do. And John Wayne was a real cowboy, too. Let's just get to those boxes, okay? I have work to do."

Blue's eyebrows arched. "Another dart game?"

"I'm practicing for the Olympics." He lifted both hands and flexed his wrists. "Got to keep these babies in shape."

She reached for the doorknob. "Don't worry about your job, Tad. I'll see that it's phased out by the time you're ready to get your gold medal."

She'd bested him fair and square on that one, and he wondered if it might not be time to offer to bury the hatchet and smoke the peace pipe. Before he could make up his mind about it, though, something hit the closed door with a resounding *whump*.

"Oh, my gosh," Blue said. "Ellie's going to fall through the door."

"You'd better get out of the way," Tad said, reaching over to turn the knob. The door hit the wall with a clatter as a whirring piece of machinery rolled into the room.

"Good morning, Tad. Your mail has arrived," the machine said with a metallic whine as it pushed its way to the desk, scooping everything before it like a snowplow. It stopped, and the top half swiveled in a ninety-degree turn. A robotic arm grasped a packet from a wire basket attached to the rear of the machine and swiveled around to the front to place the mail precisely on the corner of the desk. Then the machine moved backward across the exact path it had taken into the room, scattering the toys and papers that stood in its way. *"Goodbye, Tad. The next mail delivery will be at 2:00 p.m."*

Blue watched as the robot backed into the reception room, and repeated its performance at Ellie's desk, then moved on to Uncle Horse's office.

"That's a robot," she said with a touch of amazement.

"He doesn't like that word," Tad said, walking to the door of Blue's office. "If you want to get any mail around here, you'd better call him Zeke."

"But it *is* a robot."

"Yes, Blue. We all know the word. We just don't use it in front of him." Tad set one box on top of another and lifted them both. "And if you want your mail, you'd better leave your door open. He's not programmed for doorknobs."

Zeke exited Uncle Horse's office and headed for the glass doors leading to the hall. Tad set out on a collision course with the robot, and Blue watched, too fascinated by the four-foot-tall machine to call a warning.

There was no collision, though. The robot reached the door first, thrust out its metal arm, and the glass door opened smoothly. "Thanks, Zeke," Tad said as he carried the boxes through the doorway.

"You're welcome," Zeke answered, following Tad. The door closed behind them without a hitch.

"Strange little guy, isn't he?" Ellie said, looking up from painting her fingernails. "Scares some people silly."

With a frown Blue moved to get the last box of Tater Tossers from her office. "Is it real?"

"Sometimes I think Zeke is more real than the rest of us. He's a sight better mailboy than the last one we had. The last *human* mailboy, that is. But—" Ellie leaned forward as if to divulge a secret "—be careful. Zeke can give you a goose like nobody's business."

Blue hesitated. Could robots do that sort of thing? She didn't know much about electronics, but that seemed unlikely. Was Zeke just another one of Tad's remote-controlled toys? The idea that Tad was making Zeke pull tricks on people seemed more than likely. "Thanks for the advice, Ellie. I'll be careful to keep my 'goose' out of Zeke's reach."

With that Blue shifted the box she carried into one arm and managed to open the glass door enough to slip through. Where was the helpful Zeke when *she* needed an extra hand? Probably down the hall holding open doors for T. A. Denton.

"Blue!" Tad called to her from the end of the hallway. "Will you come on? Zeke is holding the elevator for you."

Blue shifted the box in her arms, inhaled deeply and walked down the hall. "This is heavy," she said as she stepped inside the elevator, taking care to position herself away from the mechanical monster. "Are Tater Tossers made of lead?"

"Stainless steel," Tad said, stepping in beside her. "Like all good household appliances. Let's go, Zeke."

"Going up? Going down?" The robot's electronic voice rose with the first two words and lowered with the second two.

Blue glanced at Tad over the box. "Are we supposed to answer or is he talking to himself?"

"Down, Zeke."

"Going down." The mechanized answer was accompanied by a movement of the robotic arm. The elevator proceeded downward at a snail's pace.

"Don't be afraid to talk to him," Tad said. "He's harmless."

Blue stared at the indicator panel over the elevator doors. "I prefer to have my conversations with people."

"I didn't say you should discuss politics with him. But he could be a big help to you . . . in your new position."

"I'm not as naive as you'd like to believe, Tad."

"How naive are you, then?"

Blue told herself that again he was trying to play her like he'd played the remote-controlled car. "That thing is just some sort of remote-controlled device. I don't know how you get it to open doors and operate elevators, but—"

"Infrared sensors." Tad glanced up as the floor indicator light switched from two to one. "The sensors keep

Zeke from running into walls and other obstacles and allow him to trigger an opening device in the doors . . . some of the doors, anyway. I told you he's not programmed to turn doorknobs, didn't I?''

"I believe you mentioned that." Blue smiled knowingly. "Who operates it? Where is the remote control?"

"There is no remote control."

"You don't expect me to believe it's really a robot, do you?"

Tad's sandy brows drew together in a frown. "His name is *Zeke* and he does not like the *r-o-b-o-t* word."

"Are you trying to tell me this machine is sensitive?"

"I said he has sensors, which is not to say he isn't sensitive. He's sensitive to loud noises and certain frequencies. Keep your voice moderately pitched and watch what you say when you speak to him, and the two of you will get along fine."

The elevator slowly drew to a stop at the basement level and the robot whirred. *"Mission accomplished."*

"I give up," Blue said. "How do you do it?"

"You know, I get up every morning and ask myself that same question. And every day I get a different answer." He motioned for Blue to precede him, and with a sigh she stepped forward.

Something jabbed at her hip and she jumped. She almost lost her grip on the box she held, but she managed to balance the Tater Tossers as she rubbed her hip. She glanced over her shoulder at Zeke. "That thing pinched me."

Tad laughed and stepped past her. "Don't be silly. He's an *r-o-b-o-t.*"

Blue had seldom felt more frustrated. This job wasn't worth it. She could find something else. She could— But she couldn't. She'd already tried. Rob had cut her options to one. Grizelle Gadget and Toy Company and the chance it offered her to prove herself. With a cautious glance at the lecherous bit of wire and metal that was Zeke, she moved out of reach and followed Tad.

With a grunt of relief, he set his boxes beside a concrete stairwell. Then he took the box Blue had carried and put it with the others. That accomplished, he stepped back, put his hands on his hips and surveyed the boxes in the storage area in front of him. "That's odd," he said. "I'd have sworn those were stacked flat against the wall. I wonder if Bobby moved them for some reason."

"Zeke probably did it." Blue nodded toward the robot. "He's such a helpful kind of guy."

"You're going to be surprised at just how much help Zeke can be at times." Tad frowned once more at the stack of boxes against the stairwell before he turned to Blue. "I think somebody has been messing with our Tater Tossers. I'm sure these boxes weren't spread out like this."

Blue watched as Zeke hummed and whirred his way toward her. "What's he doing?" she asked with just a hint of panic.

Tad glanced distractedly at the robot. "Oh, he's going to bed."

Blue was tired of this game. "You mean he doesn't have to have a bedtime story?"

Tad took just a second to cast a frown at her. "You know, Blue, Zeke isn't human, but the person who built him is. You might want to keep that in mind. We're all rather fond of Zeke."

Blue was ashamed of herself for being so openly cynical. What did she care if Zeke was robot or toy? "I'll make an effort to remember."

Tad's brown eyes swung to meet hers, and a spark of challenge caught her attention before it disappeared behind his lazy smile. "Good." He gestured toward a labyrinth of hallways and storage areas. "This is the basement and it's Zeke's main territory. Just think of him as an electronic Phantom of the Opera. He has a recharging station . . . that cagelike thing he's backing into now. The plug is positioned so that he connects and disconnects simply by moving forward or back. The keyboard beside the station there is for programming."

"There really isn't a remote control, is there?"

Tad lifted his sandy eyebrows. "Zeke is fully automatic and one hundred percent robot. He's about the most expensive gadget in this place."

"You're the person who built him, aren't you, Tad?"

He merely returned his attention to the stack of boxes. "I can't imagine why Bobby would have moved these like this. I've seen better stacks of pancakes."

Blue tried to see his problem. "Is it important how Tater Tossers are stacked?"

"I guess not." Tad turned toward the elevator. "Maybe one of the employees was looking for something."

"How many employees are there?"

"Fifty. We're not a huge operation."

Blue nodded, trying to piece together the political structure of the company as they waited for the elevator to return. "What do they do? These fifty employees?"

"For a vice president, you don't know much about the company, do you?"

"I've only been here two hours."

"Which is not much of an excuse . . . for a vice president."

Blue's ill humor returned . . . just when she'd thought they might have a cordial conversation. "All right, T. A. Denton. Why don't you just come right out and admit that you begrudge me this job?"

"I begrudge you this job, Blue."

She hadn't expected him to be so obliging. "Well, I'm sorry you feel that way."

"So am I."

The elevator doors opened and Tad waited—grudgingly, Blue thought—for her to step inside. She jabbed the number two button and crossed her arms at her waist. If he was miserable about her being here, it was nothing to how she felt. "Look, Tad, I know you wish I weren't here, but no matter how bad the situation is for you, it couldn't possibly be any worse for me."

He leaned against the side of the elevator and waited for it to start its slow ascent. "Don't bet the rent money on that, Blue. Don't bet the rent."

Chapter Three

"'Night, Blue. See you tomorrow," Ellie said, sticking her head into Blue's office at seven minutes after four. "Don't worry about locking up. Bobby came in this afternoon. He'll do it."

Blue stayed the impulse to check her watch against the battery-powered clock on the wall. "Does everyone go home at four o'clock?"

Ellie smiled. "Oh, no. Some people leave at three. Tad never even comes back from lunch on Monday afternoons. He goes to the zoo."

"The zoo?" Blue couldn't keep the incredulity out of her voice. "Tad spends Monday afternoons at the zoo?"

"Well, sometimes I think he goes fishing, but most of the time it's the zoo."

Blue combed her hair with impatient fingers. As far as she could tell, Grizelle Gadget and Toy Company was a zoo. She didn't see any need to go out of the office to find one. "Does anyone *work* in this place?" she asked and knew immediately it was the wrong thing to say.

"Everyone works," Ellie said, emphasizing her words with a snap of her gum. "Look, I've got to go. I'll be late for my appointment at the beauty shop."

"Ellie?" Blue hurried to make amends to the one person who'd been truly helpful. Tad was right about one thing, she needed to find out more about how things worked here before she started criticizing. "Thanks for helping me get settled in today."

Ellie's expression warmed instantly. "Hey, no prob. See ya later, 'gator."

Blue slumped back in her chair with a sigh. The zoo. Tad Denton spent Monday afternoons at the zoo. What did he do there? Take snarling lessons from the lions?

Not that he'd actually snarled at her. In fact, as much as she hated to admit it, she knew he had behaved better than she would have if their situations had been reversed. If Rob had ever told her she'd have to share her new promotion in the company with *anyone*—much less a relative of his— she'd have ranted, raved and raised such a ruckus that every employee in the McKinley Building would have run for cover.

Of course Rob would never have made such a nut-cake decision. He was a businessman to the core and she was a perfect example of what happened when one let personal matters infringe upon business matters.

With a sigh Blue rubbed away the creases her frown had formed between her brows. When was she going to be over this? When was she going to stop feeling sick every time she thought about Rob . . . and Rob's wife. It wasn't fair. A man in the same position wouldn't . . .

Face it, she told herself for perhaps the ten thousandth time. A *man* wouldn't have been in the same position. Period. End of story. She would get over it and get over the result, too. Soon she'd be able to find a decent position with another marketing firm and she wouldn't have to deal with Uncle Horse and T. A. Denton.

Which brought her thoughts full circle.

Snarling Tad.

Tad, who'd asked her for a hypothetical date before he found out she was going to be half of his vice presidency.

Tad, who was probably at this very moment plotting how to get rid of her.

Not that she blamed him. Actually, since she was trying to plot her way out of this place, too, maybe they could work together on it.

"Miranda Blue," Uncle Horse said, pausing in her doorway and searching through the pockets of his orange coveralls as if he'd misplaced something important. A frown lined his high, wide forehead. "I'm taking you home with me for dinner."

"But, Uncle Horse, it's only four o'clock."

"That late, huh?" He pulled a long, narrow rubber band from his hip pocket, snapped it and worked it around his thumb and forefinger like a beanie flip. Then he held up his hand to the light and turned it in all directions, as if he were looking for a flaw in the thin green elastic. "Marvelous invention," he said absently. "I haven't been able to think of a single way to improve it." The rubber band streaked over Blue's head and ricocheted off the wall. "Whoops," he said. "Missed."

Blue decided not to ask what he'd been aiming to hit. "I think I'll work a while longer, Uncle Horse. Maybe I can have dinner with you and Aunt Grizelle another night."

"Nonsense. There's no need for you to hang around here any longer. This is your first day, Miranda. You don't even know what you're doing. What are you going to work on?"

She couldn't have put it better herself. "That is something I'd like to talk about, Uncle Horse. Do you think you could explain just what you intend for me to do?"

"I intend for you to have a wallopin' good time."

"But—"

"No buts. A wallopin' good time. You remember that."
He waved a long, bony forefinger and shook his mane of
unruly white hair. "Now, come along. Your Aunt Grizelle would stab me with a thornbush if I didn't bring you
home for supper."

"Really, Uncle Horse, don't you think it would be better if I—"

"I've phoned for the driver already. We'll meet him out
front. I don't drive, you know. Never quite got the hang
of it." Uncle Horse pulled back the sleeve of his coverall
and glanced at his bare wrist. "And I'm not too good at
telling time because I never wear a watch. What time is it,
anyway?"

Blue sighed softly and glanced at the big, round clock on
the wall. "Quarter past four."

"Whooee. Let's get going or your aunt will be madder
than a sea otter in the circus." He turned on his heel and
walked out, leaving Blue with little choice but to follow. He
was, after all, her boss.

"WELL, WELL, isn't this nice?" Aunt Grizelle set her
glasses on the end of her nose and beamed at the assem-
blage around her dining room table. "I've been looking
forward to seeing you all day, Miranda Blue. I told Mikie
and Joe all about the time you came to visit and got so
dirty your mother screamed when she saw you. The roses
were especially lovely that year."

Mikie and Joe, a pair of nearly identical Japanese gardeners, nodded in unison. Tad, across the table, looked up
with sudden interest. "You made your mother scream?"

"I was very dirty." Blue felt she needed to defend herself for some unfathomable reason. "I hardly remember
the incident."

"Blue was *covered* with mud." Uncle Horse said. "My brother and sister-in-law had a fit. You'd have thought Grizelle had made the child eat dirt instead of showing her how to plant flowers. Henry and Anne took Miranda Blue and left the very next day. And the roses were lovely that year."

"Yes," Aunt Grizelle nodded in sweet reminiscence. "They were."

"Didn't you ever get dirty at home, Blue?" Tad sounded a bit skeptical about the whole story. "Didn't you make mud pies? You know, with water and dirt? And grass for topping. And rocks. Lots of rocks."

"I didn't play in the dirt," Blue said. Tad looked as if he couldn't comprehend a person who hadn't gotten dirty as a child. Mud pies. Please.

"So what did you do?"

Blue fixed him with a cool, quizzical stare. "What do you mean, *what did I do?*"

"He wants to know what you did for fun, dear." Aunt Grizelle sipped her after-dinner coffee with all the grace of the Southern belle she once had been. "Tad and Horace are fun loving, you know. That's what makes them interesting."

"Yes," Blue said to be polite.

"So what did you do for fun?" Tad propped his elbow on the table and his chin in his hand. "Fly kites? Play dolls?"

"I went to the office with my father."

Mikie and Joe nodded. Tad looked alarmed. "That's it? You went to work?"

Blue was sorry she'd mentioned it. "I didn't work, of course. My father's office was very large and I really...liked being there."

"You've never flown a kite?" Tad asked as if it were a great tragedy. "You've never held the string of a Sky Dancer box kite as it caught the wind and sailed toward the sun?"

"No." Blue forced a smile to show she hadn't missed having such an experience. "At least, I don't think so. I don't really remember...."

Tad shook his head sadly. "You would have remembered."

Blue decided she'd had enough of that conversation and turned toward her aunt. "It was a splendid dinner, Aunt Grizelle. Thank you for inviting me."

"Oh, it was our pleasure," Aunt Grizelle said in her spidery, high-pitched voice. "You must have dinner with us every evening now that you'll be living so close."

"I told Miranda Blue she could take every meal with us. Except I told her you didn't eat breakfast." Uncle Horse scratched the top of his head with the handle of his fork. "Since she'll be right across the garden, it'll be no problem at all. Isn't that right, Griz?"

"Of course." Aunt Grizelle concurred with a welcoming smile for Blue. "You'll be just like Tad. He lives in the pool house, too, and he's here practically every night for supper, aren't you, Tad?"

"That's right." Tad's gaze never left Blue. "The pool house is just a hop and a skip away."

Blue swallowed. "Pool house?"

"It used to be a pool house," Tad said. "Now it's a duplex. One side for me. One side for you."

Blue's gaze flew to the beauteous smile on her aunt's face, then to the wild man who was her uncle, then to the nodding gardeners and finally back to Tad's I-tried-to-warn-you expression. "I'll be getting an apartment.

Something close to the office," she said desperately. "Really. There's no reason for me— The pool house . . . no."

"Now, no arguments, young lady." Uncle Horse drained the last of his coffee and refused a refill from Rosetta, the maid. "It's no trouble for your aunt and me. We love having young people around. Why, Tad's been with us . . . forever."

"Closer to five years." Tad continued to watch Blue with that same lazy regard.

"Uncle Horse," Blue began. "It's not that I don't appreciate—"

Her uncle lifted his hand. "Enough said, Miranda. We're glad to do it. You're our only niece and we'll be pleased as Papa Abraham to have you stay with us. Isn't that right, Griz?"

"Of course, Horace." Aunt Grizelle pushed back her chair. "And now, Blue, it's time we left these gentlemen to their after-dinner sherry." She rose gracefully from the table, and all the men stood courteously as she stepped to the doorway.

Blue scooted back her chair and rose to follow Aunt Grizelle because she didn't know what else to do. This was awful. In all her nightmares she'd never imagined anything like this. She not only had to work in an office next to Tad's, now they expected her to live next door to him, too. Well, she wouldn't do it. Not for all the free meals in the Western Hemisphere.

"It's so lovely to have you with us," Aunt Grizelle said, sinking into a tapestried Queen Anne chair in the parlor and picking up her needlepoint. "We've asked your parents many times over the years to let you visit us, but there never seemed to be a good time for you to come."

There was a good reason for that, Blue thought. She was beginning to understand why her parents had never encouraged her to visit these relatives. After a glance around the room she chose a less overwhelming place to sit...a Victorian sofa. Then she turned to her aunt in earnest. "Aunt Grizelle, it's lovely of you and Uncle Horace to want me to stay in your guest house, but I really would prefer to rent an apartment. I'd just feel more... independent."

With a soft sigh Aunt Grizelle dipped her needle into the fabric. "Nonsense. I realize your mama and papa raised you to be scrupulously polite and to refuse any hint of charity. But truly, Miranda Blue, your uncle and I want you close by. Why, it's been years since we had such a divine opportunity to have you with us. It would probably break Horace's heart if you went off and rented some old apartment. Now, I mean it. This is a treat for us. It won't be any trouble at all."

Blue pursed her lips and tried to find another angle. "It's not that I—"

"I do believe I hear the men comin'." Aunt Grizelle looked up from her embroidery. "I guess Horace wasn't in the mood for sherry this evenin'. My daddy used to have a glass of sherry and a cheroot after supper every night. It was a tradition in our household. Sometimes I think Horace tells me he drinks the sherry just to please me. Of course, I'm glad he doesn't smoke cigars. He'd prob'ly set his hair on fire."

"Hello, ladies," Tad said, entering the room behind Uncle Horse and giving Blue what she considered a smug smile. She suddenly wished she had the rubber band Uncle Horse had shot at her this afternoon.

"Tad?" she said with deliberate congeniality. "Would you go for a walk with me?"

"A walk?" There was a note of surprise in his voice, a trace of wariness in his expression. "You want to go for a walk with me?"

"That's right," Blue said pleasantly, concealing the fact that she was just desperate enough to kidnap him and force him to find her an apartment thirty miles from here. "You don't mind, do you?"

"Not at all. Do you mind?" He turned the question to the elderly couple, who were—of course—all smiles.

"Oh, yes, Tad." Aunt Grizelle endorsed the idea wholeheartedly. "Do show Miranda Blue the roses. They're particularly lovely this year."

Uncle Horse nodded eagerly. "That's a bang-up idea, Tad. You take Miranda Blue out and show her the roses. They are lovely this year."

"Yes, they are." Aunt Grizelle slid the needle in and out of the fabric. "Horace and I will be out presently. It will be time for my nightly reading at eight. You're invited to listen, Miranda Blue."

A nightly reading? Blue decided it would be better not to know what that was. As she walked with Tad to the doorway, she had a more immediate problem, namely her uncle and his proposal to move her into the pool house. She quickly practiced a plea for assistance and hoped that in this instance, Tad would be her ally. Surely he would. He couldn't want her living next door any more than she wanted to be there.

"So," he said after the door had closed behind them. "Did you lure me out here to see the roses or are you going to offer me a bribe for my half of the vice presidency?"

"Would you take a bribe?"

"I doubt it, but if you make an offer we'll find out."

Blue sighed. "Please be serious for a moment, Tad. I need your help. I'm sure you realize I can't move into the pool house."

"You won't drown, if that's what you're afraid of. Aunt Grizelle saw no need for a swimming pool. So she had it filled with dirt and made it a part of her rose garden. Didn't your parents ever tell you about that?"

"No. At least, if they did, I don't remember. My parents never have had much to say about Aunt Grizelle and Uncle Horace."

"Not everyone is able to appreciate just how special your aunt and uncle are."

Blue decided it would be pointless to try to defend her parents' opinion to Tad. He was obviously prejudiced. "At the moment I'm having some problem appreciating them, myself. I asked you to walk out here with me because I'm sure you don't want to share a duplex with me any more than I want to share one with you, and I thought that together maybe we could come up with a way to avoid it."

"Why not just tell Uncle Horse thank you, but no thank you?"

"Oh, come on, Tad, do you really believe that would work?"

"If you get his attention, it might."

"There's always a catch. I can't believe this. I really can't believe this." Blue measured her steps against the cobbled path and wondered if she could find a comparable job somewhere else in the city. She couldn't afford to move again so soon, but Dallas was a big place and... Who was she kidding? Here at least she was a vice president. A vice president at Grizelle Gadget and Toy Company. Even if she had to share that position, and even if the company wasn't a Fortune 500 Company, a vice presidency looked good on a résumé. She'd have to stay long enough to earn the title, but even so that meant she could be out of here in . . .

"Can you believe this?" Tad's voice stopped her and she turned. He was standing a few steps behind her, alongside a rose bush. His hand cupped a large, yellow rosebud, the expression in his eyes coaxed her toward him. "Look at this, Blue. It's perfect right down to the way the leaf curls against the stem."

She wanted to say she didn't have time to look at a flower . . . no matter how perfect it might be. She wanted to tell him that she needed a plan, not a posy. But she didn't think Tad would like either response, so she stepped across the sidewalk and took a glance at the "perfect" rosebud. "Very pretty," she said and started to walk on, but Tad grabbed her hand.

"Would you *look* at this? Really look?" He tugged her forward. "This rose won Best of Show at the Texas State Fair last year. Aunt Grizelle named it for me. Blue Garrison, meet the Thadeus Andrew Rose."

"Pleased to make your acquaintance," Blue said to the rosebud and started to walk on.

Tad didn't let go of her hand. Instead his clasp tightened as he pulled her back for another try. "Obviously playing in dirt isn't the only thing you've missed. Now, stand still. Right here." He put both hands on her shoulders and positioned her in front of the rosebush. "You need to learn how to look at a rose, Blue."

She frowned at him . . . or was she frowning because of the warm rush of awareness that flowed down her back at his touch? "Is this a requirement for living in Aunt Grizelle's garden? Because if it is, I'd rather not—"

"This is a requirement for living, Blue. Now listen and learn."

An ambience of intimacy suddenly pervaded the evening air and Blue hadn't a clue as to where it had come from. She didn't think she wanted to know, either. She swallowed the nervous flutter at the back of her throat and tried to appear impatient with the ritual.

"Do you know how much work is involved in coaxing this one rosebush to produce this one rosebud?" Tad asked. "Aunt Grizelle can tell you to the minute, but it's a lot of work and even with every effort, there's still an element of miracle in it. I mean, look, Blue. See how the petals fold around the center? See how the color is darker on the outside and lighter inside? Look at all the shades of yellow that blend together for just this one rose."

Blue looked, even though she felt silly. It was just a flower, for Pete's sake. If Tad hadn't been standing so close to her... The truth was, he was a little too close for comfort. There was something about him...something she couldn't define...that made her feel unsure of herself and ruffled the edges of her usually rock solid self-confidence. She'd already admitted to herself...and in a vague sort of way to Ellie...that she found Tad attractive. But she'd known lots of attractive men. Even men with more prestige and power. Rob McKinley, to name one. But there was something powerful about Tad, too. She simply couldn't put her finger on what it was. Maybe her imagination had just kicked into overdrive. Or perhaps she was just overreacting to this "perfect" rosebud.

"I see it, Tad," she said, trying to inject a note of wonder into the words. "It's a very pretty flower."

Tad's sigh was deep, the shake of his head slow and pointed. "You're not into enjoying life at the moment, are you, Blue?"

Her gaze swung to his. "I said it was a pretty flower. I even said it was very pretty."

He nodded and walked farther along the path between the rose beds. Blue hurried to catch up with him. "Look, Tad, I have a lot on my mind right now. I thought you'd be foaming at the mouth to help me get out of here. It's bad enough that we have to share a job. Do you want me to be your next-door neighbor, too?"

Tad glanced at her with raised eyebrows. "Do you see me hanging on to your ankles and begging you to move into the pool house?"

"No. I see you stopping to look at the roses."

With a shrug, Tad bent to smell a softly muted pink rose. "That's because I'm not eaten up with anxiety about whether or not you move in next door to me. If you don't, I can handle it. If you do, I can handle that, too." He straightened and held his hands palm up in a gesture of acceptance. "Either way... no anxiety."

"I'm not particularly *anxious* about it. I mean, it's no big deal to me. But I just think we'd be wise to persuade Uncle Horse to forget the idea of one, big happy family."

"That's a tall order, Blue. Uncle Horse is adamant about his employees being one big, happy family. And, for now, you're part of that family. You may just have to grin and bear it."

"Look, Tad, let's get this straight. I'm here to work. Period. I am not interested in establishing relationships with co-workers. I'm not here to enjoy myself. I just want to do my job and stay out of trouble."

He looked at her and she was acutely aware of his height and the impressive bulk of his shoulders. "Is that why you left your last job?" he asked. "Did you get into trouble?"

A guilty twist in her stomach made Blue want to blurt out that it hadn't been her fault. But she did not want to get into that with Tad. She didn't want him to know how close to the truth he was. "Of course not. I just believe in keeping my business and my personal lives separate. That's all."

Tad knew she was lying. He didn't know how he knew, but he did. "Well, good luck. You're going to find it very difficult to keep to yourself here."

"Is that a threat, Mr. Vice President?"

Tad pursed his lips, debating whether to tackle that chip on Blue's shoulder or let the matter ride. He decided to keep things light. At least for the moment. "If you're trying to hurt my feelings, Blue, you're about to succeed."

"Oh, be honest, Tad. You don't want me working with you. You probably wish I was in Siberia."

"I don't wish you were in Siberia." He stroked the curled petals of a coral rosebud and then bend to inhale the fragrance. "California would be far enough away for me."

"Sorry, but I'm staying. Whether you approve or not, Uncle Horse named me a vice president, too. And I plan to do the job I was hired for."

"Believe it or not, it bothers me a lot more that you've never flown a kite."

Blue sighed in frustration. "Well, it bothers me a lot that you spent the afternoon at the zoo."

Tad lifted his head and smiled. "When's the last time you were at the zoo?"

"That's not the point, Tad. You can't— Going to the zoo is no way to run a business, and it sets a bad example for the staff. No one comes to work on time. Everyone leaves early. What kind of place is Grizelle Gadget and Toy Company?"

"An unusual place. A stimulating, exciting, always new place. You're lucky to be where you are, Blue. Sooner or later, you may even realize that."

"Oh, I'm sure you're right."

He heard the sarcasm in her tone and wished she would loosen up a little. She needed to see a few more rosebuds and a few less drawbacks in her circumstances. Blue Garrison was one uptight lady and, although he wasn't particularly happy at the way things had turned out, he wasn't *miserable*. "Lighten up, Blue. Things might not be as bad as you think."

She turned to him with a haughty arch of her brow and outright skepticism in her eyes. "Don't try to put your rose-colored glasses on me, Tad."

"Hey, forgive me for being concerned. I hereby appoint you vice president in charge of gloom and doom."

"Thank you. That's more direction than Uncle Horse has given me."

"Maybe he expects you to find your own area of interest."

"Is that what you do, Tad? Just sit around in your own area of interest, playing with whatever toy strikes your fancy?"

Tad decided he'd been too nice up to this point and it was time Blue knew where he stood. "Horace Garrison is a genius, Blue. He may seem like a spacey old man to you, he may not fit your ideal of a businessman, but don't discount his ability. And don't discount mine."

"That's not what I meant."

"That's certainly the idea that came across. I'll admit—again—that I'm not thrilled at the prospect of sharing the vice presidency with you. The office should have been mine alone. But I'm going to do everything in my power to get along with you, to find out what makes you tick, and to challenge you to do the best job you can. Even if you hate every minute of it. You're free to do anything to try and change my mind about an idea or a product or any philosophical question under the sun. But don't patronize me."

Blue was speechless. She hadn't expected he could be riled to the point of anger by her comments. He made her feel foolish and more than a little embarrassed. "I didn't realize you thought I was being patronizing. You're younger than I and less experienced in business and—"

The sincerity in her tone was the only thing that restrained his response. "You're doing it again, Blue." He moved away, past the pink roses to the red ones. "Stop while you're ahead."

She followed slowly, trying to come to terms with his accusation, wondering if she ought to apologize or just change the subject. With determination, she paused beside a magnificent burgundy-red rose, bent to smell the rich scent and brushed a petal lightly with her fingertip. "This is really beautiful. It must be part miracle. Did you see this one, Tad?"

He seemed to deliberate only an instant before he accepted the peace offering for what it was and joined her beside the rosebush. "This is Aunt Grizelle's pride and joy. It's called the Jeremy Lin." His voice trailed off and Blue looked up in surprise to see his jaw tighten before he continued. "It has the deepest fragrance of any of the roses in the garden."

Blue wondered what association, if any, this particular rose had for Tad, but she didn't want to ask. "I guess Mikie and Joe can take a lot of credit for this," she said instead.

"Mikie and Joe garden. Aunt Grizelle puts the blush on her roses."

Blue moved past the burgundy-red rose. "How does she do that?"

"She reads to them. She says literature gives them purpose."

Blue smiled at the idea. "What did she read to the Thadeus Andrew Rose to make it a winner?"

"Lady Chatterley's Lover."

Blue laughed aloud. "I see. And what is she reading this year? *Lolita?*"

"It depends on the rose. Last year the pinks got poetry, mainly Robert and Elizabeth Browning. The reds received massive doses of Longfellow. She read *Wuthering Heights* to the white roses and *Jane Eyre* to a couple of other varieties. I don't know how she makes the selections, but I've spent some pleasant evenings listening to her read aloud to her roses."

"An advantage of living in the garden, I suppose."

"It is a perk. And on that note we arrive at the infamous pool house." He gestured toward a long, low bungalow that nestled behind rows of rosebushes like a summer cottage in the Cotswolds. It was charming, quaint, just a bit odd, and Blue had an almost overwhelming urge to see inside.

But she didn't ask. How could she after all the negative things she'd said? "It's very nice, Tad. Is it bigger inside than it looks?"

"Not a lot. It was an oversized pool house. Now, it's two rather small apartments...with one bath between them."

"One bath? You're kidding."

"Nope. There's only one."

Blue looked back at the appealing little house. "All the more reason to persuade my uncle to let me find something else."

"All the more reason," Tad agreed. "Sharing a bathroom, as well as a vice presidency with me, would probably produce more anxiety than you could handle."

She couldn't think of anything to say to refute that. "I'll just tell Uncle Horse I can find an apartment on my own. He'll understand."

"Yes," Tad said. "I'm sure he will."

Chapter Four

"Where do you want this one?" Tad asked, standing in the middle of the apartment with a large cardboard box in his arms. "It's marked—" he extended the box so he could read the letters on the side "—towels."

Blue stopped trying to fit a stack of eight-inch dinner plates into seven and seven-eighths inches of cabinet space and turned her frown toward her new neighbor. "By any chance is there a linen closet in this apartment?"

"You'll be happy to know there is. It's one of many luxuries we have here at the Pool House Apartments." Tad "Mr. Helpful" Denton whistled "Tea for Two" as he carried the box toward the bathroom.

Blue pressed her lips together and told herself Tad was just doing what Uncle Horse had asked him to do. She might prefer to be at work, where she was finally getting a handle on how things worked, but her uncle had given her the day off so she could move in. Then he'd given Tad the day off to make *sure* she moved in. All in all, Uncle Horse had outsmarted them both on several angles this week and so...she was moving into the pool house.

"You want me to put these towels away for you?" Tad called from the other room.

With a sigh Blue turned from her immediate problem, intending to check the linen closet for dust and shelf paper, but she was hemmed in by boxes of kitchen paraphernalia and couldn't get out without a tremendous leap across the floor. She sank instead onto the nearest, sturdiest box and put her head in her hands. "I don't care what you do with them," she said, not caring if he heard her or not.

Tad appeared in the narrow doorway, without the box of towels. "Sounds like it's time for a break. We can head right on down to the local fast-food eatery for a milkshake and a burger or we can zip over to my place and grab something less nutritionally balanced."

"What might that be?" Blue didn't even look up, just kept her head cradled in her hands. "Twinkies and milk?"

"Graham crackers and half a bag of marshmallows. I might have a jar of dill pickles, too."

"Yum. Do you have anything to drink?"

"I'll have to check the fridge. The milk might have turned on me. I'm not sure when I bought it. But the water's always good. How about water?"

"Make mine on the rocks."

"You want to come with me? It's just next door."

Blue lifted her head. "I can't get out of here," she said quite calmly. "I'm trapped in this tiny little kitchen and I may never see daylight again."

"Well, hold the fort. I'll be back with the goodies in two shakes of a lamb's tail." With a wave of his hand, he turned and then stopped. "It is all right if I cut through the bathroom, isn't it? I know that keeping the traffic to a minimum through there is number one on your list of requirements for common decency, but it is faster and—"

Blue sighed. "Of course, Tad. Cut through. After I'm moved in, we can enforce a demilitarized zone."

With a grin Tad left and Blue listened to his footsteps as he walked through her apartment to the bathroom and opened the connecting door into his apartment. She shuddered at the thought of that one bathroom and the problems that were bound to arise from having to share it with Tad. She'd already set out some rules, some courteous dos and don'ts to make life easier for both of them. Tad had glanced at the list, but he hadn't said anything before now. Obviously, though, he had read it. She took his recent comment as agreement on his part and hoped he would be as meticulously courteous as she intended to be.

He hadn't had much to say about the new living arrangements. While she'd tried to convince Uncle Horse of the unsuitability of her living in the pool house, Tad had kept his own counsel. And then, this morning, he'd appeared with the company van, a cheerful whistle and the news that he was there to help her get settled in. He didn't mention that he was there at Uncle Horse's insistence, but Blue could figure that much out for herself. And she had to admit he'd been a lot of help... moving boxes and putting things away. She'd probably never find half of her stuff again, but at the moment she didn't really care.

She heard the connecting door open and close again and a moment later Tad had returned. "I brought Berry Cherry Kool-Aid. There was some already made up in the fridge. The marshmallows were stale, though." He stepped over a couple of boxes to offer her a tumbler and half a pack of graham crackers. Then he found himself a seat on the floor, helped himself to the crackers and surveyed the morning's progress. "Looks like we're on the downhill side now. There're only a few more boxes in the van."

"Great," Blue said with no enthusiasm for the completion of the move, the graham crackers or the drink in her hand. She tried an experimental sip of the Kool-Aid and followed it with a thirsty swallow. "I'll probably be settled in by the time Aunt Grizelle gives her nightly reading."

"I'm sure that's exactly what Uncle Horse has in mind."

Blue released a resigned sigh. "He wouldn't let me go anywhere else, you know. I tried to rent an apartment close to the office, but when the owner called to verify my employment—"

"Uncle Horse couldn't remember who you were."

"I think he gave the biggest runaround that poor woman had ever heard. Needless to say, she told me to look elsewhere for a place to live."

Tad's mouth curved slightly. "And did you?"

"No." Blue felt a little guilty about that. She wasn't usually so easily buffaloed. "I figured he'd just do it again. I would never have believed my uncle could be so devious."

"*Devious* is too strong a word for Uncle Horse. He can be pretty sly on occasion and I'll agree that he's a crafty old man, but he's not malicious. He wants you to live here in the pool house, so he can't think of any reason you wouldn't want to live here. If an idea sounds good to him, then he sees protests as polite objections, not good reasons." Tad took a drink of his Kool-Aid. "You might want to remember in future confrontations with your uncle that what you hear is not necessarily what he means to say."

"Tell me something I haven't already figured out, Tad. As far as I can see, the Grizelle Gadget and Toy Company is just one big nut house."

"A nut house that pays your salary." Tad set his Kool-Aid aside and finished off another cracker. Then he reached for one of the unpacked boxes and opened it before he raised his gaze to hers again. "You said you needed this job, Blue. So why don't you stop complaining and do the job you've been hired for.''

Blue's defensive instincts rose to the challenge. "The first thing I intend to do is instill some professionalism into this squirrelly operation. I know I'm better qualified to do that than..."

Her statement dropped into a well of silence. The look Tad fixed on her carried a heavy warning. "You're wrong if you think you're better qualified to be vice president of Grizelle's than I am, Blue. I know this company inside and out. I know how it works and why. And I'll remind you one more time not to underestimate me."

She was beginning to understand what a mistake that was. But despite the tension between them she liked his forthrightness, the steady tones of confidence and determination in his voice. His jaw tightened, and his brown eyes challenged her to prove him wrong. She found herself admiring the way his hair dipped over his forehead, softening the outline of his face.

Blue sighed under her breath and finished the last of her Kool-Aid in one gulp. It was bad enough that she had to share an apartment and a job with him. She didn't want to like him, too. "I'm sorry if I sounded patronizing again. This situation is a little hard for me to take. I'm really not always such a... a whiner."

Tad watched her in silence for a moment. "You have a Kool-Aid smile," he said.

"What?" Her hand flew to her mouth. Her eyes scanned his lips as if she might see there a mirror image of the red Kool-Aid tracks, and she hurriedly wiped her fingertips across each side of her mouth. "Did I get it?"

His mouth slanted slowly upward and then he leaned forward across three boxes, to stroke his thumb along the curve of her lips. His touch was strong, assured and altogether too smooth. Somewhere inside her a silly little feeling stirred.

"There," he said, settling back to his box seat. "All trace of your Kool-Aid break is gone. Anything else I can do for you? More crackers, maybe?"

"No. No more, thanks." Blue had to pause to catch her breath, to remember what she'd started to say. "There are a few more boxes still in the van and a whole lot of towels to be put in the linen closet."

His lazy smile remained steady, as did the look he kept trained on her mouth. Blue didn't know where to look or what to think. A moment ago he'd been angry or, at the very least, annoyed with her. Then suddenly he was smiling and wiping her mouth. Did he shift moods to unsettle her? Did he want to keep her off balance?

Whatever his secret, Tad kept it to himself as his attention dropped to the box in front of him. With a curious frown he reached in and pulled out an eight by ten frame. He turned it over in his hands and studied it.

Blue froze when she realized what he held. Why had she been dumb enough to pack the stupid thing? Why had she kept it in the first place? And how was she going to convince Tad it was nothing...a picture of two people who were merely friends?

Friends.

The word hurt her as it always did these days. She'd thought Rob was her friend. She'd thought...so many things.

"Who's this?" Tad held up a picture. "Your boyfriend?"

Boyfriend. The term sent a chill down her spine. "No, Tad. I don't have a *boy*friend. Rob was—" the catch in her voice was brief and probably all too noticeable "—*is* someone I used to work with. That's all."

"You don't look like you're working in this picture." Tad lifted an innocent gaze, although he'd have bet his favorite hat that Blue detected the shrewd intent behind his question. Someone she used to work with. Hah. "The two of you appear to be having one hell of a good time."

Blue leaned forward, as if she were trying to look at the photograph and jog her memory into providing the occasion on which it was snapped. "Oh, that was . . . at a trade show, I believe."

"Were you trading jokes?"

She straightened on her box seat. "It is possible to work and enjoy oneself at the same time, Tad."

He couldn't stop the sudden curve of his mouth. "You don't know how relieved I am to hear you say that, Blue. I was beginning to think you didn't know what the word *fun* meant. Who did you say the guy is?"

Blue hesitated. Tad could almost see the wheels of escape turning in her head. "His name is Rob. Rob, uh, McKinley."

"McKinley, huh? And you worked with him." Tad deliberately studied the photograph a moment longer. "So where do you want me to put it?"

"Back in the box. I'll deal with my personal items later."

Tad put the picture down and drained the rest of his Kool-Aid. "Then I'd better get back to the towels . . . unless there's something else you want me to unpack."

"No. The towels. That will be the most helpful thing you could do."

"I strive to be helpful," he said. "Shall I move some of these boxes before I go, so you're not trapped in your own kitchen?"

Blue glanced around the pint-sized room. "Why didn't they put a bathroom in each apartment and have the two units share a larger kitchen? This layout doesn't make any sense."

"This is Wonderland, Alice. Things don't have to make sense here."

Blue smiled unexpectedly. "If this is Wonderland, then my uncle is the Mad Hatter and Aunt Grizelle is the Duchess. Mikie and Joe must be Tweedledee and Tweedledum. Which character are you, Tad?"

"I'm the Cheshire Cat. Watch this grin fade into thin air."

It wasn't much of a vanishing act, but Tad felt he did a fair job of disappearing from her view. But once he reached the linen closet, he couldn't seem to get the image of her and that guy in the photograph out of his mind.

It had been a good picture. In the five days since she'd arrived at Grizelle Gadget, he hadn't seen anything resembling that carefree expression touch her face. She'd seemed tense most of the time. Tense and overly cautious.

Tad pulled a long strip of tape from the box marked "towels," wadded it into a sticky ball and tossed it over his shoulder. Then he pulled back the flaps and unearthed a cache of moss-green towels. Moss green, he thought. Perfect complement for the aqua tile in the bathroom. He hoped the ultimate clash wouldn't bother Blue too much, but anyone who bought just one color of towels was too structured for her own good, anyway.

With a frown Tad began stacking the towels on the closet shelf and with nothing to occupy his thoughts, the image of Blue with that man came immediately and clearly to mind.

Rob McKinley. Just someone she'd worked with. A likely story.

That was the trouble. Tad knew it as well as he knew that Blue was in love with the guy. Or at least she had been at the time that picture was snapped. She had the look and Tad recognized it for what it was. He'd been in love once himself. He still remembered how it felt.

He swallowed hard and quickly finished stacking the towels...every moss-green one of them. He didn't want to get lost in his own memories and the pain they inevitably brought. Undoubtedly Blue had experienced pain as well. She was no longer the laughing young woman she'd been in the photograph.

Had she fallen in love with her boss? Was that why she'd suddenly appeared at Grizelle Gadget and Toy? Was that the mystery?

But that hardly explained why she *had* to have this job. Especially since she obviously felt it was a step down for her. Couldn't she have found another position more to her liking? Tad frowned. He would have bet his Mickey Mouse watch that Rob McKinley had something to do with Blue's discontented state of mind.

It wasn't any of his business, he reminded himself. It didn't really make any difference what had brought Blue into his life. She was here now and he had to deal with her.

Maybe it was a good thing they were sharing a bathroom. He couldn't think how she'd be able to sustain that superior attitude once her moss-green terry towels met his rainbow-colored velours.

"WHAT'S THIS?" Tad asked, tossing a sheet of paper onto Blue's desk. He crossed his arms and waited for an explanation.

She glanced at the typed words on the paper. "It's a memo to the employees."

"Yes. And what does it say?"

One glance at the set of his jaw and Blue knew better than to ask if he could read. "It regards working hours and the misuse thereof."

"Whose *misuse*?"

"The employees," Blue answered, her voice finding the same, crisp, irritating tone Tad used. "Everyone. From you all the way down to Zeke. No one...and I repeat...*no one* seems to know that full-time employees are supposed to work a forty hour week. There's no time clock to punch here, no time sheets, and the best I can tell, no one even keeps a record of what hours the employees are here. They just show up when they please and leave whenever they're ready."

"It's called flex time, Blue. You're so damned inflexible, you probably can't understand that. But the point is, everyone works very hard around here. Okay, it isn't always an eight-hours-a-day, five-days-a-week schedule and obviously it isn't what you're used to, but it works."

"Well, at the very least, we should have some kind of time sheet to keep track of things, and a schedule so we know when employees are expected to be in."

"That would only be paperwork and take up time that could be used more productively in other areas. Why bother?"

Blue put her palms flat on her desk, pushed back her chair and stood...just so he wouldn't continue to have the advantage of towering over her. "That's a stupid question."

Tad thumped the memo with his finger. "Well, *this* is a *stupid* idea!"

"Uncle Horse doesn't think so."

"Don't try to con me, Blue. You haven't talked to him about this."

"I mentioned it to him, yes."

"And he told you to write this . . . this memo?"

Blue was on shifting sand and she knew it. The trick was to keep Tad from knowing it, too. "We discussed the way employees come and go as they please, and he agreed with me that business hours should be consistent."

"I don't believe you. Uncle Horse wouldn't agree to anything like this." Tad picked up the offensive memo and read an item aloud. "Uncle Horse couldn't work here if that were enforced. And I know he wouldn't ask his employees to do anything he couldn't do."

"Why don't you ask him?" Blue suggested.

"Oh, come on, Blue. Just admit that you were out of line with this and we'll tear up the memo and forget it."

That had happened to her organizational ideas too many times here already. This one she wouldn't back down on. "If you won't take it to Uncle Horse, then I will." She snatched the memo from his hand and started for the door. "Come on, Tad. I want you to hear this."

Tad cast her a heavy frown and then moved forward. "All right, Ms. V.P., let's go see what the prez has to say about this now."

Blue smoothed the contours of her silk skirt, adjusted the cuffs of the matching silk blouse and waited for Tad. As he passed, she lifted her chin and cast him a defiant glance. He didn't flinch. Just turned on his heel and fell into perfect step beside her. Ellie watched their progress across the reception area with unabashed interest and several severe snaps of her chewing gum.

Blue ignored the pinch of guilt on her conscience. She knew she shouldn't egg Tad into these confrontations. But he was so adamantly opposed to any idea that came from her, and she did think the company could be run more efficiently...with a few minor rules and regulations. This was the fifth time in two weeks she'd run afoul of Tad's temper. The fifth time in two weeks that she'd suggested they make this trek from her office to Uncle Horse's. And each time she wondered why she got involved in these minor power skirmishes. She didn't particularly want power and she certainly wasn't out to usurp any of Tad's. But somehow it always seemed to come to this...the two of them marching into Uncle Horse's office like contentious children sent to the principal for discipline. Maybe this time, Blue thought, Uncle Horse would actually listen, would actually take part in fixing what was wrong with his company.

Today Uncle Horse was on the floor. Flat on his stomach. In front of him, across most of the office floor space, a model train track spread in intricate loops and bends. The model was detailed with mountains, tunnels, bridges, a sawmill and a train station. On a side track one train waited as another puffed smoke and clicked along the track, taking Uncle Horse's attention with it wherever it went. Blue took a deep breath. This was not going to be easy.

"Uncle Horse?" Tad intruded on the older man's concentration. At least he tried to intrude. "Blue and I have something to discuss with you."

"Whoo-whoo!" Uncle Horse's eyes followed the engine around the outside curve. "Whoo-oo-oooh!"

"Uncle Horse?" Tad repeated his bid for attention with no noticeable effect.

"Uncle Horse?" Blue made a halfhearted effort, just so Tad wouldn't think she was unprepared for this confrontation. "Tad and I would like to talk to you about something."

The train kept on chugging. Uncle Horse kept watching.

Tad looked at Blue.

She raised her eyebrows and shrugged.

Tad gave a deep sigh and got flat on the floor beside Uncle Horse.

Blue debated her options and the washability of her silk skirt and blouse. There was no place to sit because Uncle Horse had stacked all the chairs, one on top of the other, in the corner of the room to make space for his train set. She crossed her arms at her waist and leaned against the wall. "Uncle Horse," she said decisively. "Tad and I have had a disagreement."

Tad shot her a wait-your-turn look. "She's written a memo to the employees, Uncle Horse, telling them they have to work regular hours."

"If you'll recall, Uncle Horse," Blue jumped in with her version of the story. "You and I discussed this problem at some length. You agreed that business hours should be made consistent."

"Uncle Horse," Tad stated with a confident glance at Blue. "You know we've always maintained a flexible work schedule, allowing the employees to work as long or as short a time as needed to accomplish their particular tasks. No one's complained about it and productivity remains high. There's no reason to fix something that isn't broken."

Uncle Horse flipped a switch on the control box in front of him and the idle train edged onto the track. He wiggled into a more prone position—if that were possible—and elbowed Tad in the process. "Scoot over there, Tad. Make room for Blue. Miranda, get down here where you can see this."

He patted the space on his left and Blue wrinkled her nose at the thought of her silk-clad body flat on the floor. "I don't mind standing, Uncle—"

"Nonsense. Can't see a thing from up there. Come on, now. A little dust never hurt anybody."

If she'd learned anything in the three weeks she'd been working in this crazy place, it was the futility of trying to reason with her uncle. Masking a sigh, she knelt, and with one last, sad look at her outfit she stretched out beside her uncle. "Do you really think we need to discuss this while lying on the floor?" she asked. "Wouldn't it be better to sit in chairs so we could look at each other?"

"I can see you just fine from this perspective." Tad rolled to his side and propped his head with his hand. His annoyance with her seemed now to be channeled into a droll amusement at the position they had found themselves in. "Get comfortable, Blue. We may be here for a while... unless you're willing to give in on this issue."

"Don't worry, Tad. My perspective is every bit as good as yours and my perseverance is well-known in business circles."

"Yes, but what about in train circles?"

"Watch this." Uncle Horse flipped another switch and the two model trains raced along the track in opposite directions. "You're about to see a spectacular wreck."

Blue reluctantly shifted her gaze from Tad to the toy train set. The engines were on a collision course. No doubt about that. But what was she doing here, on the floor, waiting for disaster to strike? Hadn't she learned her lesson about power and the pursuit thereof at McKinley Enterprises? Why hadn't she kept her mouth shut about the lackadaisical system of employee management here at the toy company? Everyone was happy. Even Uncle Horse, who stood to lose the most by this come-and-go-as-you-please system. Tad certainly saw no reason to change anything in the sagging infrastructure. And she didn't plan to stick around any longer than she absolutely had to. Why had she put herself and Tad on this collision course? Why couldn't she just leave well enough alone? "Stop the trains, Uncle Horse."

"Why?" Uncle Horse asked. "This is gonna be some pileup!"

"Are you sure you want to do this, Uncle Horse?" Tad asked as the trains swept toward the final, fatal curve. It was strange to find himself agreeing with Blue, but, despite their differing perspectives, in this case he did. "It might mess up some of the cars and there aren't many model trains like this around anymore," he said firmly.

"What? You both agree I should stop the trains?" Uncle Horse lifted his head as if struck by a sudden idea. His eyes bulged and Blue half expected him to yell, "Eureka!" He shook his head, nodded, then switched the levers on the control unit to Off and stopped the trains nose-to-nose, with a quarter inch to spare. "Whew. That was a close call. We almost had a whing-dinger of a crash here." He dusted his long, bony fingers together and pushed himself off the floor with amazing agility for a man of his age. "You two better get up before you get your clothes all dirty." He extended a hand to Blue. "Your mother would have a fit if she saw you down there, Miranda Blue. Dust off your pant leg there, Tad. You're a vice president, you know."

Blue picked a dust bunny from her skirt and hoped there was still room on her dry cleaning tab for one more outfit. "Tad and I came in here to talk to you about business hours, Uncle Horse. Do you think we could do that now?"

"Of course." Uncle Horse scratched his head, bringing even greater disarray to the spiked mane of white hair. "What did you want to talk about?"

"Flexible work hours," Tad said with a last slap at his trouser legs. "Blue wants to insist that every employee work a forty-hour week. No exceptions."

Uncle Horse frowned. "Hmm," he said.

"Tad won't even consider instituting a time-keeping system."

"Hmmmm," Uncle Horse said.

"Blue's prepared a memo, Uncle Horse. She says she talked it over with you."

"Well, if she says that, then it must be true." Uncle Horse walked behind his desk and picked up a pencil with a troll doll on the top where the eraser would normally be. "What do you have to say about it, Tad?"

"I say it's a stupid idea and the employees aren't going to like it. They're used to setting their own hours."

Uncle Horse began to twirl the pencil between his hands, making the doll's hair stand on end, much like his own. "That's true. And have we talked about that, Tad? You and I?"

"Many times, Uncle Horse."

"Hmm."

Blue could see this was going nowhere. She wasn't even surprised. "Tad has the memo, Uncle Horse. Why don't you read it? Then you can say yes or no and that will be the end of this discussion."

"Oh, I can't do that," her uncle said. "That's why I have two vice presidents. You and Tad will just have to come to an agreement, Blue. I can't make every decision for you. That would leave me no time to play with my electric train set."

Tad exchanged a glance with Blue before he tried again for an answer. "This is a serious matter, Uncle Horse."

"You bet it is. That's why I'm confident the two of you will work out the best solution for everyone. If you hadn't stopped the train crash, well, I might be a little worried. But together you kept a disaster from happening here and that's what's important. Isn't that right, Miranda Blue?''

"Absolutely, Uncle Horse.'' She offered the affirmation with a patient smile and a you-should-have-known-better look for Tad. "Tad and I will settle this matter between ourselves.''

"It may involve murder, but we'll settle it,'' Tad said, returning Blue's look. Then he turned to Uncle Horse. "So what you're saying here, Uncle Horse, is that no policy memo should go out unless Blue and I both agree on its contents.''

The pencil doll stopped twirling and Uncle Horse looked concerned. "I think that's reasonable. Don't you agree? Let's see a show of hands.'' His bony arm shot high in the air and Blue and Tad lifted their own appendages in sloppy assent. Uncle Horse smiled his pleasure. "There, now we're all in agreement. No head-on collisions. No whing-dinger train wrecks.'' As if that reminded him, he came out from behind the desk and plopped down, cross-legged, beside the train tracks. "I wonder what we're having for dinner,'' he said as he flipped a switch and backed one of the trains into a tunnel. "I hope it's peanut butter and jelly.''

Tad tipped his head in the direction of the doorway, and Blue stepped past her uncle and reached the reception area a few paces ahead of Tad.

"Who won?'' Ellie blew a fair-sized bubble and sucked it back between her Purely Pink lipsticked lips.

"Ellie,'' Blue began, only to be interrupted by Tad.

"It was a draw, Ellie.''

"I don't see how you can call that a draw,'' Blue protested. "Nothing was settled.''

"But we did have the foresight to stop the train wreck.''

"That's right, me and Janitor Man, defender of model trains." Blue shrugged and started for her office, curiously not upset by the loss of her memo-writing powers.

Tad watched her go and wondered how they would manage to live with Uncle Horse's new rule. It constantly amazed him that one woman could be so annoying and so damned appealing at the same time.

"You coming to the party, tonight?" Ellie asked Tad as Blue rounded the corner of the reception desk and stopped to look at a newspaper lying there. "You can bring a date."

Tad kept his eyes on Blue and only vaguely registered Ellie's question and comment. "I don't know, Ellie...."

"Oh, come on, Tad. You have to come. It'll be fun. You want me to get a date for you? I can, you know. Easy."

"I'm not interested in the 'easy' dates you come up with, Ellie."

"Okay. If you don't want 'easy,' we'll try 'not so easy.'" With a wicked wink of one eye, Ellie swiveled her secretary's chair to face the opposite corner of the desk. "Hey, Blue, you wanna come to a party tonight? It's an engagement party for me and Jim Bill, except he won't be there because he's in the Navy and out in the middle of the ocean somewhere. But you can meet all my friends, and Tad, here, really needs someone to go with him." Ellie smiled encouragingly. "It wouldn't be a date, you understand. But it would save him all the grief of showing up stag and fightin' off women for the rest of the night. He has such a problem at parties. And I do want both of you there. I mean, it is a big night for me." Ellie paused and gave her gum a confident snap. "You won't let me down, will you, Blue?"

Blue's gaze strayed to Tad's and he wasn't sure if he wanted to strangle Ellie for making such a stupid suggestion or if he was more inclined to shake her hand for thinking of the idea. Of course Blue wouldn't accept, but Tad suddenly, unexpectedly, found himself wishing she would. "Do you want to go to Ellie's party?" he asked as indifferently as he could manage. "You're welcome to ride with me . . . if you want."

Blue seemed to be considering how to phrase her regrets when Ellie gave the invitation a final push. "It's going to be fun, Blue. And don't worry about fitting in. My friends all get along real well with people your age."

Tad bit back the smile that tugged hard at his mouth. That, he thought, just about backed Miranda Blue into a corner. And it was his guess she'd come out swinging.

"Why, thank you, Ellie." Blue was obviously irritated, but to her credit she tried hard not to let it show. "I'd be delighted to come to your party and meet your *young* friends. What time do you want to leave, Tad?"

"Eight?"

"Eight." Blue gave the barest of nods and walked into her office with a decisive step.

"She's going to come," Ellie whispered with no little amazement. "I didn't think she would. I mean, I'm real glad she is, but I just didn't expect . . ." With a flighty hand, Ellie ruffled the edges of her glued-in-place bangs. "Just goes to show it pays to be polite."

Tad decided not to explain to Ellie that politeness had had nothing at all to do with Blue's acceptance. "Just goes to show," he agreed.

Chapter Five

When Ellie opened the door, Blue's first thought was that no one had told her it was a costume party. Luckily Tad's warning grip on her elbow and Ellie's effusive greeting saved her from embarrassment.

As if just being present at this party wasn't embarrassment enough.

"Come in. Come in." Ellie waved a hand toward the interior of the apartment building rec room where the engagement party was being held. "You don't know how tickled I am that you two came to my party."

Obviously Ellie was tickled pink. From head to toe, there wasn't more than a few inches of flesh not covered by hot-pink elastic. Ellie wore leotards that stretched taut to mid-calf, high, hot-pink heels, and a tunic of hot-pink leopard print with the face of a cat sketched on the front in silver glitter. The crowning glory was a hair bow made of tulle, lace and hot-pink feathers cleverly riding the crest of Ellie's bright red hair. Blue couldn't stop staring.

"I want you guys to meet my friends...before you start 'partyin' down.'" With a tug of her hand Ellie walked backward a couple of steps, pulling Blue and Tad inside the room and into the midst of a group of young people with names like Spike, Wendy, Angel, and Dewayne. After the first few minutes of introductions, Blue decided she'd have had more in common with Sleepy, Sneezy, Doc, and Dopey than with anyone at this gathering. She promised herself, though, that she'd stay and keep up the appearance of "fitting in" with Ellie's friends ... if it killed her.

Which it now looked as if it might.

Once the conversational ice was broken, Ellie indicated the kitchen and told Blue and Tad to help themselves. "We've got soda, chips, pretzels, Chex Mix, anything you want. There's plenty of room to dance in here, but we have to keep the noise level to a minimum." Ellie wrinkled her nose in disgust. "Bummer, huh?"

"I'm sure the other tenants of the apartment building appreciate the restriction." Tad had to raise his voice over the pulsating, modern-day rock music already threatening the rafters of the rec room. "Did you ever get that call through to Jim Bill while his ship was in port?"

"Yeah. Thanks, Tad. It was great." Ellie's eyes teared with emotion as she pulled Tad into her arms and gave him a big hug. Then she turned to Blue with an explanation. "Tad let me use the office phone to call Jimmy Bill shore to ship. It took forever to get through, but it was worth every minute."

Blue raised her eyebrows at Tad, but he held up his hands to lay her suspicion to immediate rest. "I'm paying for the phone call, Blue. Not the company. You can stop composing that memo about misuse of company phone lines. And don't bother to deny it. I can see the typewriter keys clicking away in your head."

"I wasn't thinking about a memo," she said as she walked behind the counter. The Chex Mix was in a big, green salad bowl. The chips and pretzels were spilling out of cellophane bags. The soda bottles were open on the counter, and ice was melting in the sink. Blue could barely recall the last time she'd been to this kind of party. Junior high, she thought. When she was fourteen.

Why had she let Ellie's remark about age push her into this situation? Why hadn't she gracefully accepted the fact that being over thirty meant she didn't have to attend teeny-bopper parties? She didn't have anything to prove to Ellie. Or Tad, for that matter. He wasn't that far from being thirty, himself. Somehow he didn't seem to fit any better with this group than she did. So what was his reason for coming?

"Want something to drink? There's plenty of soda." He moved past her, opened the refrigerator and twisted a can from a six-pack. "Sorry, I don't think Ellie made any Kool-Aid. And I doubt there's anyone here who is over twenty-one and old enough to buy beer. Except for you and me." He paused a moment. "Does that make us the chaperons?"

Blue ignored the question, took a handful of pretzels and leaned against the counter, looking out across the bar at the enthusiastic group of party-goers. "I can't remember ever being so young...even at twenty."

Tad propped his elbows on the countertop beside her. "I doubt they'd like hearing you say that. Ellie considers herself an adult and, therefore, your contemporary."

"*Your* contemporary, maybe. Ellie's made it quite clear she believes I'm well over the hill."

Tad laughed. "Twenty-year-olds can be incredibly tactless. So can twenty-seven-year-olds. How old are you, Blue? Or does it bother you to tell your age?"

"It never bothered me before I met Ellie. I'm thirty-three, old enough to know better than to agree to come to this party."

"You came because you knew it would mean a lot to Ellie and because you couldn't bear the thought of another evening with only Aunt Grizelle and Uncle Horse for company."

Blue raised her eyebrows and bit into a pretzel. "I've noticed you've made your company pretty scarce lately. You disappear right after supper and don't surface again until morning."

"I have work to do," he said noncommittally. "I'm trying to polish my memo-writing skills."

"Can we call a truce on the memo jokes? I've decided I'm not going to write any more."

"Oh, no. What will we do without them?"

Blue shook her head. "You seem to have an enormous capacity for finding entertainment. I doubt you'll suffer a great deal."

"Arguments can spur creativity, you know."

"They also spur a lot of hard feelings. I don't want to fight you, Tad." She gave a soft, mirthless laugh and turned her attention to Ellie and the other dancers in the middle of the room.

"Come on, you deadbeats!" Ellie called, waving to them in hot-pink splendor from amidst the gyrating dancers. "Are you two going to prop up that kitchen counter all night long?"

Tad set his root beer can on the counter with a clink. "I know a challenge when I hear one. Do you dance?"

"What do you mean *do I dance?*" Blue said. "Do you want to know if I *can* dance or if I *want* to?"

"Write me a memo on the subject, would you?" Tad said, walking around the counter and out of the kitchen. On the other side of the bar he leaned toward her. "If you're not out here in thirty seconds, I'm telling these kids you're too old to appreciate their kind of music."

When he put it like that, Blue didn't feel he'd left her much of an option. "You asked for it," she said as she joined him on the party side of the bar. "Roll up the rug...and no matter what kind of dance step I do, pretend you recognize it."

"What makes you think I won't recognize any step you can do?" Tad grinned and extended his hand to her. "Do I look like a fuddy-duddy? Come on. We'll show these youngsters how to trip the light fantastic!"

Blue did things on the dance floor she didn't know she could do. Somehow, in the center of all the activity, in the midst of a group of people with whom she'd thought she had nothing in common, partnered with a man who argued with her on a regular basis at the office, Blue danced her heart out. And she had a lot of fun doing it. Was it the way Tad smiled at her and dared her to mimic the steps he made up? Was it all the laughter, all the vibrant life sounds she'd missed out on lately? Was she simply releasing a year's worth of tensions and frustrations?

Whatever the reason, Blue knew she'd pay a price tomorrow. Her body wasn't used to this much exercise. Her ears weren't accustomed to the throbbing bass and blazing guitars blaring through the stereo speakers. And her feet...oh, her feet.

Fifteen minutes after the apartment manager warned them about the noise for the fourth time, Blue found herself a place to sit and slipped off her shoes. Tad was dancing with Angel...or Wendy. Blue still hadn't gotten all the names straight, and the girls both had long, silky hair and long, shapely legs and enough of a resemblance to cause confusion. Tad certainly looked like he was having a good time. Of course, the only time she'd ever seen him when he didn't look that way was when he was arguing with her.

Her lighthearted mood shifted suddenly, tipping her back toward the depression of the past few months. She hadn't realized how much the experiences at McKinley Enterprises had changed her. She hadn't realized how very long it had been since she'd laughed aloud, since she'd really and truly enjoyed herself. Probably not once in the past year. Certainly not since the situation with Rob had started to grow to monstrous proportions.

"Want me to rub your feet?" Dewayne, one of the boys whose name Blue did remember, knelt in front of her and took her foot between his palms. "I'm real good at this. After I get through with you, you'll feel like a new woman."

"You're right. I feel better already." Blue tried to slip her foot away from his massaging palms as politely as she could, but Dewayne didn't seem to get the message. "Really, Dewayne, my feet are fine. They're ready to dance the rest of the night away."

His smile indicated that this time the message was received. Garbled, but received. Blue tried not to sigh as he picked up her discarded shoe and placed it on her foot as if she were Cinderella and he, the prince. "Then, my sweet," he said with an absolutely straight face, "shall we dance?"

Blue did not want to dance. She didn't even want to stand up. But she had a feeling it would be easier to gyrate with Dewayne for three minutes than to try to tell him to get lost. Unfortunately the music changed to a ballad...the dreaded, anticipated *slow* dance, and Dewayne, with a grin as big as any lecher's, swept Blue into his arms.

"I've been wanting to do this all night," he whispered in her ear. "You're a very sexy woman, Miss Garrison."

Blue rolled her eyes. Oh, brother. "Thank you, Dewayne. That's quite a . . . compliment."

That seemed to encourage, rather than discourage him. His hands slid an inch closer to her hips, his breath came a little closer to her shoulders. "I'm not joking you. I mean it. I asked Ellie if you were dating that guy you came with . . . what's his name?"

"Tad Denton," Blue answered.

"Tad. That's it. Well, I told Ellie you were too much woman for him. I've always preferred older women. They're more mature. More experienced. More . . . *everything.*" Dewayne's lips landed on her neck. His hands slipped to her hips and Blue shifted her knee in preparation for a discretionary admonition.

"Change partners, Dewayne. Angel wants to dance with you. Right now." Tad's voice brought up Dewayne's head and startled Blue. She hadn't known Tad was anywhere nearby. Of course, with Dewayne's head buried in her neck she hadn't been able to see anything except his masses of curly, brown hair. Actually she'd been kind of looking forward to setting Dewayne straight on the etiquette of slow dancing with "mature" partners. It was a lesson she didn't think he would have forgotten anytime soon. But Tad had barged in, protecting her as if she were Ellie's age, too inexperienced to know how to cool down a hot-blooded lothario.

"I could have handled that," she said as Tad danced her away from the grumbling Dewayne. "You didn't have to rescue me."

"He was pawing you." Tad said in his own defense.

"Yes," Blue agreed, discovering to her dismay that she liked being in Tad's arms, liked being held tightly against his chest, liked moving in rhythm with his steps. He made dancing seem so effortless, and she had the oddest impulse to lay her head against his shoulder and sigh with pleasure. She dragged her thoughts back to the discussion at hand. "Dewayne *was* pawing me. And I'm quite capable of stopping that sort of thing . . . when I choose."

Tad didn't stop dancing, but his attitude took on a sudden chill. "Are you trying to tell me you enjoyed that?"

"No. I'm telling you I can take care of myself. I don't need a man to rescue me."

Tad released a long-held breath. "Maybe I didn't do it for you, Blue. Maybe the need to step in was all on my side."

"Oh, I see. You're a chivalrous kind of guy. Is that it?"

"I don't think chivalry had much to do with it, either."

Blue started to laugh, but something stopped her. He hadn't meant that. Had he? Tad wasn't actually trying to say he'd felt . . . jealous? But why else would he have felt the need to step in? Jealous? No. The idea was silly. Worse than silly. It was ridiculous. Absurd. Completely absurd.

"You know, Tad. For a moment there, you had me going. I almost thought you were serious."

He looked down at her, swept her around the corner in the final throes of the slow dance, but he didn't say a word and he didn't laugh. Blue was glad when he released her from his arms, but the feeling fled as Wendy pulled him back onto the dance floor to dance to a wild rock and roll number.

With a cool glance Blue fended off Dewayne's next move and returned to the sidelines to rest her feet and watch the party. The exchange with Tad had unsettled her, made her uncomfortably aware of a tension she didn't want to name. Dancing with him, held close in his arms, had brought out feelings she did not want to face. Watching him with Wendy generated emotions she did not want to recognize.

The music changed, but Tad didn't change partners. Rock and roll gave way to a Latin beat and the dance became a series of graceful, sensual movements. With her long blond hair and her long shapely legs, Wendy brought a mixture of innocence and worldly appeal to the steps. But Tad....

Tad made it look like seduction.

Blue watched in fascination. Other couples were doing the same steps with the same intense expressions, the same sexy moves, the same in-sync rhythm. No one else seemed to notice Tad and his partner. None of those who weren't dancing paid the slightest attention to any of it. But Blue couldn't seem to shift her attention from Tad and the sensual swaying of his body. The dance made her restless, discontented and—much as she hated to admit it—envious.

She was envious of the youth and the innocence and the great expectations represented on that dance floor. Ellie, Wendy, Angel, and the other young women had all of life stretching in front of them. Each had every right to expect a man like Tad to fall in love with her, to marry her, to share the next fifty years with her. And Blue was suddenly conscious of her own biological clock and the empty years stretching in front of her.

"Whew! Is that one *hot* dance or am I just naturally overheated?" Ellie plopped into the seat next to Blue and shook her hand to emphasize just how hot the dance was. "Tad is really good, isn't he? Everybody wants to dance with him." Ellie giggled. "The girls, I mean. The boys don't think he's all that great. At least, they never want to dance with him. Why did you let Wendy snag him away from you, anyway? You could have been out there with him right now. I mean, let's face it, this is one *hot* dance."

"Tad seems to be very good at it." Blue made the observation blandly, as if he'd been doing the polka, as if Ellie might believe Blue had paid no attention to the intricacies and innuendos of the dance. "He must get a lot of practice."

Ellie collapsed in the throes of a giant, pink giggle. "Practice," she sputtered. "I know a couple of girls who'd love to 'practice' that dance with Tad. In public or in private...if you know what I mean."

Blue did know, even without the benefit of Ellie's insinuating elbow in her ribcage, but she didn't think the subject was worthy of discussion. And despite all of that, she couldn't keep from asking Ellie for some personal information about Tad. "Does Tad date anyone special?"

"Not that I know of." Ellie's eyelashes batted up and down. "Why? Are you interested?"

"Don't be silly, Ellie. I was just curious."

"Mmm-hmm."

Blue wished she hadn't opened her mouth...and Ellie's mind. The possibility of anything romantic happening between her and Tad was about as likely as a balanced federal budget. The possibility of even a *friendly* relationship with Tad was remote. Blue wasn't interested. No matter how sexy he'd looked on the dance floor.

Ellie turned the subject to Jim Bill and the wedding, which would be "sometime in the future." Not a moment too soon for Ellie, who had dreams and plans enough for a lifetime. Blue decided that at some time in the future, when Ellie wasn't dressed in pink tights, she would bring up the subject of higher education and the myriad of choices—other than marriage—that were available to young women in this day and age.

"You two look as thick as thieves. What's going on?" Tad pulled up a chair beside Ellie's. His face showed no sign of physical exertion, no clue to the dramatic intensity of the dance he'd just danced.

Blue admired his stamina. "Ellie's telling me about Jim Bill and the wedding."

"My favorite subjects," Tad drawled. "How come you're still awake, Blue? When Ellie starts talking about the magnificent Jimmy, I usually doze right off."

Ellie slapped his arm playfully. "Just for that I ought to tell Blue the long list of broken hearts you've left behind you. She was real impressed with your *dancin'* ability, I can tell you for sure."

Tad turned a spicy-brown gaze to Blue, and his lips curved just enough to create a funny feeling in the pit of her stomach. "Don't tell me I've been wasting all that time trying to impress you with my memos when all I had to do was *dance?*"

"Ellie exaggerates." A faint heat rose to Blue's cheeks and she turned away, hoping it didn't show.

"I do not," Ellie defended herself. "At least, not much. And you are the best dancer here, Tad. You know you are."

"I know my body is telling me to stop before my muscles embarrass me by creaking and groaning loud enough for everyone to hear. Are you ready to leave, Blue? We do have to work tomorrow, you know."

Blue couldn't resist a pointed comment. "Luckily we don't have to be at the office until whenever we decide to show up."

"I knew you'd learn to like our way of doing things sooner or later."

Ellie turned her head from one to the other. "Hey," she said. "I have to go to work in the morning, too."

Tad smiled as he stood. "Yes, Ellie, we know you'll be there ready to work by eight o'clock on the dot."

Ellie looked confused. "Eight? I wasn't planning to get up *that* early."

Blue patted Ellie's shoulder. "Tad's just teasing you, Ellie. I'm sure whatever time you do get there will be perfectly all right with everyone. Thanks for inviting me to the party. I had a nice time."

Tad repeated the amenities, accepted Wendy's special good-night kiss on the cheek and walked out of the rec room into the balmy June night with Blue. The noise from the party followed them all the way to the parking lot. "You survived," Tad said as he unlocked the car door. "And it wasn't nearly as bad as you expected, was it?"

"There were moments I really did enjoy."

"One of them being when you were dancing with Dewayne?"

"That was a high point, although dancing with you ran a close second."

"Thanks. I enjoyed dancing with you, too. Nothing like a little rock music to get the old blood pumping."

Her blood felt older than Methuselah at the moment, but her heart was definitely pumping. Faster, really, than it should have been, considering that she had only watched the last dance. "You seemed quite at home with Ellie's friends," Blue said when Tad was seated next to her in the car. "Do you 'party down' with them often?"

"You may not believe this, but I'm not much of a party animal."

"Then where did you learn to dance like that?"

He gave her a little smile as he turned the ignition. "There's a dancing bear at the zoo. I picked up the steps from him."

"Does he have a partner?"

"Why? Are you in need of some lessons?"

Blue sighed. It was pointless to try to get one up on T. A. Denton. "If I'm invited to any more of Ellie's parties, I may need breathing lessons. It's an energetic group."

"And loud." Tad drove out of the parking lot of the apartment complex and turned toward home. "Every time I let Ellie talk me into going to one of these things, I swear I won't do it again. But as you said, it does have its moments."

"I'm actually glad I went. It's been a long time since I did much socializing."

"What was wrong with the men in—where did you come from, anyway, Blue?"

"San Diego."

"That would have been my first guess. You look like a California girl."

For some unfathomable reason, that pleased Blue. "How could you tell?"

"It's the way you walk...as if you have sand under your toes."

Blue wondered if Tad took anything, besides the office memos she wrote, seriously. "Thanks for telling me that, Tad. I probably needed to know."

"You're welcome," he said. "You didn't answer my question, though. Why didn't you socialize with the men in California?"

"It had nothing to do with the men in California, Tad. I spent most of my time working, and that didn't leave much room for socializing."

"You've really missed out on a lot of fun, haven't you, Blue? No mud pies, no kite flying, no parties."

"Wait." Blue held up a hand. "If you're getting ready to quote something about 'all work and no play,' you can save your breath. I'm a nineties' woman. I work because I like it, because I *choose* to do so."

Tad shot her a skeptical glance. "So, are you saying it was your *choice* to come to Grizelle Gadget and Toy Company and filch half of my job?"

The question unsettled her somewhat, but Blue decided not to lodge a protest and get another argument started. Instead she sighed. "Tad, do you know that since I met you, I have sighed more times than I can count? And that isn't like me. I'm not a sigher."

"Maybe you're really a laugher and you're just sighing to confuse the people around you."

With a shake of her head Blue turned her attention to the traffic merging and shifting on and off the highway. She had laughed tonight. She had forgotten for a while that she had nothing to laugh about.

Tad had thought he'd had her going there for a moment. He'd actually thought she might give out some information about the life she'd left behind and her reason for moving to Dallas. But Blue obviously didn't want to share her past . . . or her present. At least, not with him.

He watched for the exit which would take them to Irving and ultimately home. She probably wouldn't say much of anything else tonight. The vivacious Blue who had laughed and danced at Ellie's party had succumbed to the serious Blue who took every little thing as if it made some huge difference in the overall scheme of life. Tad liked the woman he'd held in his arms for a while this evening. And that surprised him more than anything. If anyone had told him he would be attracted to the bossy brunette, he'd have told them they'd have better odds on winning the lottery.

But he'd have been wrong. There was more to Blue Garrison than met the eye. More than he could see from a memo, either. She'd struck a chord with him tonight. She'd even brought out a protective instinct he'd thought he would never feel again.

Jealousy. For a few minutes, he'd actually been jealous of a long-haired kid with evangelistic hormones. Tad wasn't proud of himself. Jealousy was never a welcome emotion. And it sure as hell wasn't the reaction of a mature man. But he'd acted on it, nonetheless, surprising Blue almost as much as he'd surprised himself.

He shouldn't have interfered. He should have let her handle the situation.

On the other hand he'd learned something valuable. His emotions weren't dead. Feeling jealous wasn't anything he wanted to brag about, but it did indicate that he was still capable of caring about a woman. And that alone, as they said, was worth the price of admission.

"Do you have a steady girlfriend, Tad?" Blue couldn't believe she'd asked that. She'd been sitting there thinking about the evening, about Ellie, about the others, and suddenly the words were in her mouth and hitting the airwaves. "Never mind," she said hastily. "That's none of my business."

He looked at her as if considering why she'd asked the question. "I don't date a whole lot, Blue, if that's what you wanted to know. But...if you wanted to become a janitor, I might consider asking you out."

She should have expected that from him. He turned everything into a joke. "What is it, Tad?" she asked, deciding she might as well treat the subject as lightly as he had. "Do you have something against female vice presidents?"

"Only one."

"How many do you know?"

"You're it, Blue, baby. The one and only."

Blue decided to take a probably fatal step. "Don't you think it's time we progressed past the point of arguing about who should have had this job and make a few in-roads on the job itself?''

''Don't tell me you want to be treated like a...like a...*partner* all of a sudden?''

''It might make both of us more productive.''

His pause lasted through a stop light and two left turns. ''I'm willing to try,'' he said finally. ''Do you want late shift or early shift?''

''You want to be productive in shifts?''

''I want to set up a surveillance in the building at night. I thought you might be willing to help.''

''A surveillance? What for? Do you want to see if the shoemaker's elves come in at night and leave shiny new toys all assembled the next morning?''

''Ah, ah, ah. Be careful with that attitude, Blue. You're the one who suggested we should act like partners.'' He signaled another turn and waited for the traffic to clear. ''Do you remember the boxes of Tater Tossers I thought had been moved? Well, the other day I found a soft drink can in the trash container beside Zeke's station.''

Blue waited for the significance of that to sink in. It didn't. ''So what?''

''We may be flexible on a lot of rules, but we're adamant about keeping food and drink away from that computer. Especially soft drinks. One spill could ruin years of work. True, it might mean nothing. Someone might have carried an empty can downstairs and tossed it in the trash. But I don't know. Something doesn't feel right to me, Blue. I can't put my finger on what it is, but I can't shake the feeling, either.''

''So you want to stay in the building and see if anything happens?''

''Do you have a better idea?''

This was not what she'd had in mind when she'd suggested they work together instead of against each other, but she was willing to discuss it. "Are you sure this is necessary, Tad? I don't mind helping, but I thought we had a security guard for this sort of thing. Franklin. Isn't that his name?"

"That's him. Uncle Horse's token security blanket." Tad pulled into the long drive that led to the house and the apartments beyond. "I've tried to get Uncle Horse to put in a sophisticated alarm system, but Franklin's been around for a long time and your uncle just doesn't see a need to change the status quo."

"Changes, obviously, aren't Uncle Horse's long suit." Blue smothered a yawn and wearily combed a strand of hair back from her temple. "I've about decided this whole place is caught in a time warp."

"How can you say that, after hearing all that modern music and dancing all those modern steps like you did at Ellie's party?"

"I'm already paying for those dances, thank you." Blue smiled lazily and gathered her purse strap in her hand as Tad parked the car. She opened the door and stepped out of the car at the same time he did and they walked in silence, side by side, to the pool house. "Good night, Tad. See you tomorrow at work...unless you have a date with a dancing bear."

He stopped and turned to her in the dark. "Blue? Now that we're partners...I think you should consider dropping that 'big sister' tone of voice. It may, one day, get you into trouble."

"Trouble?" Blue laughed, finding it hard to believe he was serious. "And what kind of trouble would that be, Tad?"

He stood there for a second, deliberating, and Blue's heart began to pound a slow, unsteady beat. He was teasing her again. Wasn't he?

But when he stepped forward, put his hands on her shoulders and pulled her into a brief, but persuasive kiss, she knew for certain he was serious. Her knees practically buckled beneath her, he was so serious. She had to try hard to look offended and not simply stunned when he stepped back and dropped his arms to his sides.

"I am not your brother, Blue. And I'm not some kid who wants to nuzzle your neck while we dance. From now on I'd just as soon you stopped thinking of me as harmless." He smiled then...a small, rakish sort of smile. "Good night, partner. Watch out for me in your dreams."

Chapter Six

"Good morning, Blue. Your mail has arrived." Zeke's metallic whine and electronic whir invaded the quiet of the office, and Blue half turned from the window as Zeke deposited a few envelopes and a couple of catalogs on her desk. She was surprised and pleased there was that much mail for her. Her long hours of market research were starting to pay off in information. Up till now, most of Zeke's trips to her office had been just trial runs.

The robot completed his mission and turned toward the door. *"Goodbye, Blue. The next delivery will be—hiccup—will be—hiccup—will be—hiccup—"* Zeke hit the door frame and bounced away. Once...twice...

Alarmed, Blue moved quickly toward the robot.

"Tad!" Ellie yelled from the outer office. "Zeke's stuck in Blue's doorway. You'd better come and get him."

There was a flurry of sound from the office next door, and then Tad skidded to a halt in front of the bouncing robot. One glance and Tad bent, caught the robot on a forward rebound and switched him off. The robot stopped abruptly, his motor winding down with a soft whir. Tad rocked back on his heels and frowned at Blue who stood a couple of feet away. "What happened?" he asked.

"I don't know." She slipped her hands into the pockets of her skirt. "It put the mail on my desk, turned around to leave and then all of a sudden it started acting like this."

"Poor Zeke," Ellie said as she arrived on the scene. "What happened to him? He was fine just a minute ago."

Blue took a step closer, wanting to remove any doubt that she might have had something to do with the robot's malfunction. "Zeke delivered my mail and the next thing I knew it was bumping the wall and sounding like a broken record."

Ellie looked at Blue suspiciously. "You didn't call him a—" she glanced around as if someone might overhear "—*r-o-b-o-t*, did you?"

"I didn't say a word to it." Blue's attention shifted to Tad's face and his rueful consideration of the little gadget. "Do you know what's wrong?"

Tad pushed to his feet. "I could make a guess, but I won't know for sure until I can get him downstairs. Ellie? Would you get a couple of the guys from Prototype to bring up a dolly and give me a hand?"

"You betcha." Ellie walked to her desk and picked up the intercom. In a moment Tad's message was passed on to the Prototype section of the company and help was on the way.

Blue stood still, not knowing what to say or do. Zeke was a robot, and she couldn't bring herself to feel any deep-rooted concern over the prognosis. On the other hand she didn't want to appear uncaring. So she covertly studied Tad while his attention was focused fully on the robot.

It was the first time she'd seen him all morning. The first time since last night when he'd left her thoroughly kissed and thoroughly confused on the doorstep of her apartment. Her lips tingled with the memory though she had promised herself she would not think about it again. She'd

thought about it more than enough already. There was no
need to obsess over it. Tad had proved his point. There was
a certain chemistry between them. He wasn't entirely
harmless. And she would not be so careless about what she
said to him in the future.

"What are you going to do with it?" she asked just to
divert her thoughts.

"Hook him up to the main computer. Go into his pro-
grams and try to find out what went wrong." He gave Zeke
one last frown and then turned his attention toward Blue.
Her mouth went suddenly dry.

"You were up early this morning," he said. "Couldn't
sleep? Something on your mind?"

"Too much to do here at the office." Blue arched an
eyebrow, daring him to contradict her. She knew that he
thought she had next to nothing to do at the office, and she
saw no reason to dissuade him from that notion before she
finished gathering her ammunition. "I can't afford to sleep
all morning . . . as some employees can."

It was a pointed remark and Tad acknowledged the hit
with a nod. "Yes, well, some of us can do twice the work
in half the time. It's not fair, I admit it, but that's life here
at Grizelle Gadget and Toy."

Blue leaned against the corner of her desk and crossed
her arms low at her waist. She wanted to say something—
anything—about last night. It seemed only fair to set the
record straight, to tell him she thought his behavior had
been unprofessional and unbecoming . . . speaking strictly
as one vice president to another. Just a bit of friendly advice that in the future he should treat her as a co-worker,
not as a woman. But all she could do was look at him and
think about the fact that he had kissed her less than twelve
hours ago.

"Tad!" Ellie's voice boomed in the small space of the reception area. "The boys are here. Hey, Joe. Hey, Bobby." She called greetings as two men stepped past the entryway and rolled a dolly to the doorway of Blue's office.

"Hey, Ellie," one of the men said.

"Hey." The other man dropped his chin to his chest and lifted his hand in a shy wave.

"Thanks for coming up to help, guys," Tad said, moving immediately to the robot. "Let's get him on that dolly and downstairs."

Blue sat watching as the men loaded the robot and wheeled it out of the room. She listened to their comments, the male camaraderie of shop talk. "Could be a wire shorted out." "Nah, more likely it's a bad component. Or, you know, the power pack might not be fully charged for some reason." "I had a problem once with a computerized toy truck and the whole thing boiled down to power pack. Just went bad. Just stopped—"

The voices faded as the glass doors closed behind them and Ellie began talking on the phone. "Wendy? Yeah, Ellie. Wasn't that a great party last night? I had, like, the most fun. I thought we might get together at Daryl's apartment tonight, play some records. You know, just hang out. No, I don't think Tad will come. I'll ask him, but I wouldn't count on him, if I were you. Wait. Did I tell you about Lynette Wilson sending him flowers? I didn't? Well..."

Blue moved back to her desk and wished she had the nerve to close her office door. But that would create an "incident" with Ellie, and Blue did not want to deal with that. Ellie's chatter really wasn't all that distracting. It probably wouldn't have bothered Blue at all... if the conversation hadn't been about Tad.

Tad.

No. She was not going to think about him anymore. She was going to file the memory of his kiss away. Under things to forget. She'd concentrate on continuing her study of the company. She was still trying to define her "area of interest" and make the contribution Uncle Horse expected of her. The contribution she expected of herself.

Grizelle was certainly a crazy, mixed up, insane place to work. The employees did seem to be busy with something or other all of the time. And often when she spent time in the playroom, there would be a new toy or gadget on the shelves. But there were no regular reports and often no black and white stats of what idea was under production, who was working on what and when the project would be completed. She'd started to put together some standard forms that would be loose enough to cover almost any project, but detailed enough to help her and the marketing staff get a feel for what might be coming their way.

McKinley Enterprises would have closed down in a matter of hours if Rob had allowed supervision to become as lax as it was here at the toy company. But then Rob believed in keeping his thumb pressed to the pulse of his employees. Nothing went on in his company that he didn't know about sooner or later. Uncle Horse seemed happy to trust his employees' judgment and instincts.

Rob had had files thick with information and knew more about his employees' personal lives than he had any right to know. Blue had even helped gather information for those files, herself. Thinking about it now, she was sorry that she'd done that. But at the time she'd wanted to prove herself to Rob so badly it hadn't occurred to her to refuse.

With a sigh Blue picked up her mail and sorted through it. Several toy catalogs. Another selling office supplies. One selling lingerie. A notice of a seminar on marketing.

A solicitation letter with a mass-produced label addressed to the vice president and a letter from a credit card company offering to issue her, Blue Garrison, a new and greater credit limit. Blue tossed everything except the toy catalogs and seminar notice in the trash and settled in her chair to continue her market research.

In comparison, Tad's dart board was beginning to look tempting.

TAD LEANED BACK in the chair and frowned at the computer screen. There were lines of programming missing from Zeke's memory. The codes just flat weren't there anymore. If it had been only one line, maybe even several in the same sector, he might have decided it was a glitch, a malfunction somewhere in Zeke's computer itself. But this was random. A line missing here. Another line missing there. And Tad simply couldn't visualize any computer problem that would have resulted in such an illogical pattern of deleted lines.

Someone had tampered with Zeke's program. Someone with enough computer know-how to be dangerous. Someone who had no business being anywhere near the robot.

Zeke was a complex mix of computer-driven robotics, but his access code was simple. A number of the employees knew how to program data into Zeke's memory, how to update commands, how to utilize the robot in developing new ideas. That was Zeke's purpose. The robot was a tool. An expensive tool, to be sure, but Tad had never been possessive or overly protective of his invention. And until just now, he'd never felt there was any danger that the robot would be misused.

But if there was another explanation, Tad didn't know what it might be. Someone, at some time during the past twenty-four hours, had gotten into Zeke's memory banks and deleted part of his programming. It could have been an accident, he supposed. But the employees who used Zeke's capabilities knew exactly how and what to do with the sophisticated computer. None of them could have—or would have—deleted programming data accidentally without telling him.

Tad pushed back his chair abruptly and took a turn at pacing the room. No other explanations occurred to him. He'd have to talk to the employees who might have used Zeke during the past couple of days. He'd ask Franklin if anyone had stayed late the night before or if anything unusual had occurred. Not that Franklin was likely to remember, but Tad felt he had to ask the questions. He supposed he'd have to mention this to Uncle Horse, too.

Damn it. He supposed he'd have to discuss this with Blue, too. She *was*, after all, a vice president, even though she hadn't as yet completely defined what her position would be at Grizelle Gadget and Toy Company. But she was smart and soon she'd find a project that captured her time and attention. She'd find her own area of interest and, if she stayed long enough, she'd make her niche in the company.

But at the moment she was more of a hindrance to Tad than a help. And now that Zeke was involved, Tad wished he hadn't mentioned the possibility of surveillance to Blue. When it was just boxes moved a few feet here and there, a few papers rearranged on the computer desk beside Zeke's station, a file drawer left open and the contents shuffled around, a soft drink can in the trash receptacle...well, that was one thing. But now someone had tampered with valuable equipment, and the situation seemed a bit more serious.

Tad spun on his heel and reversed the direction of his pacing. Okay. So he'd tell Uncle Horse and Blue that someone had been fooling with Zeke's memory bank. Uncle Horse would worry. Blue would probably just come up with some new policy to monitor and restrict employee access to Zeke. Nothing would be accomplished, but Tad, really, had no choice. Last night Blue had said she wanted the two of them to get along better, to make the most of the position they shared.

Last night Blue had made an overture.

And then, so had he.

Tad raked his fingers through his hair at the memory. What had possessed him? Why on earth had he kissed her? Sure, he didn't like being treated as a kid brother. He didn't like the idea that Blue tried to lump him into Ellie's crowd. And most of all he didn't like... how that one kiss had made him feel.

Damn it. He didn't need this now. Especially not with a woman like Blue Garrison. It had been a long time since he'd been attracted to a woman. Oh, he'd dated some, but no one special. No one he would have considered having a relationship with. Hell, he hadn't even had much of an interest in sex for the past five years. It seemed Lindy had taken that part of his life with her when she'd left him.

He'd known that sooner or later he'd be attracted to another woman. But why now? And why Blue? And why had he started everything by kissing her?

Tad tried to dismiss the question, tried to erase the memory of how her soft lips had felt under his. He did not need this now. He had other things on his mind, other problems to tackle. And yet, when he closed his eyes, all he could see were Blue's green eyes looking at him with surprise, and all he could think of was the way his heartbeat had quickened as he'd bent to kiss her and the way he'd wanted to go on kissing her.

With a sound of disgust, Tad forced himself back to the computer desk. He would reprogram Zeke's memory, replace the missing data . . . and hope to high heaven that in the process he lost a few of his own disturbing memory cells along the way.

BLUE TURNED OFF the water and stepped into the tub filled with an ocean of bubbles and steam. As the delicious heat enveloped her body, she sighed with pure pleasure. She'd been waiting for this all day. Learning the toy business from the ground up was exhausting work.

She shook her head and ran damp fingers through her hair to loosen the waves. The steam from the bath was already coaxing her natural curl into ringlets that she'd have to work and work to brush out later. Her mother had hated curls, and Blue could remember sitting in beauty salons for what had seemed like hours to get the too-tight wave straightened. One of many things about her appearance on which she and her mother had disagreed.

Of course, if she'd had straight-as-a-string hair and her mother had wanted her to wear it curly, she'd have decided to wear it straight just for the aggravation value. But if her dad had ever stated a preference one way or the other. . . .

Blue fished through the water and retrieved a wash cloth. She leaned her head against the back of the tub and wondered why it had always seemed so important that her father notice her accomplishments and why she'd never felt as if she measured up to his expectations. He was such a dynamic man. So unlike Uncle Horse. So much like Rob McKinley.

Blue combed her fingers through her damp curls and remembered all the times she'd fantasized about the children she would one day have and the beautifully straight, beautifully blond hair they would have. Hair like Rob's.

Oh, she'd known it was a fantasy. But a harmless one, she'd thought. No one else would ever know the dreams she'd indulged in in private moments.

Now the memory of all those foolish thoughts rose to haunt her like some specter from a bad movie. And along with the memory came the guilt. The horrible guilt. She'd been the "other woman" in a love triangle. She'd been innocent, but in a way she'd been guilty, too. And whenever she remembered the awful scene with Jessica, Rob's wife...

Blue heard the phone ring in Tad's apartment and the rumbling sound of his voice as he answered. She moved, stretching lazily, catching her reflection in the mirror tiles that lined the tub. She could see the whole room reflected in those tiles, from the iridescent bubbles in her bath water to Tad's shaving supplies which took up one whole side of the counter beside the sink. His razor, his shaving cream, his toothbrush, his hairbrush.

He'd taken a shower not thirty minutes ago, and a pair of faded jeans and the turquoise shirt he'd worn at work that day hung from a hook on the door leading to his apartment. The scent of his cologne still clung to the fabric, and Blue kept catching whiffs of the fragrance. She liked his cologne, but she didn't much care for the erotic images it evoked in her otherwise well-ordered mind. And she definitely didn't like the intimacy of being forced to share his bathroom.

For probably the thousandth time since she'd moved into this duplex bungalow, she wondered what madness had possessed her when she'd agreed to take part in this arrangement.

All things considered, it actually hadn't been too much of an inconvenience. Except she was completely and constantly conscious of Tad's presence in the other apartment and she made absolutely sure she didn't go anywhere near this connecting room unless she was positive he wasn't in it. There had been a few moments of distress, but all things considered, there was no real contact between one apartment and the other. She tried not to acknowledge that there was any connection at all between the two units.

"Blue? Are you in there?" Tad tapped on the connecting door at that moment, completely ruining her mental scenario of isolated compatibility and totally destroying her composure.

She sank into bubbles up to her chin and groped for the lost washcloth. "Yes, Tad. I'll be out in a little while."

"Could you just hand out my jeans? I left something in the pocket."

Blue spread the washcloth over her chest as if somehow that might make her feel less vulnerable. "I'm in the bath, Tad. I'll be out in ten minutes or so. And I won't forget to unlock the door on your side when I leave." She'd done that a number of times, resulting in a few of the minor distresses. "Give me a couple more minutes."

"I need them now, Blue."

He could darn well wait, Blue thought, because until she had some clothes on, there was no way she was going to unlock that door. "You'll just have to wait," she said, though she could almost feel the intensity of his frown through the closed door.

"Blue, for Pete's sake. Just unlock the door and I'll reach inside and get my jeans. I won't even look inside the room. If it makes you feel any better, I'll keep my eyes shut, too. Now, please..."

"I can't reach the door from here." The mirrors would reflect the whole room in a glance and she knew good and well he would not keep his eyes shut. Nothing was so urgent that it couldn't wait ten minutes . . . or even fifteen.

He tapped on the door panel. "Blue, this is important. Open the door."

She'd be darned if she would let him bully her into rushing through what should have been fifteen or twenty minutes of relaxation. "I'm taking a bath. When I'm through, you can come in here, but not before. Now, go away."

Tad clenched his hands and quelled the urge to yell something ungentlemanly through the door. What did she think? That he wanted to get in the bathroom just to have a good look at her? He only wanted his jeans, for heaven's sake. And more precisely, the car keys in the jeans' pocket. He had to have them and he had to have them now. He raised his fist and rapped on the door again. "Blue? I have to have my car keys. Please open the door."

A splash of water met his appeal, but as it was followed by silence, he decided she was ignoring him. So much for simple courtesy. He supposed he'd have to explain. "I've got to get to the toy company, Blue. Franklin just phoned and I need to get right down there."

"What's wrong?" she asked, scrambling out of the tub and reaching for her towel. "Did someone break into the building?"

"I don't know. That's why I'm going down to check it out." Tad found he really didn't like yelling through the door. "Blue, if you don't unlock this door and hand out my keys in the next thirty seconds, I'm going to kick it in."

His last words were met with stubborn silence and Tad wondered why he'd made such a dumb threat. Under the current living conditions, taking out that door would be sheer idiocy. There was an extra key to the bathroom somewhere, but he hadn't had any use for it in so long he couldn't remember where it was. He'd thought about it on the couple of occasions when she'd locked him out of the bathroom, but he hadn't had to search for it at the time. Now, he supposed was the ideal time to locate it. He'd just turned away from the door, when he heard the jingling sounds that indicated Blue was, finally, getting his keys.

He waited impatiently, recalling the excited undercurrent in Franklin's voice when he'd told Tad about finding an unsecured window into the basement. Franklin didn't get excited very often and that, in itself, made Tad anxious. He didn't even want to think about what might happen if Franklin actually came face to face with trouble.

Tad put his hand on the doorknob, anticipating getting the keys and getting on his way.

"Tad?" Blue said from behind the closed door. "I've got your keys. I'll meet you at your car in five minutes."

"What? No. Blue, give me those keys."

"I'm sorry, Tad. This is an executive decision. I'm as much responsible for Grizelle's as you are and if there's something wrong in the building, then I have as much right to be there as you do."

Tad groaned. "Were you this much of a problem at your last job?" The only answer he got was the sound of the flip of the metal lever that would drain the water out of the tub. Great, he thought. Just great. Now he'd not only have to deal with Franklin and his Southern-sheriff routine, he'd have to keep an eye on his co-vice president as well. And all that after he'd put in a tiring day, worrying over what had happened to Zeke and trying to correct the errors.

Blue hadn't seemed all that concerned when he'd told her about the programming deletions. As he'd expected, she'd immediately suggested he should have some sort of record of who operated Zeke and when. But other than that she hadn't said a whole lot. So why was she determined to interfere now?

Tad left his apartment without bothering to close the door behind him. Maybe while he was gone, his fairy godmother would arrive on the scene and build another bathroom. He could only hope.

Blue came out of her apartment just as Tad was trying to recall the way to hot-wire a car. She carefully closed her front door and locked it before turning toward the covered carport where she and Tad parked their respective cars. "See," she said as she approached. "I made it in five minutes. Probably less."

Tad extended his hand for the keys and tried not to stare at Blue's mass of dark curls. "What happened to your hair?"

Her hand went immediately and self-consciously to the damp curls. "This is its natural state. I didn't take time to fix it. Does it look too awful? Will I scare Franklin to death?"

It was the first time Tad had seen any clear evidence of insecurity in Blue. Usually she was so together, so mantled in self-confidence that it was hard to tell if she ever doubted herself or her abilities.

"I like it," he said simply, with a great deal less enthusiasm than he actually felt. The truth was Blue looked very pretty and far too...approachable at the moment. She was fresh from the bath, and the fragrance of bath oils clung to her skin and teased him with its floral scent. And last night . . . last night he'd kissed her.

Tad bent to unlock the car door with renewed purpose. He toyed with the idea of leaving the passenger door locked and driving away without Blue, but he knew she would only follow him in her own car. He didn't know why she wanted to tag along, but he didn't think he could stop her. And Franklin had probably exaggerated about the window, anyway. "You don't have to go with me," Tad said as Blue slid into the seat beside him. "This is probably going to turn out to be a waste of time."

"I'm going along. You never know, you might be glad to have me there."

Tad knew, despite his better judgment, that he was glad to have her company. And he had no doubt at all Franklin would be all too pleased to have Blue present. "Okay, but don't say I didn't warn you that it might be a big waste of time."

"Considering how wasting time seems to be what you think I do most these days, that shouldn't be a big problem for me." She fastened her seat belt and clasped her hands in her lap.

Tad started the car.

"I WAS WALKING outside here when I noticed it." Franklin Capranelli shot the beam of his flashlight across the shrubbery on the south side of the building. "Now you can't tell me that don't look suspicious."

It was a window and it was open. Blue leaned forward, trying to get a better look behind the shrubs.

"Now, be careful, Miss Blue. We don't want your footprints in the dirt, warning our intruder off." Franklin turned the flashlight toward the ground. "That's why I didn't walk right up there and close that window myself. In case he comes back. Didn't want to leave any clues that we're onto the burglar." He pronounced the word *boogler*, in two distinct syllables, and lifted his foot so he could tap the flashlight against the heel. "These tootsies leave a print big enough to sink a well in. Ain't that right, Tad?"

Tad frowned and glanced up at the roof of the building, then back to the ground. "And you couldn't tell if there were footprints close to the window? Anything that might indicate someone had gone in this way?"

"Well, no, not exactly. I mean the dirt looked kind of scuffed up. You know, like maybe some lightweight had been walking around behind those bushes there. Could've been somebody wearing tennis shoes, I reckon. 'Course, I didn't see no sign of tennie tread marks."

Tad nodded. "Did you look inside? Under this window? Was there any indication the window was being used as an entry point?"

"Nope," Franklin said. "Nothing I could see. That's the window by the stairs, in case you don't recall. A body would have a pretty fair drop to the floor inside, but I doubt it would break a leg or nothing like that. You want to go in and have a look around yerself?"

"That's a good idea, Franklin." Tad turned toward the corner of the building and the steps down to the basement entrance on the other side. "Let's see if we can get that window closed and locked on the inside before I leave."

"I knew you'd say that," Franklin said with a chuckle. "I already brought the ladder round."

Blue followed the two men to the back of the building. Franklin was a short, skinny little man who walked with a shuffle and talked fast. She had met him before, but only in passing, and this was her first real chance to see him in action. It was obvious, though, that Franklin Capranelli didn't see much action, although he longed for it, probably even dreamed about it. But as Tad had pointed out on the way over in the car, there had been only one break-in at Grizelle Gadget and Toy Company in the past twenty years, and that one had been a mistake. The burglar had thought he was breaking into the auto parts warehouse next door.

Blue figured that word had leaked out and the would-be thieves of the world knew that any idea stolen from her uncle's company would be too difficult to sell on the open market somewhere. Just last week Uncle Horse had tried to sell her on the idea of a new toy, some kind of plastic goop he called Crazy Gravy. She'd tried to give the idea a fair assessment, really she had, but the idea sounded disgusting to her. She'd told Uncle Horse so, and he'd listened to her before he'd asked if she thought brown or gray would be a better color. To her own surprise, she'd actually given the question serious thought.

"Watch yer step there, little lady." Franklin offered the advice as they reached the stairs which led down to the basement doorway. He bounced the flashlight beam on the stairs so Blue could see the way to the basement door. When she reached the last step, she moved forward to open the door that would let them into the building. Tad was behind her and Franklin was a couple of steps behind him as she reached for the doorknob. "That door's locked," Franklin said. "I've got the key right here."

But her hand was already on the latch and the knob had moved freely beneath her touch. "It's open." Surprised, Blue glanced over her shoulder at the men.

"I locked it myself." Franklin passed Tad to investigate at closer range. "Just before I called your place, Tad. And I met you two in the front parking lot. This door should've been safely locked up all this time."

Blue's eyes met Tad's, and at that moment something moved in the graveled area behind them. It was quick, and gravel spewed in a dusty, dusky trail. Franklin whirled around and nearly knocked Blue down as he hotfooted his way up the steps and after the intruder. Tad had a second's head start, but with the advantage of being quicker, he soon outdistanced Franklin.

Just as the chase turned back toward the building, Blue realized exactly what they were chasing.

"It's the remote-controlled car," she said and then raised her voice. "Tad! It's the remote-controlled car!"

Tad slowed as he, too, got a clear look at the racer as it whipped around the corner of the building and headed for the shadows on the other side. Franklin ran smack into Tad, throwing him off balance and nearly causing them both to fall.

Blue saw a furtive movement to her left and swung toward it. "Tad," she called. "Over there."

Rubber-soled shoes made soft thuds as someone ran through the shadows at the back of the building.

"Damn it." Tad's voice carried forcefully through the night air. "He's getting away."

"Hold it!" Franklin swung his flashlight toward the sound and caught a young boy in the beam of light. "I see 'em, Tad. I got 'em. I got 'em right there."

The boy paused only for a moment, like a deer caught in the glare of headlights, and then he was running again.

Chapter Seven

"You sit down right there, young man." Franklin nudged the teenager toward an empty chair and scowled sternly. "This here is a serious matter. Real serious."

Blue raised an eyebrow in Tad's direction.

He bent forward, bracing his hands on his knees as Blue tried to catch her breath. Running after this young delinquent had been no easy task, and if Franklin hadn't stood back and waited for Blue and Tad to catch the boy, he wouldn't have been in such good shape, either.

"Give him—a—minute to cool—down," Blue said, straightening and drawing a deep breath. "Franklin? Would you mind—bringing that chair over here? That one—by Zeke's station?"

Franklin pulled the chair out of position and swung it to face the boy, who was sitting under Tad's stern gaze and looking as if he wanted to get into a fist fight with someone. Blue felt as if the kid had punched her. She hadn't run so fast nor so hard in a long time and her body was complaining. She lowered herself gingerly into the chair.

"What's your name?" she asked and received only a contentious glare for her trouble.

Franklin poked the back of the boy's chair. "The lady asked you a question, son."

Tad wished Franklin had gotten lost during the chase. It would have made this interview a whole lot simpler. "Take it easy, Franklin. He'll talk when he's ready."

"Hmmph. He'll talk to me or I'll tell the police he was uncooperative." Franklin poked the back of the chair again. "You won't like the way the police ask questions, son. No sirree, you won't like that a bit."

"Franklin," Blue said quietly and firmly. "Maybe you should take a look around. Make sure he—" she indicated the boy with a tilt of her head "—doesn't have a companion. There might be someone else still in the building. Or outside."

Franklin's pointy nose almost quivered at the thought. "You're right, Miss Blue. You're right. He might not be working alone." Franklin looked to Tad for approval. "Can you handle this without me, Tad? I'd better make sure there isn't anybody else. You know, an accomplice."

"Good idea, Franklin," Tad said. "I can handle things on this end."

Franklin gave a professional nod. "You want me to call the police first?"

Tad noticed the swift gleam of concern in the boy's dark eyes at the mention of a call to the police. Obviously the youth had some respect for authority. Otherwise he wouldn't continue to occupy the chair where Franklin had unceremoniously placed him. He could probably have gotten away if he'd made another escape attempt. Neither Tad nor Blue could have caught him a second time. "Blue and I will make the phone call when the time comes. You just make sure the building is secure."

"Okay, chief." Franklin nudged the chair one last time. "You talk to him, son, and maybe the D.A. will go light on you."

The boy slumped in the chair and stared at the floor as Franklin walked slowly up the stairs to the main offices, brandishing his flashlight from side to side, as if the lights weren't on.

"Will you tell me your name?" Tad asked. "And who your parents are?"

In answer, he received a sulky glance. Tad looked to Blue for inspiration and could see immediately that she was beginning to feel sympathetic toward the kid. Tad rested his elbows on his knees, clasped his hands and tried again. "Are you going to talk to me or shall I go ahead and call the police?"

Blue sank to the floor and wrapped her arms around her bent knees, a subtle sign that she felt no threat from this boy. "Wouldn't you rather we called your parents? Maybe we wouldn't have to call the police at all."

Tad didn't want her making concessions like that, especially not until the teenager made some sort of comment. He might look as harmless as a six-week-old kitten, but Tad didn't want to take any chances. "I'd appreciate answers," he said in a firm, no-nonsense voice.

"I don't have parents," the boy said.

"Okay," Tad said. "How about grandparents?"

The boy scoffed. "Don't have them, neither."

"Either." Tad kept his gaze pinned on the lad. "Let's start over. What's your name?"

No answer.

Tad exchanged a frustrated look with Blue. "Okay," he said. "I'll make one up for you. What were you doing in this building tonight, Walter?"

The kid shot him an irritated glance before resuming his study of the floor.

"Come on, Walter. Tell me what you were planning to steal from us. Toys? Computers? That remote-controlled car you used outside?"

The boy's chin jutted out at a defiant angle. "I didn't steal nothin'. I was just . . . lookin' around."

"Now, Walter, that's not much of a story. I don't believe that story. Do you, Blue?" With a glance Tad cautioned Blue to back him up, even though he could see she did not like badgering the boy. Tad didn't like it much, either, but he felt it was the only way to get past the youth's tough veneer.

"Didn't you break into the building to steal?" Blue asked. "Isn't that why you were in here tonight?"

The youth's dark eyes got shiny bright, but he didn't let a single tear escape. "Yeah," he said with belligerence. "Yeah. If that's what you want to hear. Why don't you just go ahead and call the police. They can put me in jail for stealin'. I don't care."

Tad observed the signs of weakening and decided to make a push for the truth. "Someone broke into this building last night, Walter. Someone turned on the computer and tried to play with the robot. Someone messed up the programming. Was that someone you, Walter?"

The boy's gaze flew to Zeke and then slowly moved to Blue before he bent his head and slumped in the chair. "Josh," he said. "My name is Josh."

Tad almost sighed aloud in relief. "What were you doing in the building tonight, Josh?"

"Lookin' around," Josh mumbled. "I wanted to see the . . . that robot."

"Zeke?" Blue said softly as her gaze found Tad's. "Are you interested in robots?"

"Computers." Josh lifted his chin a half inch, and the beginning of a weak smile touched his mouth. "Yeah. I'm interested."

"How many times have you been here, Josh?" Tad asked.

"I don't know. Six, maybe seven times." Josh glanced over his shoulder at the basement window. "I got in through there."

"How did you keep from getting caught by Franklin?" Blue rocked forward, still clasping her arms around her legs, still sympathetic and interested. "He makes several rounds each night."

"I figured out his system pretty quick," Josh said. "And I hid in those boxes over there whenever he came down here. He never knew I was anywhere around. Until tonight."

"What happened tonight?"

"He came by earlier than usual, and I didn't get the window closed. I guess that tipped him off."

"Why didn't you get out, Josh?" Tad asked quietly. "Why didn't you slip out before you got caught?"

Josh shrugged.

Blue looked at Tad to share the thought that perhaps Josh had wanted to get caught. "You said you don't have any parents, Josh, so where do you live?"

"Nowhere."

"Do you go to school?" Tad straightened in his chair.

"I'm outa school."

"How old are you, Josh?" Blue asked.

"Twenty."

Tad smiled. "And you're still waiting for your voice to change. Come on now, Walter, give it to me straight."

For a moment it looked as if Josh might retreat behind that tough-kid facade, but then he answered. Mumbled, actually, but he answered. "Thirteen. Last month."

"Old enough to know better than to break into a building." Tad stood then, using his height and authority to impress upon Josh the seriousness of what he'd done. "You could have gotten hurt, Josh. Or even killed. Franklin does carry a gun."

The boy's eyes widened a bit before he pulled off a macho shrug. "He wouldn't'a shot me. I could'a outrun him."

"You took a tremendous risk, Josh." Blue got to her feet and dusted the seat of her pants. "And you caused a great deal of trouble."

Concern immediately replaced the bravado in Josh's expression, and Tad knew then that he wasn't going to call the police.

"I didn't mean to cause trouble," Josh said. "I was just curious about what was inside a toy company and then I saw the robot. I was just playin' around, seein' if I could get it to do things."

"You came close to ruining it," Blue stated sternly. "Did you know that?"

Josh looked scared now. "I didn't do nothin'. I just tried to figure out how it was programmed, that's all."

"You got the access code pretty quickly," Tad said. "You must know quite a bit about computers."

"I learned it at school, and Gary has a computer he sometimes lets me use."

"Gary?" Blue picked up on that clue. "Is he a member of your family?"

"Nah. He's the counselor at school. Except I got moved again so I'm not at that school no more."

"Where do you live, Josh?" Tad fixed him with a stern look. "The truth, this time."

Josh hung his head and mumbled something indiscernible.

"Run that past me one more time," Tad said.

"A foster home." Josh raised his voice on the words. "I live in a stupid foster home."

"Here in Irving?"

"Yeah. But I'm not goin' back there. You can't make me."

"I'm sure someone is worrying about you, Josh." Blue's tone softened with concern. "It's after eleven and it is only courteous to let them know you're all right."

"They don't care," the boy said. "I've run away from there twice already and they never even reported it."

Tad found that a little hard to believe. Obviously Josh was determined to make his situation sound worse than it actually was. "You're not leaving us much choice in this, Josh. If you won't tell us where you live, we'll have to call the police."

"I could stay here." Josh looked around the basement. "I don't take up much space. I can sleep in those boxes over there. And I'll work. I'll work real hard. I'll make up for whatever I did to your robot. Honest, I will."

The plea almost broke Tad's heart. How sad to be so young and so unhappy.

"We can't let you stay here." Blue's voice trembled slightly, as if she, too, was touched by the eagerness of Josh's request. "This is no place for a young boy."

"I knew you wouldn't help me." Josh reverted to his earlier hostility. "You just want me out of here because you don't want to be bothered. Nobody wants to be bothered. So okay, go ahead and call the dumb police."

"Are you open to a proposition?" Tad shoved his hands into his hip pockets and rocked back on his heels. "Something like a part-time job?"

Josh looked up. "What kind of job?"

"Helping out here at the company this summer, and maybe, if it works out, you could come in after school next fall."

"Tad—" Blue stepped forward, but allowed her protest to dwindle away as Josh broke into a genuine smile, a charmingly eager, boyishly uncertain smile.

"You mean it? You're not just saying that to get me to tell you where I live?"

"I mean it," Tad confirmed. "The pay won't amount to much, but I'll be glad to show you how Zeke operates, if you'd like."

"Zeke? The robot?" Josh's voice rose with excitement. "You'd let me...you'd show me how...? Wow." Josh paused and his smile faded. "You're not just saying that. You promise? You really promise?"

"We'll have to okay it with your foster parents and with the state officials. It won't be a job, per se, because you're underage, but I think we can safely classify you as a student assistant and convince everyone that you'd be getting valuable hands-on computer experience."

"Oh, wow," Josh whispered. "I don't believe this."

"Tad." Blue obviously felt she had to interject a note of caution. "You should probably check out the legalities of this arrangement before you start making promises."

Josh swung toward Blue. "I can convince Fred and Joanne, my foster parents, to let me. I know I can. They never want me around, anyway. And my case worker is real nice. I know he won't mind."

Tad saw the worry, the concern, in Blue's eyes and knew she probably had a valid point. But he wanted to help this boy. "We'll work something out, I promise. But in return you've got to make a few promises yourself. No more breaking and entering. No more running away. You're going to have to stay out of trouble if you want to work for Uncle Horse."

Josh's dark eyes got big. "Horse? *Uncle* Horse?"

Tad grinned at the thought of the boy's first meeting with the company's founder. "Meanwhile, we've got to get you home. Blue and I will drive you...if you'll tell us where you live."

Josh looked less than happy at the idea of returning to his foster home. "I'll tell ya," he said with a sigh. "But you'll let me come back here, right? If I promise to do all those things you said?"

"Absolutely," Tad said.

"You'd better let Franklin know that you're taking Josh home." Blue made the suggestion calmly, but with one glance at the set of her mouth, Tad knew she was upset. He had a pretty good idea of what she thought. He would bet the list of rules and regulations she'd come up with would fill a small notebook. And if he knew Blue, she would undoubtedly detail each rule and every regulation to him before the night was over.

Luckily for him it was already halfway to morning.

"THEY WEREN'T ESPECIALLY friendly," Blue said as they drove away from Josh's foster home. "But they were nice enough. And they were obviously concerned about Josh. Joanne even said she was getting ready to call the police, herself."

Tad looked left before pulling onto the highway. "I understand the need for delicacy and tact in this situation, Blue. You didn't see me busting into their house and accusing them of child abuse, did you?"

"Don't be so touchy. I just said they seemed like okay people."

"You're right. They did. But the point is not how nice Fred and Joanne Knutson are. The point is, Josh Fletcher is unhappy living there."

Blue sighed and frowned at the stream of late-night traffic. The situation with Josh had her upset. Or maybe the way Tad had made those foolish promises to that young boy had her upset. "I imagine living in a foster home automatically brings some unhappiness, Tad. Even when the environment there is better for a child, the simple fact that he's in a foster home means he's experienced some sort of tragedy."

"Well, Josh is going to experience more tragedy if he doesn't get some direction really soon."

"So you're going to save him?" Blue would have liked to believe that Tad could do just that. Save Josh from any more unhappiness in life. But the fact was Tad would probably only end up hurting the boy even more. Unintentionally, true. But Josh would be hurt just the same. "You can't just step into his life, pull a few heartstrings, and make everything hunky-dory."

Tad shot her an annoyed glance. "Give me credit for having some sense of reality, Blue. Damn. I'm just going to spend a little time with the kid, show him a little something about robotics, give him someplace to be when he doesn't know where to go. Why do you have a problem with that?"

"He's in the system," Blue stated matter-of-factly, even though in her heart she wished she could deny it. "For whatever reason, he's been taken out of his biological parents' home and placed in foster care. There's a file on Josh. There's a case worker and a judge and the Knutsons, all involved in Josh's life and supervising his welfare. They're not simply going to let you walk in and make yourself at home in this boy's heart."

"I wouldn't think they'd have a whole lot to say about that."

"Because you're not considering the system and the rules that make it up."

"Rules. Ah, I knew we'd get to those before long."

She turned toward him. "What's that supposed to mean? Are you going to sit there and tell me that rules don't make a difference in this case?"

"They make a difference to you, obviously."

"And they will to Josh, too." Blue pursed her lips and wondered how she'd gotten involved in another argument with Tad when all she'd meant to do was to caution him about rushing into the situation and getting stuck between a promise and an inflexible system. "I'm only saying you should have been a bit more circumspect in the promises you made. That's all."

"I'll keep my promise, Blue. Come hell, high water or enough red tape to circle the city limits of Dallas."

"I don't doubt your sincerity, Tad. And please, don't misunderstand. I want to help Josh as much as you do. My heart went out to him the moment we caught him. I guess I'm just more cautious than you are about raising hopes that might get shattered later."

Tad was quiet for a moment. "Is that because of what happened to you? With Rob McKinley?"

Blue did not want to answer. But she knew that if she didn't, her silence would be an answer in itself. "I had my career hopes raised and then shattered, if that's what you mean. So, yes, I guess you could say part of my concern for Josh stems from my own experience. But I was an adult, Tad. I should have known better than to believe his—in promises. Josh doesn't have the wisdom yet to protect himself from disappointment."

Tad did not like the taste that her admission left in his mouth. It was beginning to sound like Blue had not only had an affair with her former boss, but that she'd done it in the hopes of furthering her career. An unpalatable distinction. "Disappointment is part of living, Blue. You can't protect anyone against it. Tonight I gave Josh Fletcher something to look forward to. And I gave myself the same gift. I'm not saying there won't be some difficulties in getting this idea approved by the authorities, but I won't be as pessimistic as you are. Of course, that is your job, I suppose. You are still in charge of gloom and doom, aren't you?"

Blue sighed softly. "Last time I checked no one here was in charge of anything. This job is driving me insane, Tad. And you're not helping any, either."

"You want me to help make you crazy?" He offered a cheeky smile. "I think I can do that."

"With very little effort at all," Blue said dryly. "I'll make a few calls for you about Josh. I do want to help and at least that would be something constructive to do."

Tad decided Blue had wandered aimlessly in the desert of Grizelle Gadget and Toy Company for long enough. It was time to point her in the direction of the oasis. "Build something, Blue. Create a new toy. Find an idea that inspires you and make it into a tangible object."

"You make it sound so easy."

"It is easy, once you get started."

"If I knew how to start, Tad, I'd already be on my way."

"Play some games. Go to the zoo. Fly a kite. Think like a child." He wasn't sure she'd ever really been a child, but maybe this job would help correct that oversight. "Stop trying to be a supervisor and try participating in this company. I think you'll be pleasantly surprised with the results."

Even at midnight in the dim light of the car, he could see the skepticism in Blue's raised eyebrows. But she didn't say she thought he was talking nonsense.

"And what about Josh?" she asked. "What are you going to do about him?"

"Exactly what I promised."

"No. I mean, what are you going to do with him once you get this part-time job business approved?"

Tad liked the way she'd phrased that. In her own pessimistic way, she was just as determined as he was. "I'll find errands for him to run. Computer games he can test. Floors he can sweep. There are a dozen things he can work on."

Blue turned toward him in the car. "How did you get started at Grizelle Gadget and Toy Company, Tad? Did Uncle Horse recruit you right out of college?" Her voice was soft and light, with none of the sarcasm he'd come to expect from her. "Or did you answer an ad for a boy genius?"

His grip tightened on the wheel, then he slowly forced himself to relax. Blue was probably just curious. She had no way of knowing how much he disliked remembering where he'd been and what his life had been like before. "Some friends of mine heard of an opening at your uncle's company and talked me into applying. You'll be interested to know that I started out as a janitor."

Blue laughed softly. "Was that when you began your secret life as Janitor Man?"

"Maybe it was," Tad said evenly. "It was definitely when Uncle Horse adopted me. He and Aunt Grizelle took me under their wings, moved me into the pool house apartment and gave me the opportunity to prove myself in the company."

"And now you're one-half of a vice president. You're moving right on up, Tad. Maybe you'll even get to be a president one day."

"Men like Uncle Horse don't retire, Blue."

"There are other places to work. You're not planning to stay at the toy company forever, are you?"

He knew that to her it was a dead-end job, a flat tire on the road to success. How could he tell her he hoped he never had to leave Grizelle Gadget and Toy Company? "My aim in life is to live every moment of every day to the fullest. That's enough ambition for me."

Her sudden silence communicated disappointment and, he imagined, a certain contempt for his perceived lack of drive.

"I see," she said. "Then why did it bug you so much when Uncle Horse gave me this job? Why didn't you just step aside and let me be the vice president?"

Ah. A good question. How was he going to explain that? "Maybe you arouse my territorial instincts, Blue."

"Maybe I just rattled that secure little cage you live in, Tad."

That was exactly what she had done, Tad realized. Rattled him. Shaken his daily routine. Made him determined to hear her laugh, see her smile. Made him angry and curious and... interested. "Is that what you did to Rob McKinley? Did you rattle his cage a bit too much?"

She stiffened, and the air inside the car felt thicker than a humid day in Houston. "That is none of your business, Tad."

"It was just a question, Blue. I'm not twisting your arm to get you to answer."

Her gaze singed a path to his, making him aware that she knew what he was trying to do, what information he wanted from her. And damn it all, she was absolutely right. He had no business asking, no business knowing, about her affair with McKinley. But the question was practically burning a hole in his gut.

"I'm sorry. That was out of line." He ran a hand through his hair and offered a half smile in apology. "Let's move on to a neutral subject. Let's talk about the new toy you're going to start working on first thing in the morning."

"Listen, Tad. I'm great at marketing. You give me something to market and I'll come up with a strategy that will knock the socks off the collective public. You're the inventor. Why can't you work on ideas and let me work on marketing those ideas? I'm sure we could get along just fine that way. But I'm not an idea person. I can't just sit down and come up with a new toy. I don't work that way."

"Mmm-hmm." Tad parked the car under the carport. "Home again, Blue. We're going to have to stop meeting like this, you know. I might start thinking you actually like my company. Do you want me to walk you to your door tonight?"

"No." She sounded definite about that. "You go to your door. I'll go to mine. We may be co-vice presidents, but let's not get carried away with this partners thing."

"You're absolutely right," he said with a smile. "You never know, I might start giving you 'ideas.'"

With a rueful glance Blue turned away, and Tad waited until she'd gotten out of the car before he leaned over and set the lock. Then he left the car and started toward his side of the pool house, noticing the way she walked, the very careful way she did not look at him as she approached the door of her apartment—the door in front of which he'd kissed her just last night. He walked past and then, turning on his heel, he came back to Blue.

She tried hard to pretend he wasn't there, but he tapped her on the shoulder to be sure she did. "Uh, Blue?"

She whirled toward him. "Now look, Tad. It's late and there is no way I'm going to let you repeat last night's—well, I'm not about to let you. So that's that." Her voice shook a little. Her eyes were wide and cautious, and Tad almost would have believed she was afraid he meant to kiss her again. Until the tip of her tongue darted invitingly across the bow of her lips.

His mouth curved in response. "And you said you weren't an 'idea' person. But much as I'd like to repeat last night's...good-night, I was only going to ask you to please remember and unlock the connecting door when you get inside." He lifted his hands in a gesture of innocence. "You won't forget, will you?"

He couldn't see her face well in the moonlight, but he was pretty sure she blushed.

"No, I won't forget the blasted door." She turned and fumbled with the lock.

"Okay, then." Tad stuck his hands into his pockets and strolled down the rosebush-lined path, whistling softly "The Man on the Flying Trapeze."

Chapter Eight

"Hey, what's this supposed to be?" Josh, who had been halfheartedly sweeping Blue's office, picked up a wadded ball of paper from the floor and smoothed it out. "Have you been doodlin' at your desk again, Miss Garrison?"

Blue turned away from the window to look at the teenage boy who in the past month had become the mascot of Grizelle Gadget and Toy Company. Tad had kept his promise. She had even helped. The red tape had been trimmed to manageable proportions, the foster parents had given grateful permission, the "system" had dispensed its blessing and Josh was now a fixture in the office. "Did I miss the waste basket again?" Blue asked. "I guess I'm just a lousy shot, Josh."

"Well, I don't think you're gonna get recruited to play professional basketball or nothing like that." The boy glanced up from his study of the crumpled paper and grinned. "But you're a 'radical' artist." Josh set his broom aside—all too easily, Blue noticed—and pulled at the edges of the paper he'd rescued. "What's this supposed to be, Ms. Garrison? It looks like Zeke. Only shorter and fatter."

Blue sighed and jammed her hands into her jacket pockets. "It was an idea for a toy robot. A build-it-yourself kind of thing. Looks really stupid, doesn't it?"

"I think it's kind of cool lookin'," Josh said. "Why'd you throw it away?"

Blue wrinkled her nose. "It's a dumb idea, Josh. I doubt that it's even feasible."

"Did you show it to Tad?" Tad *was* authority in Josh's opinion. No matter what the question, Tad had the final answer.

"He'd only toss it back in the trash," she said with a touch of impatience. "The idea isn't any good."

Josh observed her with dark, steady eyes. "You ought to show it to him, anyway."

"Trust me, Josh. He wouldn't like it."

The youth looked down at the drawing again and then turned on his heel and headed for the door. He was in Tad's office before Blue realized what he meant to do.

"Hey, Tad! Take a look at this."

With a frustrated sigh, Blue followed Josh, intent upon retrieving her trash. Just what this place needed, she thought. A teenager who thought he could play Santa Claus.

Blue was immediately ashamed of the thought. All in all she thought Josh was a nice addition to the office. He was bright, eager to please and, although he preferred working with Zeke, he didn't seem to mind doing the mundane chores Tad set for him, too. Everyone seemed happy with the arrangement so Blue kept her reservations about the future to herself. She could foresee emotional disaster. Josh was too vulnerable. Tad was too generous with his time and attention. At some point down the line there was going to be a problem. She could see it coming, even if no one else could.

"Hi, Blue," Tad said as she entered his office. He held up the crumpled sheet of paper. "What's this?"

She grabbed for it. "A dumb idea. It belongs in the trash."

Tad turned so that the paper slipped out of her reach again. "Don't be hasty now. Sometimes even the best ideas seem dumb at first."

"Right." Blue crossed her arms at her waist and leveled a solid frown on the man and the boy who stood in front of her. "That's why we're working on something called Crazy Gravy."

"And thanks to your sales pitch ToyWorld thinks it could be a big seller. They're already talking a pretty large marketing budget...and we haven't even completed all the tests yet. The moral of that story is...never underestimate an idea." Tad bent his head to examine the paper he held, and Blue struggled to subdue the impulse to tear it out of his hands and into tiny, indecipherable pieces before he could tell her what was wrong with it.

"You could finish sweeping out my office now, Josh," she suggested pointedly. It was bad enough that she had to stand there and wait for Tad's opinion, she didn't need an audience for the upcoming rejection, too.

Josh paid about as much attention to her request as Tad did. "Look at this, Tad." Josh pointed to some part of the drawing. "Doesn't it look kind of like Zeke?"

Tad didn't answer as he studied the drawing, then moved to the desk where he could better smooth out the wrinkles. Josh gave Blue a knowing look and the high sign. She wished he would go back to his broom. She wished Tad wouldn't scowl at her drawing. She wished even more that she could come up with a really good idea. Just one.

"Have you shown this to Uncle Horse?" Tad asked without looking up.

''No, it went straight from my scratch pad to the trash can. Or at least it was supposed to land in there.'' She sighed. ''Obviously I missed the shot.''

Tad looked up and smiled at her . . . a smile that caused a ripple of unrest inside her. She pressed her crossed arms tightly against her stomach. In the past month she'd experienced this queasy, tense sensation all too often. And it all stemmed from that one kiss. That one succinct and uninvited kiss which she had tried desperately not to remember. The one unexpected and tantalizing kiss which something within her would not allow her to forget.

Oh, Tad didn't mention it. But the memory was always there for him, too. It was there in the way he ran a thoughtful fingertip across his lips, the way he watched her in moments when he didn't think she was aware, the way he smiled at her . . . like now. He'd convinced her that he wasn't harmless and then—just like a man—he'd been perfectly harmless ever since.

And with the zeal of a shopper at a white elephant sale, she was on the lookout for the perfect opportunity to set him straight on the ethics of inner-office relationships, to put him back in his place and, finally, get him out of her mind.

''I can't tell a lot from the drawing, Blue,'' he said. ''Why don't you explain what you had in mind?''

''What I had in mind . . .'' she repeated, wondering if anyone in this nut house ever listened to what she said. ''Well, Tad. I actually thought about making a paper airplane, but I settled for a paper wad instead. If I'd had your Handy Dandy Paper Wad Basketball Hoop on the side of my trash container, I'd have made the shot and we wouldn't be having this discussion now.''

''If you can't hit the trash can, Miss Garrison, you sure couldn't do it if you had to loop the paper wad through a basketball hoop first.'' Josh added his jovial two cents' worth as he hooked a paper scrap into Tad's trash receptacle with flawless ease. Blue gave him a serious frown.

"Come on, Blue," Tad persisted. "Tell me what you were thinking about when you drew this little robot."

Her self-protective instincts told her to refuse to give the idea any credence at all, but in response to a direct and reasonable question her professional side took over, and she let her arms fall to her sides as she gave a resigned shrug. "I was thinking about how Josh is fascinated by computers and by Zeke, and it occurred to me that perhaps it was possible to put together a build-it-yourself robot for kids. Something that would start at, say, seven or eight years of age and expand as the child's interest develops. The basic computer might include programming that would create a pattern of blinking lights and some noise. Then, later, a component could be added to simulate movement. And another component might create a voice. And another might . . ." She let her voice trail as the idea grew to monstrous proportions. "It just gets more complicated, Tad. I don't even know if the idea is technically possible. And if it is, I'm sure the cost would be prohibitive."

"I think it sounds like a really good idea." Josh braced his hands on the side of the desk, in exact duplication of Tad's customary stance. "Tad can make it work. He built Zeke, you know."

"I *could* help you with this, Blue." Tad straightened and tucked one hand in a hip pocket.

"You don't have to humor me, Tad. I'm not going to slit my wrists because this one idea won't fly."

"Don't give up on it yet. At least, let me give it a shot."

She squared her shoulders. "It's supposed to be my idea, Tad. Mine. You already have a dozen or more projects to work on. I need something I can do myself."

"There's no rule against getting help, Blue. My gosh, you know that most of the ideas we sell are joint projects of two or more employees. Don't be stubborn. Let me help you."

Blue wanted to argue with him, partly because she wanted desperately to be convinced he wasn't simply mouthing encouragements to raise her sagging spirits. "Look, Tad, don't you really think that even if a build-it-yourself robot could be made, it would be far too expensive to market?"

"Why don't we go with this and see what we can come up with."

"Yeah, Miss Garrison," Josh chimed in. "Do it."

"What have you got to lose?" Tad asked.

Boredom. Frustration. A helpless feeling. Though she'd helped develop marketing plans for other people's work, so far none of her own ideas had met with this much encouragement. Tad certainly hadn't volunteered to help with any of them. Maybe he was serious. Maybe he really did think this idea had merit. "I suppose we could show it to Uncle Horse."

"Yes!" Josh lifted his hand in a gesture of triumph.

Tad smiled approval.

Taking the idea to Uncle Horse was capitulation, pure and simple. But the possibility that she might, finally, have come up with a workable idea was too enticing to pass up. Even if she had to have Tad's help to develop it, even if it meant spending more time with him....

Every idea had its drawbacks. And to have *something* of her own to work on, she could put up with just about anything.

Even the way she felt when Tad smiled.

"BLUE HAD AN IDEA today," Uncle Horse announced during dinner.

"How clever of you, Miranda Blue." Aunt Grizelle daintily patted her napkin to her lips. "What kind of an idea was it?"

"A brilliant idea," Uncle Horse said as if there couldn't be any doubt about it. "A really brilliant idea."

Mikie and Joe both looked up and nodded their approval.

Tad helped himself to more peanut butter soup.

"It's got a long way to go before it's *brilliant,* Uncle Horse." Blue was becoming uncomfortable with the whole thing. Maybe it wasn't a dumb idea. And maybe it did have possibilities. But it was still a long shot and it wasn't brilliant. She looked to Tad for help.

"Do you want more soup?" He held up the ladle, offering to serve.

She refused.

Mikie and Joe each extended their bowls for another helping.

Blue began to eat in earnest, actually enjoying the odd flavor of the soup and hoping her uncle and aunt would allow the subject of her bright idea to drop. This was not the place and these were not the people with whom she wanted to discuss it.

"Yep," Uncle Horse said with a nod. "Blue has done it this time. This is gonna be big. Big as Tater Tossers, I'd say."

Aunt Grizelle smiled and patted Blue's knee under the table. "You'll have to tell me all about it while the men enjoy their sherry this evenin'."

Tad looked up, caught Blue's desperate glance and decided to rescue her. Even though he was positive she'd tell him later that she'd been fully capable of saving herself. "Blue and I have an appointment right after dinner," he said as if it was a long-standing commitment. "I'm afraid I'll have to forego my glass of sherry tonight."

Aunt Grizelle looked sad. "Again, Tad? Why, you almost never take a minute to relax after dinner. And now you're runnin' off with Blue in tow. You're both workin' too hard, now. You'd better slow down and smell the roses."

Tad's smile was genuine and gracious. "Thanks to you, Aunt Grizelle, I can smell the roses every morning when I awaken and each night as I drift off to sleep. Your roses are particularly lovely this year, Aunt Grizelle."

She preened like a young girl. "They are, aren't they? I declare, every year they just get prettier and prettier."

"It's the readings." Uncle Horse speared a carrot stick with his fork. "You have a soothing voice, Griz. The roses love it and they just bloom and bloom for you."

Mikie and Joe nodded enthusiastically.

Tad met Blue's inquisitive look with equanimity. If she stuck her foot in her mouth and denied knowing anything about their "appointment," she could damn well stay and spend the evening in her aunt's and uncle's capricious company. If she was desperate enough to get out of family obligations for a few hours, she'd go along with his proffered excuse. He didn't really have any plans, but he *was* intrigued by Blue's idea of building a do-it-yourself toy robot. And he wanted to spend some time thinking about it. It would be easier if she came along so they could bounce the idea around. He could do it alone, but...

Oh, who the hell was he trying to kid? He wanted Blue's company because he wanted her company. Simple. He didn't care a whole lot about what they talked about as long as they talked. For a couple of weeks after they'd discovered Josh, he'd avoided Blue and her poker face. Though she'd pitched in to help arrange things, she'd been full of reservations about the attention he wanted to give Josh. It didn't take great depths of understanding to realize that.

But about a week ago he'd come to the rather startling realization that he missed the sparring, the delicious stimulation of annoyance and attraction their previous relationship had held. Blue awakened feelings in him that no one else had come close to touching in a very long time. Maybe ever.

Lindy had been sweetly in love with him. The feelings she had stirred were protective and warm. They hadn't fought. Tad couldn't even recall a single real argument during their two-and-a-half-year marriage. Not even at the last, when he'd tried every angle to win her response. And finally he'd lost her.

"I've got it!" Uncle Horse pushed back his chair abruptly and placed both palms solidly on the tabletop. His eyes were wide, round and wild. His hair frizzed out around his head. "What we need," he announced, "is...a talking rosebush! No, no, it won't talk. But it will grow. It'll grow when someone speaks to it. Like Griz's roses. She reads. They grow. She talks to them. They grow." He turned one palm outward in illustration and used the other to indicate a rapid growth rate. "Children like flowers. I believe they'd talk to them. What do you think, Tad? Blue? I wouldn't want to move forward on this without my vice presidents' okay."

Tad met Blue's eyes across the table as he swallowed a spoonful of soup. "It has possibilities for younger children, Uncle Horse. I can't see an older child talking to a synthetic plant.''

''Ah, yes.'' Uncle Horse nodded understandingly. ''Young Josh would be past that age, I imagine.''

Blue struggled to imagine any age group talking to a plastic flower, but then she'd had to work to get a handle on Crazy Gravy, too. ''You could tie it in with environmental awareness. Maybe package it with a booklet on how to help Mother Earth survive.''

''Great Scott!'' Uncle Horse pushed to his feet with unbounded enthusiasm. ''Another brilliant idea, Miranda Blue. Two in one day! You're hotter than a Chinese chili pepper. Did you hear that, Griz? Blue's done it again!''

Aunt Grizelle put down her soup spoon and clapped her hands together. ''How nice,'' she said. ''But do sit down, Horace, and finish your soup.''

''Soup?'' Uncle Horse repeated the word as if he'd never heard it before. ''We're talking flowers here. Toy flowers. Don't distract me now. I think we're on to something.'' With a shake of his shaggy head, he rolled his eyes, muttered some unintelligible phrases and stalked from the room.

Aunt Grizelle sighed, picked up her spoon and smiled benignly at the assembled clan. ''Horace seems to be otherwise occupied at the moment,'' she said graciously. ''Let's continue our dinner.''

Mikie and Joe nodded agreement.

Tad met Blue's eyes across the table and lifted his soup spoon in a salute. ''When you're hot, you're hot.''

''LOOK AT THIS, Blue.'' Tad came around to her side of the workbench and laid a sketch in front of her. ''What do you think of that?''

Blue lifted her concentration from her own drawing and blinked to clear her vision. Tad had brought her to the office as soon as she'd finished dinner. They'd talked about her idea for a toy robot, tossed possibilities back and forth, argued a bit about how to proceed, and then he'd suggested they each work on some preliminary sketches. She'd hardly looked up since, and her eyesight was a little blurry, but she managed to bring Tad's pencil drawing into focus. His illustration of the toy robot was to scale and much more detailed than her original. "That really looks like Zeke," she said with a wry smile. "I think you have a better picture of him than I do."

"I just have more experience than you do in translating ideas onto paper." He tapped the pencil lead against the paper. "Do you think we could break it down into three or more units? Then each unit can be broken down into smaller components. Something like building blocks."

Excitedly Blue looked up. "A snap together robot? Do you honestly think that can work?"

He leaned forward, one hand braced on the back of her chair, one hand gripping his pencil as a pointer. "If we can come up with a basic unit that's simple enough for a six- or seven-year-old to put together—something that would allow a few lights and some movement—then I don't see any reason it can't. The basic part will be the most difficult. See, this section—" he tapped one part of the diagram with the pencil lead "—has to be elementary enough to be mastered by a child, but it also has to contain the capability for expansion as the child develops more interest and skill."

Blue let her thoughts run rampant, envisioning the toy robot as she hoped it would turn out, more excited than she had been in well over a year. "I can't believe I've finally come up with an idea that might actually become something tangible.'' She paused and let her gaze slide up to meet Tad's. "You do like this idea? You're not just encouraging me because...well, because you want me to feel better about my job?"

Tad's smile was slow and Blue's response—a warm, weak sensation in the pit of her stomach and the backs of her knees—was immediate. "It's after 1:00 a.m., Blue. If I was just encouraging you, I'd have quit by eleven-thirty."

"One? It's one o'clock in the morning?" She looked at her wristwatch for confirmation. "But we just got here."

"Watch out, now. Aunt Grizelle will be telling you you're working too hard and that you need to stop and smell the roses."

Blue laughed and turned back to the workbench. "Can I borrow your answer? The one about waking up and going to sleep with the scent of roses? That seemed to tickle her."

"Be my guest." Tad leaned in to pencil a note on the top of the sketch. "I wonder if we could put together a prototype in time for that September trade show in New Mexico."

"A trade show? You mean you want to take this toy to a trade show?"

He grinned as he finished the notation. "Yes, Blue. Uncle Horse was right. This is an idea with great potential. I think it's going to work out much better than you expect."

"I don't know. Right now my expectations are riding pretty high."

"Well, the hard part is all ahead. If we want to make that September show, we're going to have to work like demons to get a prototype ready in time."

"Does that mean we go on strict eight-to-five hours?"

"We're on flex time, you'll remember. You can work until your eyesight fails and your fingers fall off."

With a second glance at her watch, she tossed a coy smile over her shoulder. "We've worked until one-thirty tonight and I'm still fresh as a daisy."

His gaze wandered to her chin and back to her mouth, and Blue was suddenly, excruciatingly, conscious of just how close he was. There were fewer than three inches of air between them. Not a safe, simple solution to the quick, short breaths that took over her lungs. Nowhere to hide, no way to disguise the awareness that flooded over her in a warm, pulsing rush.

"Fresh as a daisy, huh? Don't you mean a rosebud?"

Was it her imagination or was his voice on the breathy side, too? He didn't pull back and she couldn't...not without being obvious. A tiny sigh came from who knew where and trembled past her lips. "Now that I know...how late it is, I'll probably...wilt."

His eyes went dark and her common sense fled for cover. He leaned in and brushed her lips with his. Blue felt his hand at her back, turning her more fully around. And then his mouth covered hers in earnest, testing and tasting and tempting a response. She knew better than to give in to the impulse to wrap her arms around him, but somehow her hands were on his shoulders and moving to the back of his head. Her fingers threaded into his hair, her palms cupped the curve of his neck. Frantic shivers raced down her spine. Pleasure warred with caution. Delightful sensations smothered out a sense of panic. Tad was good at this, she thought. Too good. And she was in trouble. Big trouble.

She would have pulled back then, but he wouldn't let her. Not that she exerted much effort. She would never be able to say later that she'd struggled. Tad held her still and steady and wanting. And when his lips finally eased the pressure, ceased the demand, Blue was more disappointed than relieved. When he gave her that lazy, sensual smile, she suddenly remembered all the very good reasons why she should never have allowed him to kiss her.

"Why did you do that?" she asked.

Not wanting to frighten her, he lifted one shoulder in a careless shrug. His thumb rubbed a caressing circle against her back. "For the fun of it. Why did you do it?"

Blue wished she could say she hadn't done anything. Just flat-out deny that she had wanted him to kiss her and that she'd done anything in the way of participating. But that was the coward's way. And she wasn't a coward. Especially since he would know what a tremendous lie it was.

"I don't know," she said. "But, Tad, it can't happen again."

"Why not?"

It was a reasonable question. And it took Blue at least ten seconds too long to come up with a reasonable answer. "Because," she said. "Well... because."

"Hmm." Tad straightened and removed his hand from the back of her chair. "Because." He nodded as if that made sense. "Because."

"It's not an excuse, Tad. Really. I just... well, I feel strongly that when two people work together... there should be no... well, no..."

"Kissing?" Tad supplied. "Co-vice presidents shouldn't kiss each other. Is that what you're trying to say?"

"Yes." Blue felt silly all of a sudden. As if she were offering an excuse and not a sufficient reason. But she knew firsthand the heartache that a relationship with a coworker could bring. "We are going to be working closely together on this project, Tad. I don't want a bunch of silly emotions getting in the way."

He considered that with a slight frown. "What happened to you, Blue? What happened to make you so afraid?"

She stood then. Stood and walked away from the drawing board, trying to ignore the twist of guilt and the rising pangs of disappointment and depression. She was away from all that now. Nearly a year down the road. And there was no way she intended to dredge it all up again just to answer Tad's offhand question.

"Nothing happened to me, Tad. I simply have more experience in these situations than you do. And I've learned that it isn't a good idea to get involved with a co-worker. Not even with the best of intentions."

"Did you have an affair with your boss, Blue? Is that why you had to leave McKinley Enterprises?"

"No." The denial came out explosively. Quickly. Too quickly. She could see in his eyes that he didn't believe her. And somehow that hurt. "My reasons for leaving McKinley are none of your concern, Tad. From now on I'd prefer that we kept a professional distance between us. I want your help on this new project. I need your input and your assistance. But that's it. Please, don't try to be my friend. And don't kiss me again."

For a long moment Tad looked at her in silence, but although the look made her fidgety, Blue held her position and his gaze.

Then he smiled. Damn him. He smiled.

"So," he said. "Is it all right if I drive you home or do you want to call a cab?"

She sighed. "There's no need to carry this to ridiculous lengths, Tad. Of course we can ride home in the same automobile."

"Well, good. That's settled then. We are allowed to travel together. As long as we maintain a professional distance. I understand." He reached over and switched off the high-intensity light over the workbench. Then he swept his hand toward the door of the office. "You go ahead. I'll follow at a discreet, very professional ten paces."

Blue wanted to argue with him. Why did he make a game of everything? He'd probably tease her unmercifully about the "professional distance" thing. And he'd kissed her "for the fun of it."

But then, what had she expected him to say? He'd kissed her because he'd fallen desperately in love with her?

Stupid thought.

Silly.

She turned on her heel and walked regally to the doorway, deciding that she wouldn't give him the satisfaction of knowing his teasing attitude had distressed her in any way. "Do you really think we can get a prototype of Little Zeke ready for that trade show, Tad?"

"I don't know. We can certainly give it our best shot." He followed her from the office, flipping off the lights as he went. "I guess it will depend on just how closely we work together. And I'm referring to a 'professional' closeness, Blue. A true 'working' relationship. Just so there's no misunderstanding...."

"Mission accomplished, Tad." Blue didn't even glance over her shoulder at him. She knew she'd only see his laughing smile. "I'm sorry I ever tried to make you understand."

He laughed softly as he dimmed the lights in the reception room and stepped forward to open the glass doors into the hallway. "Understanding your position does not mean I agree with you. Lighten up, Blue. Do you want to go with me and Josh to the movie tomorrow night? You can sit in the back row. We'll sit in the front. That'll be enough distance, don't you think? You'll have to get your own box of popcorn, though. Otherwise, we'd have to throw the box back and forth across the movie aisles. And that might interfere with our enjoyment of the movie. But, hey, if that's what it takes to maintain professional distance.... Never let it be said that Tad Denton wasn't willing to help out his co-vice president.''

Blue didn't answer. She just marched down the hallway ahead of him, hoping he wouldn't catch up with her and witness the traitorous, blasted little smile of amusement that tugged at the corners of her mouth.

Chapter Nine

The little robot whirred pitifully, shuddered and sat frustratingly still in the middle of the table.

"Come on, Little Zeke." Josh bent, brushing the straggly brown hair out of his face before bracing his hands on his knees and getting eye to eye with the toy robot. "You can do it. Show your stuff."

Ellie snapped her gum. "What's the matter with it? I thought you said it was ready for demonstration."

"Hmmmm." Uncle Horse paced the length of the table, hands clasped behind him, studying the toy from every angle. "Hmmmm," he said again.

"It walked and blinked its lights on and off just a little while ago." Blue looked at the assembled employees gathered in the playroom for Little Zeke's debut, wanting them to know this was just a glitch, just a minor setback. She turned toward Tad. "It worked earlier, didn't it, Tad?"

"I saw it, Miss Garrison." Josh immediately was her ally.

"Don't panic, Blue." Tad stretched half across the table so he could make an adjustment to the bottom building block of the toy computer. "This kind of thing happens all the time."

"He's right, Blue." Ellie plopped herself in a chair at the far end of the table and crossed one leg over the other. "Once we were testing a remote-controlled tow truck, the Red Max, and it worked perfectly. Not a single glitch. Then when the head wizard and all the clone wizards from ToyWorld showed up, the truck played dead. Wouldn't budge. The winch wouldn't turn. The toy just sat there. But Tad got it to work. And he'll fix Little Zeke, too. He can do anything with toys. Can't you, Tad?"

"Sure." Tad shifted, made another adjustment with a screwdriver the size of a toothpick. "I studied with Santa and his elves."

"You want me to switch it on again, Tad?" Josh was almost on top of Tad, trying to see what was going on. "I'm ready when you are."

Blue kept her smile in place despite the raw tension in her stomach. If this thing didn't work . . .

"Okay, Josh. Try it one more time." Tad stepped back to watch the result. With a maximum of self-importance, Josh flipped the switch. The robot hummed. The row of lights across the top blinked brightly. The toy rolled forward as smoothly as a luxury car, stopped, rolled backward and played two full bars of "Yankee Doodle."

Ellie clapped. Josh laughed aloud. Uncle Horse danced a jig. Blue looked at Tad and smiled a genuine smile in triumph.

His smile came more slowly, tucking in first at the corners of his mouth and then moving upward, lighting the cinnamon depths of his eyes. It had in it a measure of triumph, tempered by a few lines of weariness. But it was the undiluted affection in his eyes that grabbed the tension in Blue's stomach and gave it a different twist.

In the month and a half that they'd worked together, day after day, night after night, on the robot, she'd learned to appreciate his intelligence, his skill, his talent, his incredible optimism that it would all, in the end, come out right. And now the toy worked. Together she and Tad had taken the seed of an idea and cultivated it, made it into something real.

Little Zeke, as the toy robot was to be called, was a series of parts that snapped together like oversized plastic building blocks. The electronics were encased in the central unit and there were ports for later, more complicated, additions to the computer itself. The toy would be a challenge for most youngsters, but it wasn't too difficult to put together. Its lights and movements would appeal to young children as well as older ones. Josh, at fourteen, was completely entranced by the robot, although Blue supposed the attraction for him might possibly be entwined with his growing affection for Tad and for herself.

Affection. Attraction. Two innocent words. When she used them in reference to Josh they evoked harmless, nice and warm feelings. When she switched the reference to Tad, *harmless* flew out the window, *warm* turned into an uncomfortable heat, and *nice* became an indefinable ache inside of her.

He hadn't kissed her again. He'd maintained a respectful, professional distance . . . and had teased her unmercifully about it. And now he smiled at her across the table, over the top of the toy they'd built, and her knees went weak. She found herself wanting him to breach that professional distance, to sweep aside her feeble protests and laugh away her every doubt.

But she was painfully aware of how easily feelings of admiration and esteem for another person could be mistaken for deeper emotions—emotions upon which a relationship might be built. She'd made that mistake once. She wouldn't make it again.

"What do you think, Uncle Horse?" Blue dropped her gaze to Little Zeke as she solicited her uncle's approval. "Do you think this little robot will be a hit at the New Mexico Product Convention?"

"All depends on how many of the manufacturers can hum 'Yankee Doodle,' I reckon." Uncle Horse scratched his head. "Hey, Tad, why don't we program this little gadget with a mix of tunes? A sampler. A 'Sing along with Zeke' sampler." Uncle Horse nodded as he snapped his fingers, enchanted with the idea. Then he frowned all of a sudden. "What songs are popular with kiddos these days?" he asked the gathering at large. But his wide-eyed gaze settled on Josh.

"Rap music, Uncle Horse. That's what you ought to put in it. That'd be so bad." Josh swung around. "Can you do that, Tad? Can you get Little Zeke to do rap?"

"I don't think that would be a big selling point," Blue said. "Remember, it's the parents who spend the money."

"But it's the kids who whine and beg for the toy." Ellie slid from the table and dusted her hands across her hips. "When Jim Bill and I have children, they won't act that way. My kids won't be allowed to throw tantrums."

"Your kids will probably throw rocks." Josh grinned and ducked as if he thought Ellie might throw a rock at him.

Ellie just made a face and headed for the doorway. "I'm out of here, guys. See ya tomorrow."

Tad glanced at his watch. "Josh, I promised Joanne that you'd be home early enough to get your homework done before supper. She says you've been giving her a few problems about that."

"I haven't, Tad." Josh's words rushed out in self-defense. "Mostly I get it done at school. But she won't believe me. She says all kids have homework and I shouldn't try to get out of doing it by lying."

"So you have no homework to do tonight?" Tad asked.

The boy's chin dropped several notches. "A little. But not much. Really, Tad. I'll get it done. Let me stay a little longer. Please?"

"Come on, Josh." Blue patted his bony shoulder. "I'll take you. I think Tad and Uncle Horse want to work on Little Zeke's musical repertoire, so I'll drop you off on my way home."

"I can stay longer," Josh assured her. "I can wait for Tad."

"Not this time, sport." Tad picked up the toy robot. "I've got a little more work to do before I can leave. You go with Blue and get all of your homework done. That's part of our deal, remember? You don't want Joanne and Fred to start insisting that you go straight home after school, do you?"

"No." Josh scuffed his feet and mumbled something about stupid homework and a stupid house.

Blue ignored his dissatisfaction and moved to Tad's side. "I'll come back after I've dropped Josh off," she said.

"Go on home, Blue." Tad carried the toy to a workbench and placed it in Uncle Horse's waiting hands. "We won't work very late. In fact, knowing your uncle, I'm certain we'll be home before dinner." He leaned close to whisper. "I'll try to keep him from programming in any rap music."

Blue smiled. "Good idea. After all, we do want this product to sell."

"It will, Blue. The merchandisers will whip out their fountain pens so fast the ink will melt. Isn't that right, Uncle Horse?"

Uncle Horse was engrossed in taking apart the toy robot, and his nod was vague and unrelated to the conversation.

"I'll see you at dinner then."

"Yes. Dinner." Tad turned to assist Uncle Horse, and with some reluctance Blue left with Josh.

"I WISH TAD would have let me stay." Josh shifted restlessly in the seat. "I would have had plenty of time to get my homework done later. But, no, I have to go home and do it before supper. I don't have much to do, anyway. And it's easy stuff. I can have the math done in probably two minutes."

Blue kept up her side of the discussion by driving and not interrupting Josh's spiel of complaints. At moments like this, when he didn't get his way, he claimed to be the most mistreated adolescent on the face of the earth. From past experience Blue knew his frustrations would vent themselves before they reached the Knutsons' home, and she listened without paying a lot of attention.

"Fred hates it when I say stuff like that," Josh continued, his tone already settling into a more pleasant pitch. "His and Joanne's kids must have been pretty dumb in school because Fred's always saying that math is too hard for kids to learn. He doesn't like it that I'm good at math and it doesn't take me long at all to figure out a problem. Were you like that, Ms. Garrison? I'll bet you were really good in school."

"I never liked math," she admitted with a rueful smile. "But I studied and managed to keep a decent grade. It was very important to my father that I make *A*s, so I suppose I was a good student because he expected me to be."

"My father wanted me to be good in school, too. If he hadn't had that heart attack, I'd probably have straight As."

Josh's remarks often bordered on fantasy. Blue knew his background because Joanne Knutson had told her. Josh's father had abandoned the family when Josh was barely a year old. His mother had died of pneumonia three years ago, and soon afterward Josh had been placed in the Knutson home. Josh, like many foster children, sometimes tampered with reality to make it more palatable. Blue understood. There were moments in her own history that she would fictionalize if she could ... mostly those moments that involved Rob McKinley.

But she couldn't rewrite the past and neither could Josh. A fact which Blue believed the youngster was learning, step by painful step.

"Making straight As in school isn't a true measure of success, Josh. Be the best you can be. That's all anyone expects from you."

"Yeah, everybody says that. But then they get mad when the grade isn't an A."

"Well, this year I'll bet that will change. I know you're trying very hard, Josh. The Knutsons know that, too. I think you'll be pleasantly surprised when your first nine weeks' grades come out."

"Maybe." His tone was doubtful, but there was a marked shift in the set of his shoulders, a certain self-confidence that hadn't been there a moment before. "Little Zeke is real cool, Ms. Garrison. I'd give you an A, if I were the teacher. Of course, you had Tad's help and he can do just about anything with a computer. That's probably because he's good with math, like me."

Josh wanted so badly to align himself with Tad. And considering the situation, the boy's adoration was understandable. A whole new universe had opened up for Josh during the past few months, and Tad was at the center of it. For better or for worse, Josh could see no flaws in his hero.

There were times when Blue worried that the boy was headed for certain disappointment and other times when she shared Tad's confidence that everything would be all right. She'd enjoyed tagging along on the trips to the zoo and local museums he'd arranged for Josh. She wanted to believe that Tad could work miracles. Not only with a toy robot, but for her and for Josh as well.

"He's quite a guy," she said because Josh seemed to expect her complete agreement. "But if it wasn't for you, Josh, Little Zeke would never have been built. Thanks for saving him from the trash can."

"Hey, no problem." His youthful jaw tightened with pride. "I knew you had a good idea."

Blue smiled and for several seconds they rode in silence.

"How come Tad isn't married?" Josh asked casually as if the question had just popped into his mind.

"I don't know, Josh," she said just as casually. "He's never discussed that with me."

"Oh." Another mile passed in silence. "Do you think he wants to have kids someday?" As if he were aware of her sudden discomfort, Josh turned toward her in the car. "I mean, don't you think he'd be a great dad? He knows how to treat kids so they feel important and he likes to have fun. Don't you think a guy like that would want kids?"

"I guess he might," Blue said noncommittally. "I really don't know."

"But don't you think he would? Don't you think he'd be a really good father? Don't you think he wants to be somebody's dad?"

Blue didn't want to express an opinion. For one thing she didn't want to encourage Josh to think that *he* could be Tad's kid, Tad's son. That was the danger in this situation...that Josh would exchange one fantasy for another. A fantasy just as false, just as unattainable as idealizing the father who had abandoned him.

And she didn't want to think about Tad in a personal way. For the past couple of months she'd managed to create and maintain a professional relationship with him. She didn't want to jeopardize that with thoughts of who Tad might marry and what his children might look like. There was danger in that kind of thinking, too.

"You'll have to ask him about that, Josh. I really can't give you an answer."

A measure of Josh's eagerness faded, but then he seemed to recover. "Well, what about you? Are you going to get married and have kids?"

"Oh, Josh," Blue said with a nervous little laugh. "I doubt it. I'm involved with my career and, well, I've just never met Mr. Right." She didn't want to perpetuate the myth of one ideal mate, one perfect man, but she simply couldn't think of anything else to say at the moment. "I guess I'm just a dyed-in-the-wool career woman."

"Does that mean you can't ever have kids? Women on TV have careers and kids all the time." Josh watched her expectantly and Blue felt as if the future of the whole women's movement suddenly rested on her shoulders.

"A lot of women on TV and in real life do manage to combine having a career with having a family. I'm just not one of them, that's all."

"Why not?"

Blue wanted to tell him it was none of his business, but he was just a child, after all. And he was only curious. "I waited too long, Josh. Certain choices have to be made in life, and the choices I made when I was younger...well, they canceled out some other choices I might have made. Like having children.''

''But Mrs. Reed, my math teacher, is going to have a baby and she's got to be forty. Maybe even older than that.''

''It isn't age, Josh,'' Blue said, even though she knew it was partly a lie. Her mother had been thirty-five when Blue was born. She'd always felt that her parents were too old. Too old to play with her. Too old to appreciate her youth. She wouldn't bring a child into the world and then be too tired to enjoy motherhood. ''There are other reasons. Personal reasons.''

''You could adopt a kid.'' He turned to look out the side window. ''People do that all the time.''

Blue's heart settled in her throat. ''Maybe I could,'' she said, and hoped she wasn't raising unfair expectations. But what else was she supposed to say? She wasn't a mother. She didn't know how to handle moments like this. ''Look at the time, Josh. Four-forty. You'll be home in plenty of time to get that homework done. Won't Joanne be pleased?''

Josh's frown demonstrated his opinion of the idea. ''She'll just find chores for me to do. She thinks I'm a slave.''

''While you're slaving away, try to think of new things for Little Zeke to do. Okay?''

Josh brightened a little with the assignment and Blue stopped the car in the Knutsons' driveway. ''Okay. I'll see you tomorrow at the office. And I'll think of some songs, too.''

''No rap music,'' Blue warned.

''Ah, you're no fun.'' Josh made a face as he got out of the car and shut the door. He waved and walked toward the front of the house where Joanne Knutson waited with a smile.

"I'M SURPRISED that the roses are still blooming," Blue said as she and Tad walked to the pool house after dinner. "It's already the middle of September."

"They'll continue to bloom until the first frost. Pretty, aren't they?"

Blue smiled. "They're particularly lovely this year."

"It's Aunt Grizelle's voice that they respond to, you know."

"So I've heard. I hope the toy market responds as well to Uncle Horse's Talk-to-Me Rose. I think he's more excited about that little plastic flower than about any other project in the works right now."

"He likes the ecology tie-in. That was a stroke of genius on your part, Blue. I think we're going to have at least two real successes on our hands at the trade show."

"I hope Little Zeke is a hit. Not just because it's my baby, either. We've worked so hard on it, I'm not sure I can stand the thought of no one else liking it."

"Don't worry. It'll sell itself. Uncle Horse and I made an adjustment to the switches so there shouldn't be any more delays when it's turned on. And it won't be difficult to put in a sampler chip that will replace 'Yankee Doodle' with a medley of tunes. They'll have to be short, but then our target audience has short attention spans, so I think we'll be all right. Are you pleased with it?"

"Little Zeke?" Blue looked at him in surprise. "Are you kidding? I'm so proud of that little toy that I can't wear anything with buttons, for fear they'll pop right off. Aren't you excited about how the robot turned out?"

"I'm excited. But Little Zeke is your baby. I only assisted at the birth."

Blue's cheeks felt warm all of a sudden. Everyone seemed to be talking about babies today. "I appreciate your help," she said sincerely. "I couldn't have done it alone."

Tad accepted her thanks with a nod and began to whistle softly as they walked past the last row of rosebushes to reach the pool house. Blue had decided earlier that Tad should know about her conversation with Josh that afternoon, even though he probably would dismiss her concerns as melodramatic or overly imaginative. If Tad had seen the danger in his relationship with Josh, he'd never let on. But that possibility didn't diminish her need to warn him of what was coming.

"Tad," she said. "I wanted to talk to you about Josh. He and I had an interesting conversation on the way to the Knutsons'. I . . . think you should know what he said."

Tad stepped beneath the overhang that served as a porch for his apartment. "He said he wants me to adopt him. Is that it?"

As usual he'd taken the wind right out of her sails. "How did you know that? Has he already broached the idea to you?"

Tad studied the tips of his tennis shoes before lifting his gaze to meet Blue's. "He's dropped a few hints. I know how thirteen-year-old boys think. I figured the question was bound to arise sooner or later."

"I hope you have an answer for him, Tad. One that he'll understand."

The lines around Tad's mouth tightened. "What did he say this afternoon?"

"He asked me why you weren't married. He wanted to know if you wanted to have kids of your own. He asked me if I thought you'd be a good father."

"What did you say?"

"I told him I didn't know why you weren't married, that we had never discussed the subject. I tiptoed past the question on having children and told him he'd have to direct his next inquiry to you."

"Did he ask why you aren't married? Did he want to know if you plan to have children?"

The setting sun cast an autumn glow across the rose garden. The fragrance of the flowers wove a subtle and sweet intimacy between them. Blue didn't know why the discussion about Josh seemed suddenly personal. "He asked. I told him I'd made other choices."

"I'll bet he really understood that."

She shrugged. "I explained the best I could. He's going to get hurt, Tad. He's starting to believe he can belong to you. I told you early on this was a setup for disaster."

Tad leaned back against the door and crossed his arms at his chest. He looked tired, Blue thought and felt an instant and inexplicable desire to hold him, to soothe him with pats and soft whispers, to kiss the lines of weariness at the corners of his mouth.

"What were the other choices you made, Blue?"

"What?" She pulled her imagination into line and her gaze away from his lips as his question registered in her mind. "Choices. Oh. I told him I'd chosen to have a career, that I'd waited too late to have children."

"That's nonsense."

She smiled slightly at the strong way he'd phrased it. *That's nonsense. Nonsense.* As if a woman could simply say, I choose to have a child. It was just a bit more complicated than that. "Well, that's what I told him and he, in turn, told me there was no reason I couldn't adopt a child, if I wanted to."

Tad nodded. "He's setting us up as his parents, isn't he? I can't believe he's really that unhappy with the Knutsons."

"He's not that unhappy. He just wants a family of his own, Tad. We all want to belong somewhere, to have someone who loves us. Josh is a little young for a romantic interest, so he's fantasizing about the family he'd like to have. Joanne and Fred are nice enough, but they're foster parents. They don't really belong to him, and Josh knows he doesn't really belong to them, either. You're his hero, Tad. It's only natural that he wants to think of you as the father he never had. The question is, what are you going to do about it?"

Tad straightened with a smile. "Nothing. I know it's hard for you to believe, Blue, but fantasy isn't a bad thing. Josh is a bright kid. He can recognize the difference between what is real and what he wants to be real. A little bit of daydreaming won't do him any harm. I'm going to continue to be his friend. I'm going to teach him as much as I can about computers. I'm going to enjoy his company and continue to have fun with him."

"And when he asks you to adopt him? What then, Tad?"

He leaned forward and took her hand into his. "When and if the question is put to me, I'll answer it. In the meantime, Blue, I know you'll figure out just what I ought to say."

"That isn't fair, Tad. I'm only trying to prevent a disaster. I'm concerned because Josh is becoming so...so attached to you."

"The feeling is mutual. He's a great kid—bright, funny, eager to learn. I'm not insensitive, Blue. I know there's some risk involved in being Josh's friend. I just happen to think Josh was more at risk before we took an interest in him.''

Blue looked at Tad, admiring his willingness to get involved, wishing she could be as optimistic, as worry free about the consequences. ''Be careful, Tad. It's an enormous responsibility to have someone look up to you and admire you so much that they'd do anything to please you.''

''Are you speaking as an observer or from personal experience?''

''It doesn't matter. Just . . . be careful.''

His eyes dropped to her lips and returned to meet her gaze with a soft, questioning regard. ''Be careful with Josh? Or with you?''

Blue swallowed and made a feeble attempt at removing her hand from his. ''Josh, of course,'' she said in a shaky, breathy little voice. ''I can take care of myself.''

''Sure you can.'' He smiled then, but he didn't let go of her hand. ''That's why you're here in Dallas and your heart's still out in California.''

''Don't be silly, Tad. My heart is right where it's supposed to be.''

He lifted his hand and slipped it inside the left side of her blazer, placed it above her breast and pressed lightly. ''Are you sure it's here?'' he asked.

Blue shrugged in an effort to dislodge his hand, to escape the tantalizing feel of his touch. ''Don't, Tad.''

''Shhh. I'm trying to detect whether or not your heart is beating.''

Oh, it was beating, all right. Too fast. Too erratically. She did not want his hand to stay there. She did not want to feel so breathless, so completely at the mercy of the tumult within her body. She wanted to be in control. But Heaven help her, she also wanted his hand beneath her blouse, against her skin, on her breast. She wanted his lips on hers. She wanted . . . oh, but she wanted. . . .

Tad understood how she felt, even though she hadn't said a word. He allowed his impulse to take command and guide his hand downward until he could cradle her breast, until the rich fullness of her filled his palm and stirred his desire. He'd been fighting these feelings for too long now, and her idea of professional distance was about to kill him. Surely Blue was tired of the pretense, too.

He took a last irrevocable step forward, and the unhurried journey of his mouth to hers gave her time to draw back, time to escape if that was what she wanted. But she didn't move. She just waited there, her eyes shadowed, her lips slightly parted. She sighed softly as he captured her trembling lips beneath his own.

Her kiss was uncertain but powerful. A ripple of pure and undiluted yearning crested inside him and broke into waves of intense emotion. He couldn't recall the last time he'd felt this hot, sweet flash of desire. But he knew at once that it had been far too long. By the way Blue shivered when he eased the pressure against her lips, he thought she felt much the same way. It was time to put an end to this charade and to call her bluff on all the ridiculous restrictions she'd placed between them.

He lifted his head and let his hand slide away from her breast. Desire still ruled in the emerald depths of her eyes, and he basked for a moment in the delicacy of shared anticipation. "Come inside with me, Blue."

Her lips parted, but he didn't hear any protest. Okay, so he knew she had reservations. He knew she was emotionally vulnerable. But hell, so was he. Life was too short, and indecision stole too many special moments as it was.

"Come with me," he said again. "Celebrate today's success. Enjoy this moment. Right now. Share it with me."

He allowed himself a slight, softly pleading smile. "I promise to keep Janitor Man in the closet."

Her lips curved and she lifted one eyebrow. "Janitor Man?"

Tad gave a small shrug. "Well, if you'd rather be with him...?"

"I think I already have my hands full with you."

His smile went past the limits of acceptable enthusiasm, but...who cared? "Hold that thought," he said as he turned to open the door.

Chapter Ten

Blue stepped past Tad into his apartment, knowing that she ought to think twice—probably ten or twelve times—before she did. Celebrate with him? She'd end up in bed with him. She knew it. He knew it. Janitor Man might be the only one who didn't know where this was heading. And if she had a grain of sense, she'd bolt for safety. But instead she stood there, like an idiot, and took in the differences between his apartment and hers.

There weren't many. The apartments weren't big enough to support much individuality. A computer took up one whole corner of his living room and another sat on the dining table. There were all kinds of toys scattered about, and pictures and graphs decorated the walls. His apartment looked a lot like his office, and Blue had a flash of realization that something was missing from both places. Then she realized what it was. History. There were no old photographs, no souvenirs from the past, nothing much to indicate who he'd been a few years before. That only proved that he lived for the moment, not yesterday. And that hardly came as any surprise.

"Can I get you something to drink?" Tad came up behind her and stole what small measure of composure she'd managed to regain. "I don't have champagne, but there is a little bit of wine."

A nervous laugh issued from her throat. "Are you going to ply me with wine and take advantage of my lowered resistance?"

"That wasn't my intention, but now that you mention it, it sounds like a damn fine idea." He came around her, walked into the kitchen and opened the refrigerator. "Let me know as soon as your inhibitions drop."

She took a couple of steps after him, thinking she was going to need a drink before this was over. "Are you ever serious, Tad?"

"I try to look on the lighter side whenever possible. Besides when I'm serious, I scare you."

"No, you don't," she denied immediately. "What makes you think that?"

"The way you tremble every time I touch you."

"I don't."

Raising his head, he looked at her over the open refrigerator door. "Do you want me to prove it?"

She didn't.

Maybe she did.

She definitely wanted this impossible tension to end. What did he expect her to say? A simple yes? Could she do that?

"Yes." The word came out muted and indistinguishable. She swallowed a wellspring of caution and tried again. "Yes."

Tad straightened, an expression of genuine surprise on his face. The refrigerator door swung shut with a whoosh. "Yes?" he said hoarsely. "Did you say, *yes?*"

She was beginning to think better of the idea, wondering if he'd just been teasing her all along. But he didn't give her a chance to reconsider. In one step—the kitchen was really ridiculously small—he had her in his arms, had his lips on hers, had her trembling with need.

This was all wrong. Giving in to this—this physical attraction—was probably the worst possible thing they could do. It couldn't have a happy result, couldn't possibly bode well for the future of their working relationship. So what was she doing with her arms around him? What was she doing kissing him back? Why didn't she pull away, say she'd only been teasing and get the hell out of there?

Because she'd already made the choice to stay. Blue knew there was no point in denying it. Especially not when the tender pressure of his lips evoked an unequivocal surrender. Somewhere between the time her eyes had met his over the robot they'd invented and the moment he'd kissed her on the porch, she'd decided that when the opportunity arose she'd grab it. Maybe she was lonely. Maybe her body was simply starving for human contact. Maybe she only wanted to feel loved. Whatever the reason, she knew she was a goner, and she lifted her hands to cradle the back of Tad's neck.

If Tad had any second thoughts, he hid them well. In fact, Blue could hardly believe he hadn't planned every step of the seduction, he handled it with such finesse. The kiss he had initiated with such slow, persuasive insistence escalated to an intoxicating intensity. The embrace that had begun with tenderness tightened into a dual knot of desires...her hands tracing the muscled curve of his spine...his hands finding all sorts of pleasurable holds...his tongue teasing hers...her lips parted and inviting.

By the time he brought one hand up to cup her breast, Blue felt as though her emotions had already been thoroughly ravaged, beautifully plundered. And then he invented a whole new series of sensations for her, and she realized her emotions had barely left the starting gate. When he stopped kissing her and lifted his hands to her shoulders, she heard a soft moan of protest and knew it had to have come from her.

His brown eyes held steady on hers. He was still smiling as he traced the inner lapel of her blouse, from collar point to top button, sending spidery tingles along her skin. She wanted his finger to dip lower, to just touch the swell of her breasts, but he brought his hand back up to the base of her throat and then let it drift downward again. A sigh shuddered past her lips.

"May I take your jacket?" he asked quietly, politely, ignoring the fact that her breathing was heavy and hard. "I think you'd be more comfortable without it."

"You might be right," she managed to say as she started to struggle with the linen jacket.

His hands stopped hers and then gently and firmly **pushed** the material off her shoulders and guided it over her arms.

"Oh," she whispered when he tossed it aside. Then she reached for the middle button of his shirt and deftly unfastened it.

"Oh." He looked down at the front of his shirt with some surprise.

"I think you'd be more comfortable without this, Tad."

"I'd never argue with a vice president," he said as she undid his shirt and ran her palms inside the opening, creating a tug of material against the waistband of his jeans, creating a need he hadn't felt in too long, creating a definite tug on his heart.

Miranda Blue had unforeseen talents, he realized. His skin fairly burned beneath the gifted touch of her hands. Her flair for sensual stroking brought a faint sheen of perspiration to his chest. His heart pounded like a bass drum.

He hadn't thought Blue would ever lower her professional guard long enough to let him discover the passionate woman inside. Kisses were one thing. So was a scintillating attraction to each other. But this was something else again. Something surprising. Something exceedingly sweet. Something splendid. And he intended to enjoy every second of it.

Blue had been a shock to his system from the first. Everything she'd done, everything she'd said, had gotten under his skin in one way or another. And now she was in his arms, kissing him like a woman who knew exactly what she wanted and how to get it.

He couldn't see a single thing wrong with that.

Lifting his hands, he cupped her face and tilted her head so that she had to look at him. Her eyes were shiny with unspoken tensions, and he swallowed hard at the thought of how very pretty, how very desirable she was. He wanted her. But he wanted to make it special. A magic hour in a world of too much reality. Blue needed that. She deserved it.

He leaned forward and pressed his lips to hers, tenderly, possessively, hoping she would understand just how careful he meant to be. Of its own accord his hand drifted to her throat and down to the lowest point of bare skin. With no difficulty at all he released the top two buttons of her blouse, slid his hand beneath the silk and found his way to the lacy covering on her breast. She inhaled sharply as he made contact and then she sighed with new pleasure. Tad thought he might have sighed, too. But really, he wasn't thinking clearly enough to notice at the moment.

Blue was having trouble thinking at all. She felt as if she were just one big blush. She was hot, so very hot she was afraid she might begin to melt. Tad's thumb circled the puckered center of her breast, sending spirals of pleasure echoing through her body. She buried her hands beneath the folds of his shirt . . . the one she'd meant to strip from his shoulders . . . the one she hadn't quite managed to remove as yet. Delight coursed through her when she felt the tautness of his muscled chest, the thudding of his heartbeat against her palm. This might be all wrong, but oh, glory, did it feel right. She hadn't felt so *right* in years.

When his hand stole downward past her hip and slipped under the hemline of her skirt, she stumbled. Not literally, of course, since she was standing perfectly still. But she jerked, startled by her sudden, heated response to that one touch. Tad moved, gathering her quickly and efficiently lifting her into his arms. His lips grazed her temple with a murmur as he carried her into the bedroom.

She didn't hear or care what he'd said. His touch was the only thing that mattered. Her need the only concern she could focus on.

He laid her on the bed and stripped off his own shirt. Without breaking the hold of his gaze, he removed the rest of his clothing before he turned his attention to removing hers.

In moments the silk blouse was a heap on the floor. Gone, too, was the linen skirt that matched the jacket he'd tossed carelessly somewhere in the outer rooms. A lacy bra, thigh-high nylons, bikini briefs, and a sensible pair of low-heeled shoes were all that was left of her professional appearance. There wasn't even a tatter left of the professional distance she'd tried so futilely to maintain.

Tad seemed perfectly happy with the change. The loss of restrictions and good sense didn't appear to bother him in the least. In fact he looked almost mesmerized as he stood beside the bed. Blue had to smile at the hard swallow he took when she lifted her right knee and began to roll down the hosiery. It was moments like this, she decided, that gave a woman a real sense of power.

Tad didn't waste much time before he answered her challenge. He knelt beside her and finished undressing her with tender delight. Then, as he wrapped her in his arms, holding her tightly, possessively, he showed her that power plays had no part in this seduction.

He touched her and she responded. He moved and she followed. He asked and she acquiesced. But he exercised no power other than pleasure, no demands other than the promise of a sweet fulfillment. Passions mingled. Tension built to a fevered pitch, banked to a slow, aching desire and then crescendoed in a frenzied rhythm of need. Blue was besieged with new sensations and the strong feeling that she belonged here. Here with Tad, in his arms, possessed by his tenderness, open to his special gift for living.

When the waves of release finally swept through her, she clung to him, wanting the magic to continue, wanting to belong just a little longer. He tensed, trembled with release, and then slowly, lovingly, he brought their lovemaking to a gentle end.

He rolled to his back, pulling Blue with him, nestling her between the curve of his arm and the curve of his body. With a sigh she lay her head on his shoulder and let the soft warmth of satisfaction fill every part of her being.

"'But, soft! what light through yonder window breaks? It is the east, and Juliet is the sun! Arise, fair sun, and kill the envious moon....'"

Somewhere beyond the window, outside in the garden, Aunt Grizelle read to her roses.

"The pinks," Tad said, his chest rising and falling comfortably beneath her head. "She's reading Shakespeare to the pinks."

"'See, how she leans her cheek upon her hand!

O! that I were a glove upon that hand,

That I might touch that cheek . . . !'"

"*Romeo and Juliet,*" Blue whispered, wishing Aunt Grizelle had chosen to read something else to the pink roses . . . something with a happy ending.

Tad's arm tightened around her as if he sensed her sudden doubts. He offered reassurance with a stroke of his hand through her hair. Blue didn't know what she ought to do next. It was too early for sleep. They'd already had dinner. Should she just get out of bed, gather up her clothes and go home? Should she lie here and wait for Romeo to climb up to Juliet's window? She didn't have any training for this particular situation, and she felt completely awkward and uncertain.

Funny. Five minutes ago she'd felt perfectly wonderful.

"'That which we call a rose—'" Tad quoted softly in unison with Aunt Grizelle's distant voice "'—by any other name would smell as sweet.'" His sigh was deep and contented. "So, Miranda Blue, tell me about you."

She stirred against the solid mass of his body, but she didn't gain any distance or any great perspective. "What do you want to know?"

"Tell me what happened to you at McKinley Enterprises. Tell me about the guy in the picture."

Blue had thought there was a certain convention about "sweet nothings" being whispered back and forth after two people made love for the first time. That's what usually happened in books and movies. In her own limited experience with intimacy, she seemed to recall that some small talk bridged the gap between lovemaking and the new direction of the relationship. Obviously that didn't hold true with Tad. He wanted to know all about her past . . . and Rob.

"Nothing happened," she denied out of habit. "And I really would rather not talk about it."

"So, which is it?"

She frowned. "Which is what?"

"Either nothing happened and there's nothing to talk about or something happened and you don't wish to talk about it. You can tell me, Blue. We're friends."

Friends. The word chilled Blue. She didn't want to be friends with Tad. She didn't want to talk to him about Rob or McKinley Enterprises...or anything else. "I don't think so, Tad."

By the tone of her voice Tad realized he'd made a tactical error. He'd believed that now that they'd shared a beautiful and barrier-destroying intimacy, there was no need for secrets. No reason to hold back the private hurts and broken dreams of the past. He was prepared to bare his soul, to tell her about his wife, Lindy, to tell her about his son, Jeremy. But apparently Blue wasn't in the mood for sharing. Obviously she hadn't been quite as moved by the experience as he. "Sorry," he said, trying not to sound wounded. "I just thought—"

"Forget it." Blue moved from the circle of his arm to the edge of the bed. "We shouldn't have done this, Tad. It will ruin our working relationship. This was so—I can't believe I—"

"Whoa, there." Tad managed to get hold of her arm before she was out of reach. "Lie back down here and tell me what in hell you're talking about."

She didn't lie down again, but she did turn to look at him. Her green eyes were wide and frightened, as if she'd committed a crime and only now was aware of the consequences. Tad couldn't imagine why his innocent question had evoked this reaction. Unless she was still in love with the other guy. The thought choked him.

"Look, Tad." Her voice trembled with sudden anxiety. "Let's forget this happened, okay? It was poor judgment on both our parts." The fright in her eyes gave way to cool decision. The tremor in her voice firmed with new resolve. "I'll get my things and go to my apartment and we'll act as if—"

"Wait a minute." Tad sat up in bed, still keeping a good grasp on her arm. "You know, Blue, if you didn't enjoy it, you can just say so. I thought making love to you was...." *Beautiful. Special. The beginning of something more.* Tad couldn't say that now, though. Not in the face of almost certain rejection. "I thought it was...fun. I thought you enjoyed it, too. My mistake." He shrugged as he released her arm. "There's no need to take it so seriously, Blue."

He'd wounded her. He could see it in her eyes. Not frightened now. Not even shiny, but dull with hurt. He felt awful, but damn it, he'd thought she wanted a way out. A graceful exit. "Blue...?" he began, but she was already off the bed, already picking up her clothes, already... gone.

Tad fell back against the pillow and wondered what had gone wrong. It was all too obvious that bringing up her past had been a dumb thing to do. Also obvious was the fact that she must still care a great deal about that McKinley guy, even though he'd hurt her.

And now, ass that he was, Tad had hurt her, too. All because he'd thought... It didn't matter what he'd thought. Blue wasn't thinking along the same lines, so...okay. He'd bow out of the picture, go back to the other side of that professional distance she was so fond of and try to talk himself out of the idea that he might—just might—have been a little bit in love with her.

BLUE SLAMMED the bathroom door, threw her clothes in a heap on the floor and turned on the tap. *Fun.* He'd thought making love to her was *fun.* That was Tad's only pursuit. *Fun.* Why had she thought—even for a split second—that he could be serious?

What was it in her nature that drew her into these impossible relationships? First Rob. Now Tad. Men she worked with. Two men, who in different ways had been her mentors. Two men, who in different ways expected her to be someone she wasn't. Two totally different men, yet with that one simple common denominator—neither one of them really wanted her.

Rob had wanted the challenge she represented. She'd been the forbidden fruit. The one person in his life who told him no and meant it. Someone so much like himself that he'd wanted to change her.

And Tad. She supposed she was a challenge to him, too. She was too serious, too structured, too ambitious. And he'd wanted her to be different, more like he was, more spontaneous. Fun. With Tad there'd been no wife to bring up a moral issue. They were both independent and over the age of consent. So, in a moment of weakness, she'd said yes and he'd made love to her...*for the stupid fun of it.*

She grasped the tap and gave it another sharp twist. Hot water gushed into the tub, sending scalding steam across the tile, streaking her face with sudden perspiration. Of all the dumb mistakes she'd made in her life—and really there weren't that many—this was the worst. She was embarrassed. It wasn't as if she'd been in love with Rob. She'd loved his image, envied his success, been dazzled by his power.

But Tad. Well, what was it she loved about him? Not his image, certainly. He still dressed like a...well, like a janitor. And his success? Well, he wasn't a failure, but he wasn't the chief executive officer, either. And power? Ha! The only power he had came from a battery pack.

Who did he think he was anyway? He'd thought making love to her was *fun!* He'd said he could be serious and then he'd coerced her into his bed. He'd seduced her and...

Blue fanned the steam away from her face and opened the cold water tap. Then she turned to the fogged-up mirror. Okay. So it hadn't exactly been one-sided. She would accept responsibility for her participation in this... this fiasco. If only she'd had a little more experience, if only she'd known how to handle the aftermath of passion, maybe he wouldn't have asked about the past, brought Rob McKinley right into bed with them.

Blue groaned at the memory and her own ridiculous overreaction. Why couldn't she have passed it off as unimportant? Why couldn't she have found some way to make a graceful exit? Why had she made a big deal out of nothing?

Because she'd been scared.

That was it, of course. In the past few years she hadn't had intimate experiences with men because she was afraid of losing her edge, losing the power, the status, she'd gained through her career. She'd imagined herself in love with Rob because he'd been everything she wanted and he was married, safe. But then she'd lost everything, anyway.

And now there was Tad. Tad, who had helped her piece her life back together, who had encouraged her to use her creative powers for her own enjoyment, who had expected her to find her own area of interest and pursue it, not for the sake of success, but simply because it pleased her. And surprisingly enough, success had followed.

Little Zeke. Her creation. With Tad's help, of course. But still hers in a way nothing had ever been hers before.

Tad had taught her to trust her instincts. He'd teased her, badgered her, argued with her and kissed her. He didn't care about her career. He cared about whether or not she was enjoying herself. She'd thought she was safe with him, too, so she'd said yes to him and lost again.

Blue grabbed a washcloth from under the cabinet, tossed it into the tub and then followed it, allowing the hot bath to swallow her body in its warm embrace. His touch had felt so good. She could still feel the weakness he'd created inside of her, still remember the swirling wonder of sensation and emotion.

Tad had done a terrible thing to her. He'd stolen her edge. He'd forced her to rediscover a childlike delight in living—a delight she'd nearly forgotten she possessed. And he'd let her fall in love with him . . . for the fun of it.

Blue sank up to her chin in the bath water, wishing Tad would tap on the door, wishing he would open the door, wishing he would tell her something, anything to wipe out the last ten minutes and take them back to Romeo and Juliet.

. . . *A rose by any other name* . . .

Okay. She wouldn't name this emotion *love*. She'd call it . . . *infatuation*. Or maybe *misguided regard*. Yes. That sounded good. She'd come to regard Tad with respect and some admiration. She'd misinterpreted those feelings as something more personal. It had happened before, but it wouldn't happen again. Twice burned and all that.

From now on she'd be more careful. She'd resurrect a professional distance between herself and Tad if it killed her. But she would survive. She would overcome. She was a woman of the nineties. A successful career woman. Having a relationship with a man was not necessary for her happiness. Not in the slightest.

She only hoped her heart was paying attention.

Chapter Eleven

"Is it okay if you and Tad have rooms on the same floor or should I make a separate reservation for you at a hotel across town?" Ellie lounged against the door frame as she stood poised to write Blue's instructions on a steno pad. "It's all the same to me, you know. One hotel or two hotels. One room or two. I'm just the secretary. I don't have to know what's going on. I do what I'm told to do and I don't ask any questions." She blew a small bubble and then sucked the gum back into her mouth with an aggravating pop. "You and Tad still on the outs or what?"

Blue laid down her pen. "Tad and I are not, as you put it, 'on the outs.' We're merely very busy getting ready to go to the product convention. As for the hotel accommodations, I thought you'd taken care of that weeks ago."

"I did," Ellie said with some satisfaction. "But with the recent drop in temperature around this place, I thought I should double-check. You're scheduled to leave tomorrow, you know. So this is the last day to make changes in the accommodations. If you don't want to be next door to Tad, you'd better speak up now or I won't be responsible for what happens."

"For Pete's sake, Ellie." Blue pushed up from the desk, annoyed by her secretary's goading. "I don't give a damn where the hotel room is located. Tad can be next door, down the hall or ten flights up for all I care. If you've made the reservations, then forget about it and worry about something else. Okay?''

Ellie took a minute to scribble some notes on the steno pad. ''You're sitting next to him on the plane,'' she said in an exaggerated drawl. ''That could be dangerous. Frost could accumulate on the wings and the plane could crash. Attitude affects everything, you know. I probably ought to notify the FAA of the chill in the air.''

Blue had thought that during the past week she and Tad had done an excellent job of concealing the fact that they were barely speaking to each other. ''You're imagining things, Ellie.''

''If you say so.'' Ellie made another scribble on the notepad. ''It could be my imagination that something happened between you and Tad last week and since then neither one of you has had a nice word to say to the other.'' The snap of her gum punctuated the sentence. ''And it could be my imagination that the tension in this office is as thick as my grandmother's cheesecake. And it could be my imagination that some of the employees in Production have set up a departmental wager as to what the atmosphere will be like when you and Tad get back from New Mexico.'' This time the snap of gum was accompanied by a shrug. ''But don't give it another thought, it's probably just my imagination.''

''Ellie . . .'' Blue pursed her lips and tried to behave as if there couldn't possibly be any truth to the allegations. She was very glad that neither Tad nor Uncle Horse were in their offices at the moment. ''I hope you were smart enough not to place any bets.''

The telephone rang, and with a sly smile Ellie slipped the notepad into the crook of her arm. ''It's not nice to fool

Mother Nature,'' she said, and then she turned on her heel and went to answer the phone.

What was that supposed to mean, Blue wondered. Ellie suspected that something had transpired, but she didn't—couldn't—know exactly what. So she was fishing for clues, angling for an explanation. There wasn't really a betting pool in the Production Department. And Ellie didn't know for sure that anything was wrong. She was guessing, that was all.

Blue resumed her seat and picked up her pen. She wanted to complete the schedule of projected production costs for Little Zeke before—

"That does it! I have had it!" Ellie's voice, raised in frustration, and the simultaneous slam of the telephone receiver brought Blue up out of her chair again. She walked to the door of her office to meet Ellie's angry glare.

"Do you want to tell me what's going on?" Blue asked.

"What could be going on?" Ellie said. "Just because I do a little yelling doesn't mean anything is going on. It must be your imagination, Blue. Nothing is wrong. Everything is fine. Just hunky-dory.''

Tone of voice alone gave the lie to her statements, and Blue wondered how to calm Ellie down. "Are you okay, Ellie? Is there something you want to talk about?''

Ellie reached under her desk and grabbed her oversized purse, which she promptly slapped down in the middle of her desk. "Something *I* want to talk about? Now where did you get that idea? You can't tell me what's going on between you and Tad, but you expect me to pour out my problems with—" She clamped off the last words, but it wasn't hard for Blue to fill in the blank. Jim Bill. There was trouble in Ellie's paradise.

"I'm going home," Ellie announced with a determined lift of her chin. "You can tell anyone who asks that I'm not here and I don't know when I'll be back. And if that woman from the junior college calls back, you can tell her I am not interested!''

Junior college? Blue crossed her arms as Ellie hiked her purse strap over her shoulder and started toward the door. ''Ellie? Wait.'' Blue stepped forward. ''Why are you getting calls from a woman at the junior college?''

Ellie offered her best don't-be-dumb look.

Blue concealed a smile. ''Are you thinking about going on to school? This would be a great opportunity to—''

''Hold it. I've already heard this spiel. I'm getting married and I don't have to go to college. Period! End of discussion! My future is decided. I am not going back to school.'' The purse strap slipped from her shoulder and she jerked it back into place. ''No matter what Jim Bill says.''

This was getting interesting, Blue decided. ''Let's go downstairs to the snack bar, Ellie. I'll buy you a soda and we'll ... talk. Okay?''

''If you think I'm going to talk about this, you're mistaken.'' Ellie gave a little sniff. ''I mean, you won't talk to me about what happened with Tad and so you can't expect me to tell you—'' another sniff and an angry sigh ''—about Jimmy.''

With belated intuition, Blue realized that this had been Ellie's aim all along. She'd had a fight with her boyfriend and she needed someone to talk to. And it was always better to talk to someone who could understand, preferably someone who had also just had a fight with a boyfriend. Blue didn't feel qualified, exactly, but she thought she could certainly lend a sympathetic ear. ''Let's go downstairs,'' she suggested again.

Ellie eyed her with mingled caution and curiosity. ''Will you tell me what happened with Tad?''

"Every sordid detail," Blue said. She wouldn't, of course. But Ellie would never know that.

In no time at all they were seated at one of the three tiny tables by the snack bar. Blue had a cup of coffee. Ellie had a cherry cola, a bag of chips, a candy bar and a blueberry muffin. She had, she confided to Blue, been a little off her feed lately. Blue nodded her understanding and confided that she hadn't had much of an appetite, either.

Ellie's eyes lit like firecrackers. "Oooh, it must be bad if you couldn't eat. What happened?" she asked. "You and Tad did have a fight, didn't you? What was it about? Are you still mad? Men are the pits, aren't they?"

From there Blue had only to make concurring noises as Ellie poured out her own problem. Jim Bill, it seemed, was having second thoughts. Not about marrying Ellie, of course, but about getting married before he finished his term of enlistment. Wouldn't it be better, he'd been telling Ellie, if she went to school while he was away. Then, once he was out of the navy, they could marry and finish getting their educations before they started a family. It was a good, practical idea, he'd told Ellie.

And when she'd told him to run his idea, along with his skivvies, up the ship's flagpole and see who saluted, he'd said a few choice words about her maturity level—remarks that Ellie felt were uncalled for and unfair, especially since she'd spent two hours before his phone call baking cookies to send to him. Chocolate chip cookies. His favorite. And hers. But she hadn't eaten a single one so that *he* could have them all.

"Men," she said in conclusion, "are jackasses."

In the interest of being supportive in this woman-to-woman discussion, Blue agreed without a qualm. "You're right. Men are more trouble than they're worth."

"I didn't say *that*." Ellie quickly backed off her position. "I mean, just because he got this one stupid idea doesn't mean I don't love him anymore. I do. If I didn't, I wouldn't care whether we got married tomorrow or ten years from now. But I do care, so there's no reason not to get married when he gets leave in December like we planned."

Blue sighed. "Can I have the blueberry muffin?"

Ellie pushed it across the tabletop. "I love Jim Bill. I want to be with him. I mean, look, Blue, I'm engaged to him. I ought to be wherever he is. Except I can't be on the ship. They won't allow that. But he has two more years before he gets out and that's twenty-four months, seven hundred and thirty days that I could be right there with him whenever he didn't have to be on the ship. Doesn't that make sense to you? More sense than me bein' here and him bein' there. Texas is a long way from Virginia, you know. And when his ship docks he's going to want me to be there and he's going to want to get married right then. I know he will. He just isn't thinkin' real clear at the moment."

"He's thinking about your future, Ellie, which shows a great deal of maturity on his part. Postponing the wedding for a couple of years will give you the opportunity to go to college without any extra responsibilities to worry about and your marriage will only be stronger for it."

"Oh, yeah. Like hell it will. It'll be a whole lot stronger if I don't give him a chance to find himself a girl in every port." Ellie picked up the can of soda and swallowed two long gulps. "I'm not stupid, you know. Sailors have a reputation for being great lovers, and Jim Bill is just about the finest specimen of male that ever walked the earth. It's only natural that other women will try to steal him away from me. That's why I need to be with him instead of sitting in some stuffy classroom."

Taking a small bite of muffin, Blue debated the wisdom of tackling this discussion. But...oh, well, why not? "You know, Ellie, if Jim Bill is the kind of guy who wants to have a girl in every port, you'll be much better off with a college degree than with him."

Ellie ripped open the candy bar wrapper. "Yeah. Well, if he's met somebody else, I'll scratch her eyes out. Just as soon as I get through beating him to a pulp. And I won't need a college degree to do either!"

"If that's the way you talk to him, you'll be lucky if he even wants to see you in December."

"Hmmph. He'll want to see me." Ellie sank her teeth into the chocolate bar. "I know my Jimmy."

Blue removed the paper from around the muffin, one pleat at a time, wondering why she'd thought she could reason with a lovesick nineteen-year-old. "Well, I wish you would consider going to school, Ellie. An education is a valuable thing to have, and a little life experience is not going to hurt your marriage."

"You have an education," Ellie said with a shrug, "and life experience. But you're not all that happy. In fact, how do you know you wouldn't be happier right now if you'd married your high school sweetheart when you had the chance?"

"I didn't have a high school sweetheart," Blue replied patiently.

"College boyfriend, then. There must have been some-body who wanted to marry you, somebody you turned down so you could have a *career.*"

"That is not the point, Ellie. The point is you should get an education. Jim Bill is mature enough to see that, and if you don't, then you're not as smart as I think you are."

Ellie stuffed the last bite of candy into her mouth and eyed Blue speculatively as she chewed. "Okay," she said around the mouthful of chocolate. "I'll think about college. Now you tell me what happened with Tad."

With a frown Blue quickly invented a story. "We had an argument about the toy robot and whether it was ready to be presented at the trade show. I won. Little Zeke is going."

Ellie looked skeptical. "You never win an argument with Tad."

"This time I did."

"And now you're not speaking to him?"

"Something like that."

"That's childish, Blue. If you're going to argue with a man, at least argue over something important."

A smile curved despite her best attempt to hide it. "I'll keep that in mind, Ellie. Maybe while we're in New Mexico, Tad and I can find something of importance to argue about."

Ellie grinned and popped a stick of chewing gum into her mouth. "Swear you'll tell me everything when you get back or I'm calling the hotel and rearranging your room reservations. You might just find yourself locked in a closet with Tad 'The Hunk' Denton."

Blue laughed. "Spare me that, Ellie. I am, after all, a career woman."

"Yeah, well, we all make mistakes. But hang in there, Blue. Life experience may have a few surprises for you yet. Who knows? You might meet a sexy sailor in the hotel lobby."

"If his name is Jim Bill, I'll let you know."

Ellie gave her gum a ferocious snap and stood up. "That isn't funny, Blue. That isn't funny at all."

TAD TAPPED on the bathroom door. "Blue? I'm bleeding. Open the door."

The mascara wand slipped in her hand and left tracks on her eyelid. Blue frowned at her reflected image. They were going to miss the plane. He'd had the bathroom first and now she was never going to be ready in time. "I'll be out of here in a minute," she said tersely.

He replied with a second, firmer tap on the door. "If I don't get to a styptic pencil pretty quick, you're going to have to take me to the hospital instead of to the airport."

Blue licked her fingertip and tried to erase the smudge of mascara before she reluctantly reached over and opened the door for him. At least, she thought, she was already dressed.

Tad wasn't. "You're not even dressed," she said as her gaze took in the expanse of bare male chest, which suddenly took up more than half the mirror space.

"I'm *bleeding,*" he said. "I took off my shirt so the blood wouldn't get on the collar. Somehow that just seemed the prudent thing to do."

Blue lifted an eyebrow. Sharing this bathroom with Tad was not the prudent thing to do at five o'clock in the morning. Probably not at any time, morning or night. His presence unnerved her, her mouth felt cottony dry, and she tightened her grip on the mascara wand. "There's hardly more than a drop of blood on your neck. You could have waited until I was finished in here."

"Easy for you to say. You're not the one who's bleeding." He rummaged through the drawer on his side of the sink and eventually came up with the styptic pencil. With a nod in her direction he turned on the tap and moistened the stick before placing it on the minuscule cut on his neck. "I cut myself shaving," he explained. "I thought it had stopped, but when I put on my shirt, I noticed it was still bleeding."

"Lucky thing you discovered the leak before you lost too much blood."

He leaned in, closer to the mirror...and to her. "That's me. Mr. Lucky."

Blue stepped back rather than try to apply the rest of her makeup with him in the room. "Am I in your way?"

His grin was slow and sure. His gaze locked onto hers in the mirror. "Nope. I think it's kind of nice to share a mirror with you. Especially when your hair's all damp and curly."

"I haven't combed—" Her hand flew to her hair, but she stopped herself from fiddling with it, trying to smooth it out. "We're going to be late unless we hurry."

Tad examined his neck in the mirror. Blue tried not to stare at his bare shoulders. He caught her in a weak moment, though, and smiled as she tried to disguise the hungry look that probably showed all too clearly in her eyes. "All I have to do," he said, "is put on my shirt. Then I'm just waiting on you."

"If you'd get out of here and let me finish, we might still make our plane." Blue lifted the mascara wand in a gesture that she thought clearly told him to move out of the way.

He didn't seem to get the message, although he did sidestep to give her more room in front of the sink. "We'll make it, Blue. You worry too much."

"I don't know why Ellie booked us on such an early flight."

"Meanness, I expect. She's got a mean streak half a mile wide. Poor Jim Bill doesn't know what he's in for."

"Oh, I think 'poor Jim Bill' has a pretty good idea. Ellie's been upset lately because he wants to postpone the wedding until he gets out of the service. He's trying to get her to go to college."

Tad craned his neck again to see if the scratch had stopped bleeding. "What did Ellie have to say about that?"

"Take three guesses, but the first two don't count." Blue decided she wasn't going to let Tad make her any later, even though he took up too much space in the mirror and was far too much of a distraction. The sight of his muscled chest and broad shoulders drew her eyes again and again to his reflection. The very nearness of him made her feel restless and made the blood pulse through her veins like a hot, sweet tide. There was no way she could finish putting on her makeup with him standing beside her, sharing the mirror and this too-tiny room. She'd just give her eyelashes a quick once-over—to demonstrate that she was not bothered by his presence—and then she'd get the hell out of the bathroom.

Tad finished his inspection of his cut and watched her brush mascara across her lashes. She was nervous... either because she was running late or because he was standing beside her. He thought it was probably the former and hoped it might have something to do with the latter. Either way he wasn't much inclined to let the moment end. She hadn't said this many words to him since the evening they'd made love. She was still angry about that, although he hadn't yet figured out why. He was hoping this trip would provide some answers. At least it offered an opportunity for them to discuss the problem. They were going to be together, almost day and night, during the next four days. He was determined to produce a warming trend in their relationship.

Blue's gaze flicked to his in the mirror and shifted immediately back to her own image. "Are you going to get ready to leave? Or are you just going to stand here and watch me smear my makeup?"

"I'm ready to go," he said with an easy smile. "Except for my shirt, but I want to hear more about Ellie and higher education."

"I can tell you on the plane."

"What if we're not sitting together?" Tad folded his arms, loving the intimacy of sharing this morning ritual with her, loving the way she looked, the way she leaned toward the mirror, the way her mouth formed that little *o* while she darkened her eyelashes with mascara. "What if I'm in first class and you're in coach? It could happen, you know. You'd better go ahead and tell me about Ellie now. I'm not sure I can wait until we get to Albuquerque."

"There's not much to tell. Jim Bill made the suggestion and Ellie told him where he could put it."

"She wasn't receptive, huh?"

Blue put on a soft rosy shade of lipstick and Tad wished he might be allowed to kiss it away. She pressed her lips together to set the gloss, and a warm sense of desire uncurled deep inside him. "She hung up on the woman who called from the junior college. And I had to part with a couple of dollars to get her to tell me what was going on."

"You bribed her?"

With a frown Blue reached for her hairbrush. "I bought her a soda, but since she'd been 'off her feed lately,' as she put it, I also had to spring for chips, candy and a blueberry muffin. She let me have the muffin."

"Along with an earful of all Jim Bill's many faults."

"He is the finest specimen of a male ever to walk this earth," Blue said dryly. "In Ellie's eyes that pretty well overshadows any faults."

"I can see where it would."

"She did say she'd consider going to school, though. So maybe there is hope for her yet."

Tad nodded, fascinated by the movement of the brush through Blue's hair. The curls lengthened before his eyes and straightened into her usual smooth style. The hair was velvet dark around her face and her eyes seemed extra large and deeper green than normal. He wanted badly to touch her, to sink his fingers into the lustrous strands of hair and feel the dampness and the texture for himself.

"I like this," he said quietly.

"What?" She pulled the brush through her hair one more time before laying it aside. "Having to hurry to catch a plane? Or making *me* have to hurry?"

"Watching you. There's something alluring about watching a woman get ready to go out."

She turned toward him briefly, her eyes wide with a sudden tension, but then she turned back to the mirror and used it as a buffer zone. "If you're waiting for me to ask you to zip up my dress, you'll be disappointed. There isn't a zipper and I was able to manage the buttons on my blouse without any problem."

"I might need help with my shirt," he said. "I am injured, you know."

"If you're looking for sympathy, you've come to the wrong place."

"Sympathy wasn't what I had in mind."

Her gaze slipped to meet his in the mirror and then darted back to her own image as she smoothed the arch of her eyebrows with a fingertip. "I'm sure you can manage to button your own shirt, Tad. And since you never wear anything except the most casual clothing, I know you can't need help with cuff links or a tie. So unless you want me to tie your shoelaces, I can't imagine why else you're still standing here."

Tad had his foot propped on the counter before the last word was out of her mouth. With a flick of his fingers he had the laces of his shoe untied. "Would you mind?" he asked politely. "My neck hurts when I bend over."

She looked at his size-eleven foot, and he watched the smile that struggled for control of her mouth. She won, though, and the smile was confined to a twitch at the corners of her lips. "Tad Denton," she said evenly. "You are the most—"

"Captivating man you've ever met. Don't bother to deny it, Blue. I can see in your eyes that you know it's true." He leaned forward and retied the shoelace himself. "'I am what I am and that's all that I am,'" he quoted with a grin. "And that, in case you didn't recognize it, Ms. V.P., is the theme from 'Popeye the Sailor Man.'"

She laughed then, a pure crystalline delight of sound that quite put the finishing touch on Tad's morning. "Ellie told me I might run into a sailor," Blue said as she gathered up her makeup and stashed it away in a travel bag. "She'll be so relieved to hear that his name is Popeye."

Tad didn't follow the line of Blue's amusement, but he decided it wasn't important to know why she had laughed. What was important was that the tension between them was eased and the road now open to a mutually enjoyable four days. "You know, Blue, if you don't get a move on, we are going to miss that plane."

With an arch look she tucked the makeup bag under her arm and turned toward her door. "You worry too much, Tad." And with that she left him with his foot still propped against the sink, his neck streaked with the powdery residue of the styptic pencil, his good humor intact and his hopes high. When he went to get his shirt, he left the connecting door open.

Maybe, he thought with some optimism, it would still be open when this trip was over.

GOING ON A BUSINESS TRIP was, like everything else in
Uncle Horse's life, a cause for celebration and ceremony.
He viewed Blue's and Tad's departure as an occasion and
had invited any and all of the employees to participate.
Uncle Horse, Aunt Grizelle, Josh, Ellie, a half dozen other
employees who had worked on either Little Zeke or Talk-
to-Me Rose, were on hand for the scheduled six o'clock
departure. The waiting area for Gate 23 was crowded with
well-wishers, and the enthusiasm of the group flowed
around Blue like so many bright-colored streamers.

"You take good care of Little Zeke," Josh said, his hair
still tousled from sleep, his eyes shiny with excitement at
being included in the send-off party, as he took Blue's
hand. Only for a moment, of course. At thirteen he didn't
want to be observed in the giving or receiving of affection. "And take care of Tad. Don't let him have too much
fun without me. Okay?"

Blue smiled at the boy and squeezed his hand before allowing him to draw it away from hers. "We'll be working,
Josh. I don't think there'll be much of an opportunity for
having fun."

"Tad always has fun," Josh said.

Blue couldn't have put it better herself.

Ellie walked up to Blue and slipped a pack of chewing
gum into her hand. "Chew this during takeoff and land-
ing. It'll keep your ears from closing up. And remember
what I said about arguing with Tad. I have a substantial
amount of money riding on the outcome of this trip."

"Ellie . . . ?" Blue's reprimand was cut off by the
boarding call, and Uncle Horse came to take both of
Blue's hands into both of his.

"This is it, Miranda Blue," he said with his usual wild-
eyed urgency. "You and Tad should let these products sell
themselves. And the two of you should just enjoy being

there. The important thing is to have a good time and not spend your time worrying. Remember . . . work is fun, and fun is fun, and there's no reason not to have fun when you work.'' His bushy white brows wiggled up and down. ''It's simple, Miranda, and I trust you to uphold the Garrison family tradition.''

Blue smiled lamely. *Heigh Ho. Heigh Ho. It's off to work we go.* Her uncle didn't know the first thing about the Garrison family tradition. The problem was he didn't know that he didn't know. ''I'll do my best for you, Uncle Horse,'' she said. ''And for the company.''

Aunt Grizelle nudged her husband out of the way and patted Blue's arm. ''Now, Miranda, eat slowly while you're away. Don't just gobble a sandwich. Take time for a real meal. It eases the stress of being away from home.''

Blue nodded and was glad when Tad touched her shoulder and indicated that they should board the plane. The goodbyes were loud and cheerful and at the last minute, Josh ran forward for a last, long hug. ''I'll take care of Zeke,'' he told Tad. ''Don't worry about a thing.''

''I won't, Josh,'' Tad assured the boy. ''Not with you in charge.''

''Keep Ellie's spirits up.'' Blue leaned closer to whisper in Josh's ear. ''And tell her your plans for college. She wants to know *everything* about it.'' She winked at Josh's skeptical look. ''Trust me.''

''Goodbye. See ya Monday afternoon.'' Josh waved his arms high above his head, and Tad and Blue paused just before entering the plane to wave back.

''I can't believe this,'' Blue said. ''They're all acting like we're going off on a vacation or a trip around the world or something.''

''Or a honeymoon.''

Blue couldn't believe he'd said that. "I hardly think they'd get up at this hour of the morning to see anyone off on a honeymoon."

With a shrug Tad waited for her to go ahead of him down the aisle. "Stranger things have happened," he said.

Blue couldn't think of a single reply.

Chapter Twelve

People were everywhere. People in business suits. Men wearing silk ties in Windsor knots. Women with scarves at the necks of their white or pastel blouses. Men in pin-striped shirts and high-gloss shoes. Women carrying briefcases and wearing sensible heels. The look of success. The low hum of productive conversation. Concise notes jotted in pocket diaries. Appointments penciled in. Business cards exchanged.

A surge of adrenaline pumped through Blue's veins as she waited in line to register at the hotel. Behind her Tad sat on his suitcase and read a paperback mystery. "Look at all the people, Tad. There must be a couple of hundred right here in the lobby."

"One hundred eighty-three," he said as he closed his book and glanced up.

She was impressed. She hadn't thought he was paying any attention. "Are you sure?" she asked with another visual scan of the lobby. "Did you count them?"

"I didn't have to. I just looked at the top of the page. Wonderful inventions, books. Not only can you read them, they automatically number each page so you never lose your place. Clever, huh?"

With a sigh she turned around and moved herself and her luggage a step closer to the registration desk. "Be careful you don't lose your place in line, Einstein," she said over her shoulder.

"I'm with you every step of the way, so don't get trampled in the rush to get a room."

"Do you suppose all of these people are staying in this one hotel?" Blue couldn't resist wondering about the people she saw. A little more than a year ago, she'd been one of them. A mover and a shaker. A good-sized cog in the wheels of one of the biggest marketing firms in the country. Now she was on the other side. A rubber band in the gears of a wind-up toy. "Do you think they're all here for the product convention?"

"Either that or Elvis has been spotted in the restaurant."

Blue shot him an annoyed look. "Are you going to be like this all weekend?"

"What can I say? When I get away from home, I'm just one wild and crazy guy." He yawned and got to his feet. "And if I don't get to a bed pretty soon, I may have to stretch out for a nap right here in the lobby."

Two people at the front of the line moved and Blue closed the gap. Only one more person stood between her and registration. She could handle another five minute wait. "I think we should check in with the trade-show people right away. We'll want to get our booth assignment and start setting up as soon as possible."

Tad looked at her in alarm. "How many of these things have you been to?"

"Enough," she said coolly. "Why? How many have you been to?"

"More than enough." He ran a hand through his attractively disheveled hair. "Don't be so eager, Blue. You're on the other side of the game now. We're here to sell our ideas. All we have to do is put the prototypes on the table, sit back and let the free-enterprise system take care of the rest. Don't worry, Little Zeke will do fine.''

''May I help you?'' The desk clerk cleared his throat as he extended a pen and a registration form across the marble desk. ''Do you have a reservation?''

Blue gratefully accepted the interruption and stepped forward to register.

''Really?'' She heard Tad say behind her a minute later. ''Well—'' He drew out that one word into four syllables. ''As a matter of fact, I am from Texas. Dallas. The 'Big D.''' A casual glance showed Blue that Tad had struck up a conversation with a young woman in a lavender jumpsuit, who was in line behind him. He appeared to be making quite a hit, too, with his Texas drawl and cowboy charm. Blue decided if he said even one shucks! or gol'durnit, she would pretend she'd never seen him before in her life. But, no. As best she could hear, he managed to elicit the information that Lavender Jumpsuit was a buyer for Oracle, a big name in the toy industry. Another question and he had her name and a promise to look him up later. Blue turned for a better assessment of the woman, but the desk clerk claimed her attention again with a crisp, ''Mmm-hmm.''

''Your key, Ms. Garrison,'' the young man said pleasantly. ''Enjoy your stay with us. May I help you, sir?''

Tad smiled and stepped forward. ''See you later, Blue,'' he said, before he motioned the woman from Oracle to precede him. ''I think she was here first,'' he told the clerk, and then he propped an elbow on the registration desk and prepared to wait his turn with a lazy smile and a wealth of charisma.

Blue picked up her bags and headed for the elevators. How did he do it? she wondered. How did he wear an old pair of jeans and a pullover shirt and not style his hair, much less carry around an appointment book or a fountain pen, and still charm the socks off everyone he met? Blue didn't understand it. But she thought she just might keep an eye on him during this trip. She might learn something. On the other hand maybe she would be the one to teach him a thing or two. There was no denying that he had more experience as an inventor, but she was certainly no novice at selling a product. She could hold her own at this tradeshow and maybe by the time it was over, Tad would have a greater appreciation of her abilities.

The thought made her smile as she handed over her bags to a bellman and stepped inside the elevator.

Twenty minutes later, as she slipped her suit jacket back on and prepared to go downstairs again, Tad knocked on her door. "Blue? Are you in there?"

Where else would she be? she thought. But she opened the door with a gracious smile and met his studied frown. "Don't tell me you're locked out of your room?" she said. "Sorry, but I can't help this time. No connecting door."

"I'm two doors down." He indicated the direction by a tilt of his head. "I think you'd better come with me."

"I'm not going to your room, Tad."

"Good, because I'm not going there, either." His gaze ran over her, taking in every detail of her navy suit. "Don't you have something else to wear? Something that you won't mind getting dirty?"

She looked down at her skirt. "I have plenty of clothes," she said with a tinge of irritation. "I prefer to look like a professional, that's all."

"Suit yourself." He lifted one shoulder in a careless shrug. "But you may look like a dirty professional before this is over."

"Why? Do we have to set up our own booth?"

Another, more noncommittal shrug followed. "You never know what you might run into."

Blue looked him square in the eye, trying to decide what he had up his sleeve, but he didn't blink and she couldn't decipher the glint in his smoky-brown eyes. "All right," she said reluctantly. "I'll change. Are you going to wait for me? Or shall I meet you downstairs?"

"I'll wait." He crossed his arms and leaned one shoulder against the door frame. "I'll wait forever or ten minutes, whichever comes first. So, take your time."

Then he smiled and she closed the door.

"WHAT DO WE HAVE to do?" Blue asked as she followed Tad into the waiting elevator. She'd compromised on the clothing issue by changing into a pair of gabardine slacks, but she'd kept on the silk blouse and draped a maroon blazer over her arm. That way, she'd decided, she wouldn't look *too* underdressed to mix with the business suits in the lobby, but she wouldn't care if she got a little bit of dirt on the outfit, either. She ran her fingers around the waistband of the slacks to be sure the blouse was completely tucked in. "I can't imagine why the booths wouldn't already be set up, but I've never been to a trade show as an exhibitor before. Did you talk to a representative about this? What did he, or she, say we have to do? I can't believe we'd actually be expected to put up a booth."

With arms crossed Tad rocked back on his heels, looking supremely unconcerned. "Relax, Blue. You don't have to do anything if you don't want. I can handle this by myself. I'm good at it."

"We're in this together, Tad. If you can do it, then I can, too. So we'll just go downstairs and find out what needs to be done."

"It may not be nearly as bad as you think."

She offered a frown to his good humor. "I'm sure you'll think it's great fun, whatever it turns out to be."

"I know it'll be fun, Blue. I've done this before."

An odd feeling scurried past her racing thoughts, but didn't linger long enough for her to label it. She was excited, nervous. She wanted to mingle with the people who also were at the hotel to participate in the product convention. She wanted to exchange information, find out if anyone here knew any of the people with whom she'd once worked and with whom she'd since lost touch. She wanted to swap shop talk with someone who knew and loved the field of marketing as she once had. No one at Grizelle's seemed to really understand. She wanted to feel the way she'd felt then ... in charge, in demand, in control.

The elevator doors opened and she stepped out decisively. "I suppose we should ask someone at the desk who's in charge of this trade show." She glanced over her shoulder at Tad. "Or do you know where we're supposed to go?"

"I know." He touched her elbow, steering her through the still-overflowing lobby. "Stick with me, kid."

They followed a corridor, past the gift shop and the coffee shop and a shoe-shine station. Tad led her past the glass doors that led into the indoor pool area and a workout room. It wasn't until he opened a door that led out into the midday sunlight that Blue realized he was up to something. "Tad," she said simply. "Where are we going?"

"I'm not exactly sure, but the taxi's right over here and the driver said he knows the perfect place."

She stopped dead in her tracks. "The perfect place for what?"

"It's a surprise." He stepped forward and opened the taxi door with a grand gesture. "And you did say that we were in this thing together and that if I could handle it, so could you."

Which meant nothing . . . or almost anything. Blue hesitated, her better judgment telling her she should not get into that taxi . . . not unless she was willing to forego her plans for the afternoon and participate in his. "What are you up to, Tad?"

"About six-one, but I might grow another inch or so before my next birthday. Come on, Blue. The meter's running and our expense account only goes so high."

"You're not planning to stick Uncle Horse with the cost of a sight-seeing taxi ride, are you?"

"This is legitimate, Blue. Uncle Horse would approve." He waved encouragingly toward the back seat of the cab. "Trust me."

The taxi driver rolled down his window. "Give the guy a break, lady. He's got somethin' real special planned for ya. Get in and let's go."

That, in itself, should have made her turn tail and run for cover. But Tad looked so eager, so entreating, that she hesitated. And in that instant she lost her bargaining power.

"You won't miss anything here this afternoon, Blue," Tad said in a last-ditch appeal. "Honestly, there's nothing to do except stand around and chitchat with people you don't know, trying to pitch a product you can't display until tomorrow morning. You'll have a much better time if you come with me."

She couldn't deny it, much as she wanted to. Her earlier desire to socialize vanished all too easily beneath his persuasive smile. With a carefully contrived frown, which she hoped would let him know of her displeasure at being tricked, she did what she really wanted to do and got into the taxi.

"THAT'S IT!" Tad shouted. "Run into the wind with it, Blue. Run!"

She ran, holding the string tightly in her hand, looking up and over her shoulder at the Sky Dancer kite that was just about to catch a ride on the Albuquerque air currents. Tad loped a few paces behind, coaxing, instructing, trying with verbal support to get the kite up in the air. When it bobbed, then fell to the ground, Blue sighed with disappointment and walked back to Tad, taking up the slack kite string as she went. "I'm not good at this, Tad. You do it."

"Nope." He bent and picked up the kite, turning it in all directions, inspecting it for damage. "If I do it, you won't know what it feels like. You'll get the kite up, Blue. It's just a matter of time."

"Before I keel over from oxygen deficiency?" She collapsed on the grass of the local park to which the taxi driver had brought them and looked up at Tad. "You should do this sort of thing with Josh."

"It's more fun to watch you run." He laid the kite on the ground and sank down beside her, wrapping his long arms around bent knees. "Don't give up, yet. You'll get the hang of it."

"I can't believe I'm out here doing this. I'm supposed to be working. So are you, as a matter of fact."

"Who said I wasn't? Teaching you to fly a kite is turning out to be more work than I expected."

"Well, thank you, Mr. Kite Master. I didn't ask for this, you know. I'd have been perfectly happy back at the hotel getting ready for the trade show."

"Once you feel the tug of that kite string in your hands, you won't be so sure about that." He shook his head and looked at the few other people in the park. "Flying a Sky Dancer is a wondrous thing, Blue. Wait. You'll understand."

She wasn't sure she would ever understand this man and his unusual outlook on life. But for the moment the park was quiet, the sun was warm and bright, and she was content to sit and catch her breath. "Josh is right, Tad. You should have children so you'd have someone to play with in the park."

His gaze continued its investigation of the perimeters of the park until it slowly came back to her. "I had a son, but he died."

If he'd reached over and slapped her, Blue could not have been more stunned. "A son? You had a child?"

Tad plucked a blade of grass and pulled it between his thumb and forefinger. "His name was Jeremy and he would have been six years old in November."

She didn't know what to say. "Oh, Tad. I...didn't know."

"Not many people do. I don't talk about it very often."

"It must still be very painful for you." She knew it sounded trite, but she was at a loss. So she reached over and laid her hand on his arm. "I'm sorry."

He looked down at her hand, her fingers splayed ever so slightly across his skin, the slightest tension in her fingertips. He covered her hand with his. "There was a time when the pain was unbearable, and it got worse before it got better." He paused, preparing himself to take the memory out of storage and expose it one more time. Never an easy task under any circumstances. And now, somehow, more difficult because it was important to him that Blue should know about his past and understand his motivation for living. "Jeremy died in his sleep when he was four weeks old. SIDS, Sudden Infant Death Syndrome, was listed as the cause of death. I used to know the statistics on how many babies die of SIDS each year, but I've let the information slip away from me. I just know that one night we put him to bed and when Lindy went in to check on him four hours later, he was dead."

"Lindy? Your...wife?" Blue's fingers were digging deeper into his arm, and Tad found the pressure oddly comforting.

"Yes." He released his inner tension on a shaky sigh. "She died five months to the day after Jeremy's death. She...committed suicide."

Blue's quick intake of breath revealed her shock. Her grip on his arm went slack. A mist of sympathetic tears glistened in her eyes. "How tragic. I'm so...sorry."

There was no "right" reaction to the kind of story he'd just shared with her, no "best" way to express sympathy. He'd received many such expressions at the time of the tragedy, and a few since then, but no one had been more sincere than Blue was at this moment, and he knew she hurt for him as much as anyone ever had.

He lifted her hand and entwined his fingers with hers. "I stopped living after that. Within six months I'd lost my job, my house, my car, everything...except the memories. And those I tried to drown in a bottle. I spent the days in a stupor and the nights dead drunk. Luckily I had a couple of friends who refused to let me kill myself that way. They told me that if I insisted upon committing suicide, too, I should at least stay sober long enough to make the decision. Either they said the right things, or I was in no condition to resist. Whatever the reason, I allowed them to clean me up inside and out and send me to a job interview at Grizelle Gadget and Toy Company. Uncle Horse hired me on the spot because he said I had more reason to live than anyone else he'd interviewed. It took a while before I understood what he meant, but once I did, losing my wife and son became a turning point in my life and not the end of it."

Blue sat quietly, listening, reevaluating her understanding of this man, changing her estimate of his experience and his courage. "That must have taken a lot of courage."

He smiled suddenly. "Courage? I don't think so. It was more like an obligation, my responsibility. Lindy and Jeremy died before they had a chance to live. Jeremy was only a month old. Lindy was barely twenty. And the only way I could figure out to somehow avenge their deaths was to enjoy life enough for three people, make sure that every minute counts, every second is special. It seems like such a small thing to do for them. And I like to think that somehow they know I haven't forgotten." He shrugged then, and Blue accepted it as a way of discarding the heavy mood.

"You make me feel like a fraud, Tad," she said. "All this time I've bitched and groaned about losing my job at McKinley Enterprises as if it were the end of the world."

He squeezed her hand and released it. "Losing is losing, Blue. The life you knew and had planned for died. You have a right to grieve for it."

She appreciated him saying that, even though she knew there was no comparison between her loss and his. "I'm sorry I've given you such a hard time over the past few months, Tad. It was inexcusable of me."

He brought his gaze to meet hers, and there was a depth of emotion in his eyes. "Remorse is not necessary, Blue. I didn't tell you about Lindy and Jeremy to elicit your sympathy. I told you because the subject came up and because I wanted you to know. Don't feel sorry for me. I'm long past the need for that." His expression changed then, softened a little, and his lips curved in a half-smile. "Actually I think you're making progress. At first you were patronizing. Now you're sorry for all the nasty things you've said to me. Next thing you know, you may realize you actually enjoy my companionship."

She was too full of mixed feelings to think of a snappy rejoinder, but she did manage a weak smile. "I thought you were going to teach me to fly a kite, Mr. Denton."

"You're right." He picked up the Sky Dancer box kite, got to his feet and extended a hand to help her. "Let's get this baby in the air. Believe it or not, you're going to thank me for this."

"Sure I am." She took his hand and he pulled her up to her feet. She could have gone right into his arms at that point. One step forward and she would have been positioned against his chest, her arms ready to wind around his neck, her lips in line for his kiss. She knew by the glint in his eye that he recognized the opportunity, too. But he didn't take it and neither did she.

Somehow the moment seemed too full already.

"AND THEN I thought it was going to fall, but it caught the current and went higher and higher...." Blue laughed with the exhilaration of her experience. "I couldn't believe how high it went. I bet you've never seen a kite go that high before, have you, Tad? It was great!"

Tad held open the door leading into the hotel. "Didn't I tell you it would be? You should listen to me more often, Blue. Your life would be a hell of a lot more fun."

She brushed a strand of hair from her eyes and thought idly that she probably looked a mess. She knew for certain that there were grass stains on her slacks, maybe on her elbows, too. She was wrinkled and rumpled, wind-blown and recklessly excited by her success. "Do I look awful?" she asked as they started down the hall toward the lobby and the elevators beyond. "I mean, should I jump in the pool before I walk through the lobby?"

"You look great," Tad said in the offhand way of a man who looked very little different going in than he had going out.

She grabbed for his arm. "Tad, really. We're here on business. Do I look too disheveled? Wouldn't it be better if I, at least, tried to comb my hair or something?"

He stopped and turned toward her. With a couple of quick movements he smoothed her hair, wiped a smudge from her cheek and gave her a wink of reassurance. "I think you look great, Blue. Prettier than any other woman at this whole trade show."

"You haven't seen all the women at this trade show, yet."

"True, but you're the prettiest one in this hall."

With a sigh Blue decided she wasn't likely to see anyone in the lobby who would recognize her, anyway. "They should have put the elevators in the back," she said.

"Would you stop it?" Tad put a hand at her back and urged her forward. "Who cares if you look a little wind-blown? It's a small price to pay for the fun you had this afternoon."

"You're absolutely right." She lifted her chin and stepped quickly and purposefully into the lobby.

Halfway across the wide area, she heard someone call her name and felt her confidence deserting her like air from a deflating balloon.

"Blue? Blue!"

She would have recognized that voice if she'd heard it cheering from the other side of the stadium in the midst of the Superbowl. With a quick, indrawn breath, she spun around to face Rob McKinley.

"Blue! I thought it was you." He advanced toward her, purposeful, powerful, more handsome even than she'd remembered.

"Rob," she said in a slightly hesitant voice. "How are you?"

"Couldn't be better." He reached her and immediately grabbed her hands and lifted each in turn to his lips. "You can't imagine how happy I am to see you. Where have you been? You just dropped out of sight, disappeared. No one knew where you'd gone. I was afraid I might never find you again."

She tried for a careless laugh and managed one that she hoped only sounded hollow to her. "I didn't know I was lost."

"I guess you weren't...except to me." Rob's smile curved appealingly, and Blue was sorry to feel the erratic response of her heartbeat. He was probably the most dynamic man in the building, undoubtedly the most charismatic, and everything about him, from his Armani suit to the style of his hair, emphasized the image of a successful man. That was Rob. Image. Pure and simple. There was no depth of character, nothing beneath his polished exterior. She could see that now.

"Have dinner with me tonight, Blue," he said as he released her hand and glanced at his watch. "I have to meet a client for cocktails in a few minutes, but I'll be free in an hour. Meet me in the restaurant at seven. No, I'll need to go back to my room first. Why don't you meet me there? We can have a drink and then go down to the restaurant. That will give us more privacy, anyway."

Across the room someone else called to Rob, and he waved to indicate that he'd heard. "I'm on the twelfth floor, Suite 1201. I'll be waiting for you at seven." With a quirk of his brow that Blue recognized as meaning *no arguments,* he turned and left her as easily, as purposefully as he'd approached her.

Only then did Blue remember Tad and, with a small rush of panic, she turned to look for him. He stood a few feet away, holding the kite, waiting for her with some noticeable lack of patience. She could hardly blame him. She hadn't even thought to introduce him. But then she hadn't even had the presence of mind to leave Rob standing in the lobby talking to himself, which is what she should have done. And now she had to face Tad, apologize for her poor manners, try to pretend that seeing Rob again had had no effect on her whatsoever.

"That was Rob," she said uneasily. "A...guy I used to work with."

Tad nodded, but didn't comment.

Blue wondered if she should come up with at least a lame excuse for not having introduced the two men. But under the regard of Tad's solemn brown eyes, she decided to tell the truth. "I'm sorry I didn't introduce the two of you. Frankly, I was so...surprised to see him that I wasn't thinking very fast."

"No problem." Tad turned toward the elevators and waited for her to fall into step beside him. He had rarely felt so helpless, and he was completely unable to see any humor in this twist of fate. *A guy I used to work with,* she'd said. As if he were no one of importance. No one special. But the look on her face...

Tad jabbed the button and waited impatiently for the elevator to arrive.

"He...invited me to dinner."

Tad's gaze shifted to hers as the elevator doors slid open. She stepped inside. He followed. "That will be nice," he said and stuck his free hand into his hip pocket to keep from making a fist. "It's always nice to visit with old friends."

With a sigh Blue leaned against the mid-high rail. "He isn't exactly a friend. He used to be my boss."

"Is he the guy you were...involved with?" Tad did not want to know the answer, but he couldn't keep from asking the question. "The guy in the picture?"

"Yes. I mean, we weren't involved—"

The way her voice broke made Tad's heart sink. "You don't have to explain to me, Blue. And you don't need my permission to have dinner with him. You do whatever you want."

The expression in her eyes made him feel a little like a traitor. But what did she expect? His blessing?

"If I decide to have dinner with Rob, would you join us?"

"Why would I do that?"

"Because I asked you."

The elevator opened and another couple entered. Tad stepped back, giving the tail of the kite another loop over his arm to keep it out of the way. When the elevator stopped again, he followed Blue into the hallway and walked in silence to her door. "Look, Blue," he said, steeling his heart against any appeals. "Don't involve me in this. Rob McKinley is your past. Either have dinner with him or don't, but leave me out of it. I can't sit there and watch you reminisce with him. I just . . . can't.''

He would have walked away then, but she touched his arm and held him by an emotion he did not wish to feel. "Wait, Tad. It's . . . not that I'm—''

A man came out of a door across the hall and walked toward the elevators. Blue's gaze followed him before returning to Tad's. "Come in with me. Please. Let me explain.''

Dread welled in his throat. Of all things, he did not want to hear her confession. "That isn't necessary, Blue. And, really, there isn't time. Not if you're going to meet him.''

"I guess that is the decision I have to make, isn't it? Whether or not I'm going to have dinner with him? Whether or not I'm going to his room and . . .'' Her voice trailed away, but was steady again, quiet and resolute.

Tad came very close to telling her that he'd accompany her, he'd do anything she asked. But that wouldn't be fair. Not to her. And not to him. He handed the kite to her. "Here,'' he said. "A memento of the first day you flew a Sky Dancer.''

She took it with a quick smile. "It's mine to keep? Really?''

"Really.'' He smiled, too, and then he brushed his knuckle across the underside of her chin, turned and walked away.

"Tad?'' she called after him.

He stopped reluctantly, made a half turn toward her. "Yes?''

"Thank you. For the kite. And the afternoon. I'll . . . never forget it.''

Tad lifted his hand in a gesture of acceptance and went

on to his room, wondering how he was going to get through the next few hours, wondering at what moment, when exactly, he'd gone and fallen in love with Miranda Blue.

Chapter Thirteen

After a glance up and down the hallway to see if anyone was watching, Blue tapped on the door. Not that it mattered who saw her. Not that she cared. She was just a little nervous, that was all. She wasn't accustomed to going to a man's hotel room. Actually, at one time, she'd gone in and out of Rob's various hotel rooms without blinking. But that had been business.

This was not.

She lifted her hand and tapped again, harder this time. What if he wasn't here? What if he'd made other plans? What if...?

The door swung open and Tad looked at her in surprise. "Fire drill?" he asked.

Her nervousness faded. "Monkey business," she said. "May I come in?"

"When you put it like that, how can I say no?" He held the door and waited for her to step inside.

His room was a replica of hers, except that the watercolor prints over the bed were of a lily and an orchid. The prints in her room were of a lilac and a rose. She set her evening bag on the dresser and clasped her hands as she turned to him. "Do you have plans for dinner?"

"I was kind of thinking about ordering a pizza." His tone was noncommittal, cautious, as if he wasn't sure what she expected him to say.

"Pizza sounds good. Would you mind if I joined you?"

He pursed his lips and put his hands in his hip pockets. "That depends. How many pieces will you eat?"

"A couple. Maybe three. Maybe four, if you order extra cheese."

He looked her over. "Would I have to put on a tie?"

She glanced down at her black sheath dress, black hose, black heels. She wasn't exactly dressed for pizza. She brought her gaze up to meet his. "I won't say anything about clothing, if you don't."

"Fair enough." He nodded. "Can I ask one question, though?"

"One question," she repeated. "Okay."

"Is some guy in an Armani suit going to pound on my door and try to punch me in the mouth?"

Blue's lips curved in a slow smile. "I had no idea you knew what an Armani suit looked like."

"You didn't answer my question."

"He can't punch you if you don't open the door."

"Good point." Tad moved to the bed and the phone on the bedside table. "What kind of pizza do you want?"

"The works . . . with extra cheese."

He punched out the number of a pizza delivery service listed in the phone directory and gave the order. Blue walked to the window, pulled back the sheer curtain and looked out at the buildings and streets of downtown Albuquerque. Before today she'd never been to New Mexico, and she'd never flown a kite. She'd also never dressed for a dinner date and ended up ordering pizza before.

At this very moment she could have been with Rob, in his suite, ordering an elegant dinner. For a good twenty minutes after coming upstairs, she'd actually considered his invitation. Pride had urged her to go. It was appealing to think that she could show him she was doing well—quite well—since the fiasco at McKinley Enterprises. She would love nothing more than to see regret in his eyes and know that *he* knew he'd made a mistake in letting her go.

But she wouldn't have been able to pull it off. He would have behaved exactly as he had downstairs, as if nothing had happened, as if they were old friends meeting after a long separation, as if he hadn't stood back and let her take the blame for something she hadn't done. And she would have stood silent, but getting angrier by the minute, just as she had before.

"Thirty minutes," Tad said as he replaced the receiver. "Do you want something to drink? There's a soda machine at the end of the hall and there's ice in the ice bucket."

"Thanks. I'll drink water."

"I can order something from room service, if you like. Wine, maybe?"

"No, really. Water is fine."

Tad nodded and moved to fix a glass for her. Blue felt awkward suddenly and knew that Tad must be wondering why she was there. He had every reason to ask for an explanation...but he hadn't and probably wouldn't. She loved him for that.

"Tad, I—" She searched for the right way to say thank you. "I appreciate your letting me horn in on your evening this way. You probably would rather be able to watch TV and have your pizza all to yourself."

He shot her a rueful, sidelong glance. "Oh, yes. I really hate it when a beautiful woman barges into my room and makes herself at home. It's a bummer."

"I guess I should explain."

"You don't have to." He handed her a squatty glass filled with water and a few ice chunks. "But I'll admit that I'd feel better if you lied and said I wasn't your second-choice as a dinner companion."

"You're my first choice, Tad. Second choice would have been my own solitary company."

"And Armani Suit doesn't figure into this, some-how?" He took a sip from his glass. "That's a little hard to swallow, Blue, even considering that I did tell you to lie."

"It isn't a lie. I'll admit that I thought about accepting his invitation. I imagined myself waltzing in, looking like a million bucks and making him sorry for the way he'd treated me. But it was only a mental exercise. I never intended to go."

"Which is why you're all dolled up and looking like a million bucks," he said with a good dose of skepticism.

She looked down and then brought her eyes up to meet his. "Maybe I wanted to impress you."

"You know you don't have to dress up to do that, Blue." He made the ice cubes clink against the side of his glass. "Did you come to my room because you needed a place to hide? Are you afraid he's going to come looking for you?"

Blue stood uncomfortably, wishing the pizza would arrive and ease the thick tension that had entered the room. "I'm here because I wanted to spend the evening with you."

Tad turned from her and set his glass on the table. He pulled out one of the chairs and asked her with a lift of his eyebrow if she cared to sit. When she shook her head, he settled into it and propped his feet on the bed. "Cut the line, Blue. I saw the look on your face when you saw him downstairs. The day you moved into the pool house, I saw the picture of the two of you together. It's the same guy.

And the look on your face was the same, too. Rob McKinley is not, and never was, just 'someone you used to work with.'"

"No," she admitted with a long sigh. "He's president and CEO of McKinley Enterprises. For a while I was his right-hand man, his star pupil, his ardent worshiper. Wherever he went, I was right beside him, ready to bask in the glow of his wisdom, eager to have his approval and intent upon capturing some of his knowledge and talent for myself." She sank to the edge of the bed, facing Tad. "No, that isn't right. It wasn't his knowledge or his talent that fascinated me. It was his power. Power is deceptive. It can be attractive and very, very seductive."

"And you were seduced." Tad's voice went flat, and her tension shot higher.

"By power, yes. By the illusion that I could somehow share his position, his authority. I imagined…oh, all kinds of things. To be recognized by my peers, to be in demand as an expert in my field. I don't know what all I thought. I was wrong. About Rob. About myself. About the things that really mattered."

She clasped her hands around her glass and stared at the ice in the water. "I know you think we had an affair— everyone thinks that—but I never had sex with him. Don't get me wrong. I wanted to, I would have, but he was married. And that just happens to be a taboo for me. I wasn't going to break up his nice little family."

"If you didn't have an affair with him, what do you have to feel guilty about?"

"I broke up his family, anyway. I fooled myself into believing that I could be in love with my boss and no one would ever know. I thought as long as nothing physical happened between us then everything else was all right. We spent days together, nights together, weekends. We traveled together. All under the guise of business, I'll admit, but still it was time...endless amounts of time that rightfully belonged to others. Rob and I had secrets, private jokes, insider smiles. And of course other employees talked about it, gossiped about us, wiggled their eyebrows and hid their snickers behind winks and knowing looks. I went on pretending that I had the world by the tail and that, somehow, someway—I never quite got the fantasy fleshed out—his existing family would disappear and Rob and I would marry and have beautiful children of our own.''

"Did he know how you felt?"

Blue looked at Tad and frowned. "I'm sure he did. He isn't the least bit stupid, and it was to his advantage to have me head over heels in love with him. That way he possessed every ounce of my energy. All of my abilities were at his disposal twenty-four hours a day. Work was his focus and mine. It was all intertwined in a nice, neat arrangement. Work and Rob. Rob and work. What could have been better? I thought I had the greatest job in the world."

"Until?" Tad prompted.

"Until Jessica, his wife, began to feel threatened. When I first started working in the executive office, she was very nice to me. We're the same age, and she used to tell me that she envied me because I'd chosen a career. She'd been a dancer and was quite good. At least, Rob said she had been. They have two little girls, beautiful children. Anyway, as many women do after a few years of marriage, Jessica began to feel she wasn't really a part of Rob's life. She was just his background, an accoutrement of his success. Gradually she got less friendly. Eventually she got hostile. Finally she confronted me, in Rob's presence, and accused me of having an affair with her husband. It was the most humiliating experience of my life. And Rob never said a word. He didn't back up my denials. He didn't come to my defense. He didn't even say I was a valuable employee. He didn't do anything.''

"He fired you."

Blue massaged the back of her neck, enjoying the cold feel of her fingers against her skin. "No. He told me that under the circumstances I should resign, and when I refused, he just told me to think it over. Being the somewhat stubborn person that I am, I decided to ride it out. After all, I hadn't done anything wrong. I hadn't actually had an affair. But the writing was on the wall. Rob didn't have time for me anymore. Projects were moved to other employees. I wasn't included in meetings. Clients stopped calling and didn't return my calls. The people I had worked with avoided me. And when I began to think about looking elsewhere for work, I realized that my *reputation* had preceded me.''

"You mean other marketing firms wouldn't hire you because they'd heard rumors?"

"Well-founded rumors, Tad. I *looked* guilty. I'd always been with him at meetings, when he wined and dined clients, when he socialized with other professionals in the industry. He'd spoken of me then as his partner, as the one person without whose help he couldn't run the company. Then, suddenly, he dropped me. Of course people believed we'd had an affair, and it had ended on a sour note. Rob McKinley is a big player and since he didn't comment on the rumors, he made me the scapegoat. He went home to soothe his wife's suspicions and I was left to field propositions... none of them related to business.''

Tad watched her over the rim of his glass. "You must have been very angry."

"Fire-breathing dragons had nothing on me in those first couple of weeks. But when I realized my career was sinking faster than I could bail water, I decided to resign. Rob said he wished me well and that he wished things had turned out differently. And that was it. My brilliant career was over.''

"I'd say your brilliant career merely took an unexpected turn.''

She smiled wanly. ''You're always the optimist, aren't you, Tad?''

He dropped his feet to the floor, stood and walked to the window. ''If Rob McKinley ruined your life, Blue, why were you so happy to see him again?''

Happy? Blue thought. She'd been surprised, stunned even, to see him so unexpectedly. But happy? No, she didn't think so. ''I was just surprised, that's all. Seeing him caught me off guard.''

"All the more reason to think your reaction was an honest one.''

"I don't hate him, Tad. For a while I really tried to blame him for everything, but I always came back to the same conclusion. He was no more and no less culpable than I. I think he should have handled the situation differently. I *know* that I should have.''

Tad continued to look out the window. ''That's always the temptation, isn't it? To look back and say 'if only I'd done this' or 'if only I'd done that.' To believe that somehow we should have foreseen the future and kept disaster from happening.''

He understood because he'd been through it, Blue realized, and she stepped forward to touch him, to let him know that she cared about his loss, too. ''I'm sorry,'' she whispered.

With a slight movement he turned his head and looked down first at her hand on his arm and then into the earnest sympathy in her green eyes. ''You've said that already, Blue. Now tell me why you knocked on my door tonight, instead of his."

Blue swallowed. Tad could see the tension filter through her expression, attenuating the sympathy and changing it to uncertainty.

"I had a sudden craving for pizza?" She was obviously making an effort to lighten the mood, but Tad resisted. He wanted more. He wanted a hint of how she felt about him. He wanted to know if she were here hiding from her past or looking for her future.

"Pizza was not on your mind when you put on that dress, Blue."

Her hand dropped from his arm, but her gaze held. "Isn't it enough that I'm here, Tad? Here, and not there?"

He supposed it would have to be. She'd told him nothing, given him nothing to hold on to. But she *was* here with him. That counted for something. In sudden hunger, he pulled her to him and crushed her mouth beneath his. There was no fun allowed in the embrace. Not this time. His emotions were too jumbled, his reason all clouded with unmistakable desire. He wanted Blue in his arms and in his bed. To hell with her reasons for being there. To hell with her past. Heaven was more the destination he had in mind. And with a little luck he might be able to make her forget that she was in love with another man.

His hands reached greedily for her, his body pressed ravenously against hers. He felt breathless and hot and troubled and knew that he ought to slow the pace of his passion, the reckless racing of his pulse. But then she placed her hands on his hips and exerted a steady pressure to hold him against her. It was heaven . . . and hell . . . and a whole new world of feelings.

His arms slipped around her and drew her nearer, his lips parted hers and won an impassioned response. He pressed her to him, felt her breasts firm against him, felt her warm breath in his mouth. The tremor that coursed through her transferred itself to him and he wasn't sure he would ever be able to satisfy his need for her. When had she become so important to him? When had his happiness gotten all tangled up with her?

It took two tries, but he managed to slide the slender strap of her dress from her shoulder. His lips found refuge in the newly exposed area, and she sighed in his arms as he traced the hollows of her neck and shoulders with his tongue. His heart began tapping so hard against his ribcage that he almost thought he could hear its pounding. And then Blue's hands came up to cup his chin and lift his head.

"Tad," she whispered breathlessly. "The pizza's here."

He realized, then, that someone was knocking on the door. With some effort he straightened, ran a shaky hand through his hair and gave her a little smile. "I'll get it," he said. "You wait here."

"Don't worry. I will."

He turned, grabbed his wallet from the dresser top and gathered enough presence of mind to ask who was at the door before he opened it. In a couple of minutes, he had the pizza box in his hands and had sent the delivery man on his way.

The smell of Italian food permeated the air. "Hungry?" he asked as he moved the ice bucket to make room for the box.

"Yes."

"You are?" He knew he shouldn't let his disappointment show, but how could she want pizza now?

"Maybe," she suggested with a slow smile, "it would be best to finish what you started before you open that box."

Relief washed through him like a warm, summer rain. She wanted him, too. "Are you trying to bribe me?" he asked. "Because if you are..." He advanced toward her.

"Because if I am... what?"

"Your dinner is going to get cold."

"I've always loved cold pizza," she said as they sank together onto the bed and slipped into each other's arms.

"Come on over, girls and boys! See Little Zeke the robot toy!"

Little Zeke strolled forward on the table, blinked his lights, raised and lowered his robotic arms, reversed and repeated the whole process.

"Come on over, moms and dads! You will see that Zeke is bad!"

"I still can't believe you programmed Little Zeke with rap music," Blue said to Tad, although she was careful to keep her voice low so it wouldn't carry to the crowd gathered in front of their booth. "Couldn't you be happy with plain old 'Yankee Doodle'?"

"It was Uncle Horse's decision," Tad said. "And it's certainly getting a lot of attention, isn't it?"

She couldn't refute that. The crowd around their booth had been steady for three whole days. People loved Little Zeke. From eight in the morning until ten or eleven at night, at least one person was always standing in front of Grizelle Gadget and Toy Company's booth, fascinated by the toy robot. Everyone at the trade show, from other exhibitors to the general public, wanted to see what Little Zeke could do. She and Tad took turns manning the booth while the other one had breakfast, lunch or dinner, and they tumbled into bed at night too tired to sleep.

The fact that they tumbled into bed *together* probably contributed more to the lack of sleep than weariness, Blue thought with a smile that she kept all for herself. It had been a hectic three days, a delightful three nights, and she hadn't felt so good in a long time.

The only cloud in the sky was Rob McKinley and, like the sound of a woodpecker in a distant tree, the worry about when he would approach her again kept tap-tapping at the far side of Blue's mind. She'd seen him several times, had even made eye contact once, but he hadn't come near her since their meeting in the lobby. He'd left messages for her at the desk, had even slipped a note under the door of her hotel room, but he hadn't made an effort to approach her at the booth. Not yet, anyway, but he would. Blue knew him too well to think otherwise.

And while she didn't want to think about Rob or wonder why he was here and what he wanted from her, a part of her longed for the confrontation. To be able to look him in the eye and tell him she had no interest in anything he had to say, that she'd made a new life for herself and no longer yearned for her old life. He wouldn't believe her, of course. And she knew she wouldn't be able to believe it entirely, herself, until she'd settled things with Rob.

"Toy company alert." Tad passed her in the narrow confines of the booth and indicated with a shifty eye movement that the representative from Oracle Toys was, once again, walking toward their booth. "I think she wants to negotiate."

"We're only here to demonstrate the toys," Blue said with a pointed arching of her brow. "Negotiations have to go through our home office."

"Well, what if she wants to make an offer on the key to my hotel room?" He tossed the question out quietly, casually, so no one else could hear his teasing. "Who's going to deal on that?"

"I'll bargain with her. You have nothing to worry about, Tad. Nothing at all."

"Women have been saying that to men since time began. I don't know why we still fall for it." He stepped to the other side of the booth and offered to demonstrate the Talk-to-Me Rose to the Oracle representative.

The woman accepted with a smile that made Blue want to jerk the toy flower out of Tad's hands and demonstrate its amazing powers of growth, herself. But of course she didn't. Jealousy was beneath her. It was also a warning sign that she had lost all remnants of professional distance. An unsettling thought, at best, and one she didn't dwell on. Since that first night when she'd knocked on Tad's hotel door, she'd made a pact with herself . . . she would borrow Tad's philosophy of living one day, one moment at a time and not worry too much about what tomorrow would bring. When she returned to Dallas, she could fret about consequences and the future. For now, she was just enjoying herself.

"She's interested," Tad said, coming to stand beside her again as the Oracle representative moved on to another booth. "We're going to get more offers for these two toys than we can sort through in a month. Since you stand to make a pretty decent bonus off this trip, I think you should take me out to dinner to celebrate." He smiled lazily. "It is our last night together, you know."

Last night together. A little chill ran down her back, but she kept the pleasant curve of her lips steady. "Since you stand to make a decent bonus, too, why don't you take me out to dinner?"

He pursed his lips as if considering. "Well, okay. I think wining and dining you will qualify for my expense account. And don't plan to write me a memo about frivolous expenses, either. You're the one who has an entire hotel room that you're using strictly as a clothes closet."

"Maybe I should remedy that."

He nodded. "You're right. You can invite me to your room tonight. After our celebration."

"After our celebration," Blue agreed as she turned to accommodate another approaching customer.

Chapter Fourteen

"I'm sorry, Blue." Tad looked at her over the top of his menu. "No pizza."

"That's okay. There's still some in your room upstairs."

"I'm thinking of having it framed and keeping it as a memento of our first trade show together."

She let her gaze drop back to the menu, suddenly and belatedly bemused and a bit shy about the new intimacy of their relationship. She suspected she was more than a little in love with Tad, but she didn't want to ask for or make any commitments at the moment. If this was just a weekend fling for him—an affair for the fun of it—she didn't want to know. At least, not yet. Why risk spoiling what little time remained to them.

"I'll have the salmon," she said. "With rice. What about you?"

"I'll be on the dessert menu. Tad à la mode. You'll have to consider me an after-dinner treat."

She lifted one eyebrow in a dare. "In that case, I'll just have a small salad and we're out of here."

"Ah, a woman of easy virtue and a cheap date, besides. I think I love you, Miranda Blue."

Her eyes met his for a sliver of a moment, and awareness flowed over and around her like thousands of confetti streamers. Was there any possibility that this once he wasn't teasing?

"Hello, Blue." Rob's voice effectively burst her bubble of possibilities and drenched her in a wave of memories. "May I join you?"

"Rob," she said and was alarmed to hear the dismay in her voice. Her gaze flew first to Tad. She noticed the tightening along his jawline, the tension in the way he gripped the menu. Then she looked up at her former employer. "Hello, Rob," she said in a steadier tone. "Tad Denton, this is Rob McKinley."

Tad rose... reluctantly, Blue noticed... and offered his hand. "It's nice to meet you."

"Tad Denton. Tad Denton." Rob repeated the name as he accepted the handshake with a smile. It was his habitual way of cementing a new name and face into his memory. Blue had watched him do it hundreds of times. She'd learned from him how to use recognition of another person to her own advantage. And she realized how shallow, how self-serving it sounded.

"I'm so pleased to meet you," Rob said. "I hope you don't mind if I join you. Blue and I are old friends and it's been over a year since I last saw her. I've been trying to find a minute free so we could talk, but you know what a rat race these trade shows can be."

"Yes," Tad agreed as he resumed his seat at the table. "Makes me wish I had a rat trap."

Rob laughed easily and pulled over an extra chair. In less than a minute he was seated at their table and the waiter was hovering to find out if another place setting was needed. Blue knew she'd waited too long to protest and wondered what had kept her silent. Rob was going to ruin her and Tad's celebration . . . and she had no one to blame but herself.

She lifted her glass of water to her lips and sipped before turning to Rob. "Have you enjoyed the trade show?" she asked politely.

His expression was one of studied amusement. "Trade shows are not high on my list of preferred activities, as you well know, Blue. But I suppose this one has been fairly productive for me. After all, I did find you here."

"So you did." She looked at Tad, thought how handsome he looked in the suit he called his "trade show best," with his hair combed back and falling forward across his brow. How genuine he was, how special. "Who came with you on this trip?" Blue asked Rob, not because she especially cared, but simply to prove she could ask it casually. "Pete? David?" She paused for effect. "Jessica?"

Rob called the waiter to the table with a lift of his hand and ordered a bottle of wine. A good wine, of course. An expensive wine. She was not impressed. Tad caught her eye and raised his water glass, reminding her, either by intent or accident, of that night in his hotel room when they'd had pizza and water. No wine, but plenty of intoxicating kisses. She smiled and Rob reclaimed her attention.

"Pete no longer works for me. David is in New York on business for the firm. And Jessica is . . . well . . . we divorced three months ago."

Blue turned to him in surprise. "Divorced? I'm sorry to hear that, Rob."

His lips formed a rueful curve. "I thought you might be happy about it, Blue. You provided the catalyst for it."

"That's not something I could ever take pleasure in knowing, Rob, and I'd appreciate it if you didn't credit me with giving you an excuse to end your marriage."

"I'm sorry. That was tactless of me. Of course you had nothing to do with it. The divorce was inevitable from the beginning."

Blue settled the surge of anger his words had evoked and told herself she would not lose her composure in front of him, or in front of Tad. "How are your little girls?"

"Beautiful, as always. They live with their mother, of course, but I see them as often as I can. Unfortunately, because of my work, that isn't very often."

"Children grow up so fast," Tad commented.

"Yes," Rob agreed with a shake of his head and a sad smile. "Divorce is hard on them."

Blue found it interesting to realize that Rob didn't have any idea of what Tad had meant. He would see his daughters once in a while, give them a few minutes of his time, and tell himself it was all he could do. He would probably never understand that he could have done so much more.

"You'll never guess who has proven to be a crackerjack at her job," Rob said with a laugh. "Remember Lucy? The young woman from Cal State who drove you crazy with her ideas?"

"Oh, Lucy." Blue rolled her eyes and sighed. "How could I forget her? She was the one who wanted to mail a complimentary pair of underwear to every female in California as an advertising gimmick. Luckily for us the client thought she was only joking."

Blue and Rob laughed together, and Tad struggled to overcome an attack of jealousy. The two of them, Blue and Rob, had a history together, mutual acquaintances and shared experiences that Tad couldn't hope to match. His stomach knotted with tension and he wondered—not for the first time this weekend—if Blue was still in love with the man.

He didn't want to think so, but already, within ten minutes of the time Rob had sat down at their table, she was relaxing, swapping memories with him, asking questions about people they both knew, about the marketing field in general. Her earlier nervousness was fading, her movements were steady and her tone of voice reflected an interest she hadn't shown before. Tad knew she was conscious of his presence at the table, and she made an attempt to pull him into the conversation from time to time. But he had no basis for joining in. So he listened politely and told himself he'd known from the beginning that she wouldn't stay in his life forever.

He'd known about Rob McKinley, had known that Rob was a special man in Blue's life. And, despite his mistreatment of her, it was not inconceivable that she would forgive and forget the past. Tad accepted that. What choice did he have? He could hardly stand the thought of losing Blue, but she'd never made any promises to him, never indicated that she would stay in Dallas and work at Grizelle Gadget and Toy Company for the rest of her life. On the contrary she'd made it quite clear that she was only there out of necessity. Her job there was only an interlude in her career, a stopgap measure that would eventually no longer be needed. She would move on, as surely as the roses would die back when winter came.

Blue laughed at something Rob had said and Tad smiled. She was beautiful. Her eyes shone with all the mystery of emeralds. Her hair swung across her cheek, and she kept pushing its dusky strands back, away from her face. He'd loved being with her. He'd loved going to sleep with her in his arms and waking up with her beside him. He had packed as much enjoyment into these four days as he could, and now that it was almost over, he knew it hadn't been nearly enough. With a strange sense of resignation, he reached for his glass of wine. The wine Rob McKinley had ordered, paid for and poured. Tad had a feeling it was going to taste very bitter.

"And has David made the progress you'd hoped?" Blue asked. "With Pete gone, you must be very short-handed in that department."

"We are. That's why I'm so glad to have run into you here, Blue. I've had inquiries out, trying to locate you, but I hadn't had much luck." Rob leaned forward and Blue drew back, aware that she didn't want to hear what he had to say next. "Is there any way I can persuade you to come back to McKinley Enterprises?"

"No," Blue said firmly. "No."

Rob held up his hand as if he could deflect the answer. "I know I have no right to ask and no reason to expect you would want to return, but don't say no right away. Think about it for a week or so. I can promise you a vice presidency up front, a sizeable increase in salary, benefits, more decision-making power, and almost anything else you care to name. I realize I made a mistake in letting you go before, Blue, and if it makes any difference, I apologize for handling the situation so poorly. Please, just think about the offer. That's all I ask."

Blue's gaze met Tad's across the table. She couldn't interpret the message in his smoky-brown eyes, but his smile was full and encouraging. Did he think she was actually going to consider the offer? "I'm not interested, Rob," she said decisively. "Thank you, but no."

Rob nodded as if expecting that response. "I won't beg, but I won't withdraw the offer right away, either. You think about it and, if you change your mind, give me a call." He pushed up from the table and turned his charm toward Tad. "So nice to meet you, Mr. Denton," he said. "Any friend of Blue's..." Leaving the cliché to dangle, he picked up his wineglass and lifted it in a toast. "To you, Blue. And to your future success. Keep in touch, won't you?" With that, he bowed slightly and, taking his glass with him, he walked away from the table, leaving the rest of the wine and a tight silence behind.

"I can't believe him," Blue said, half to herself. Had Rob actually thought she'd jump at the chance to come back to him. Was he so arrogant that he hadn't thought she could change? "Rob hates the word no. He never backs off on a first refusal. He'll just wait a little, then push a little harder, up the offer a little more, dangle some other juicy carrot. He's a master of the game. I've seen him do it dozens of times."

Tad thought by the look on her face as she watched Rob walk away that she admired that ability, too. It appeared to Tad that Rob McKinley held the winning hand in this game. He'd placed his bet, given Blue the opportunity to call his bluff, to uphold her pride, to feel avenged and vindicated. And he'd left the table with his hand still intact, when all the bets were down. But the game was far from over. There would be another offer, another round of bidding, and the next time Rob walked away from the table Tad expected he'd take Blue with him.

"We didn't drink to his toast," Tad said, forcing himself to smile as he lifted his glass. "To you, Blue, and to your success."

"To success," she repeated and took a drink.

Tad hesitated only a moment before he tipped up the glass and drained every bitter drop.

ROB HAD RUINED their celebration.

Blue knew that without knowing exactly how or why. It was hard to pinpoint whether the strain emanated from Tad or from her, but the tension could have been an elephant sitting on the dinner table between them for all its lack of subtlety. And it certainly succeeded in crowding out the good feelings that had ushered in the evening. Oh, they were gay enough after Rob's departure, and the conversation flowed as smoothly as the wine had gone down, but something had changed. And she didn't know what it was or what to do about it.

Her appetite had all but disappeared by the time the waiter brought the food, but she ate, anyway. Tad talked about Little Zeke, Oracle Toys and Josh. He spoke of being ready to go home and smell Aunt Grizelle's roses again. He mentioned Ellie, wondering idly if Jim Bill had persuaded his betrothed to enroll in school. He said it seemed like he'd been away longer than four days and that trade shows always left him feeling out of sync and eager to get back to work. He talked about projects already in production and ideas that were still on the drawing board. What he didn't talk about was her.

And although she didn't know what she expected him to say, she knew that she wanted him to say something, to confirm what she was feeling, to offer her some hope that this new facet of their relationship could continue once they returned home.

But she wouldn't ask and he didn't volunteer.

The dessert tray came and Tad ordered a chocolate torte. Blue ordered coffee.

"That'll keep you awake," he said when the waiter had left.

"That'll give you nightmares," she replied.

He ate the next bite with relish. "This is worth the sacrifice. Want some?" He offered a morsel of cake to her on the end of his fork. "It's killer chocolate."

"Thanks, but I'll stick with insomnia."

"Good. You can finish all the packing while I toss and turn and fight a giant cocoa bean in my sleep."

"Just call in Janitor Man. He'll clean up your dreams for you, and you'll be rested and ready to help pack in the morning. We do still have to box up Little Zeke and Talk-to-Me Rose before the flight home." Blue sipped her coffee. "Do you think there will be as big a crowd at the airport to welcome us home as there was to send us off?"

"Probably bigger, considering that we're scheduled to arrive at a decent hour. I still haven't forgiven Ellie for putting us on that 6:00 a.m. flight."

"It worked out all right and it really wasn't her fault. You're the one who wanted to get here early enough to fly a kite."

He smiled then, a slow, tantalizing uplift of his lips. "Don't forget to pack your Sky Dancer."

"Not a chance. It's my one and only souvenir of this trade show."

"Oh, don't be modest, Blue. The kite pales next to the job offer you received."

"And turned down," she added hastily. "I have no intention of going back to work for Rob."

Tad ate another bite of cake in a doubtful silence.

"You don't believe me, do you?" Blue leaned forward, anxious to correct his thinking on the subject. "It's true. I will never go back to work for Rob."

"Never is a long time."

"Listen to me, Tad," she said and heard the note of desperation in her voice. "I mean it. I will *never* work for him again."

Tad scraped some icing from his plate and took a moment to savor the last of the chocolate torte. "Okay," he said.

"Okay, what?" She was impatient with his obvious skepticism. Why didn't he believe her? After the last few days, how could he think she would even consider going back to Rob? "Okay, you believe me? Or okay, you don't care one way or the other?"

"How about, okay, it's none of my business?"

None of his business? He didn't mean that. "Well, technically, no, I guess it isn't, but—"

"Stop right there, Blue." Tad laid his napkin on the table and motioned to the waiter. "There is no qualifier on this. What you do or don't do about this job offer—and any future job offer—is none of my business. The decision is yours and I don't figure into it."

The waiter presented the bill and Tad signed it, while Blue sat wondering what he'd just said to her. Of course the decision was hers. But he could at least express some relief that she wasn't going to rush off to California without a second thought for the relationship they now shared.

Or was he trying to let her know, in his own way, that these few days didn't add up to a relationship? The thought filtered through her like an early-morning frost, leaving her feeling chilled and vulnerable.

"Let's go upstairs." Tad rose and pulled back her chair.

She picked up her purse and stood, smiling politely at the waiter, wishing she had the courage to ask Tad, point-blank, how he felt and what his intentions were. But even if she'd been brave enough to ask, there was no opportunity on the trip upstairs. The elevator carried other guests to other floors and private conversation was out of the question.

When they reached her room, Tad took the key and opened the door, but he didn't follow her inside. A premonition of loss and an accompanying sense of panic swirled hopelessly in her stomach as she turned to face him. "You may come in, Tad." Her voice shook a bit, and the sound was far removed from the teasing tone she'd tried for.

He shook his head slightly.

"I thought we'd decided to stay in my room tonight."

He didn't smile. "That was before your past came back to haunt you."

Her heart began a futile pounding in her chest. "This is all because of Rob, isn't it? I told you I'm not—"

"You don't have to tell me anything, Blue. I don't need an explanation. I don't want one." Tad inhaled sharply and ran a restless hand through his tawny hair. "Look, all I'm trying to say is that you should, at least, think about the offer. You *will* think about it, no matter what you're feeling right now. From the moment you arrived at the toy company, you've been plotting to leave. You like structure. You like companies that run on reports and schedules and memos. You like big business. So, here's an opportunity to get your career back on track. And you won't even have to share the vice presidency."

"I'd be one of several there," she said matter-of-factly. "Do you want me to take the job, Tad? Do you want to be the one and only vice president of Grizelle Gadget and Toy company? Is that the point of this conversation?"

His jaw tightened, but he continued to lean against the door frame, half in her room, half in the outside hallway. "I never wanted to share the vice presidency with you in the first place and you've never made it a secret that, as far as you were concerned, the position was all mine the moment you got a better offer."

"Maybe I don't consider Rob's a better offer."

"Maybe you should."

"It isn't. And that's final."

"You can change your mind, Blue."

Her lips tightened as she emphasized each word. "I won't change my mind."

"Okay."

"Okay." She tossed her purse onto the bed in frustration. "So are you coming in or not?"

"Not. You have a lot to think about, and I have a chocolate nightmare to deal with."

That was the last straw, she thought as she kicked off her shoes. "Damn it, Tad. Will you stop playing games with me? For the past three nights, we've share the same room and the same bed and now, suddenly, it's just...over? All because Rob offered me a job? A job, which, I'll say one more time, I refused firmly and decisively."

"Yes. I was sitting right there and I heard you. But I wasn't convinced that you meant it, Blue, and neither was McKinley. These past few days...and nights...have been great. I've enjoyed every moment, but I wouldn't want you to let them influence your decision."

"And why would you think they would?" Anger factored into her emotional equation. "I am quite capable of knowing what I want and what I don't want and, believe me, a few nights of sex isn't going to deprive me of that ability. You flatter yourself if you think *you* had anything to do with my refusal of that job offer."

"Good," he said crisply. "Then we don't need to talk about this anymore."

"No. We don't need to talk about this ever again."

"Okay."

"Okay." She stood, barefoot, looking up at him and trying to figure out how she'd ever let herself get involved with him. He didn't even know how to fight for what he wanted. But she did. "So, for the last time, are you going to your room or are you staying here?"

"I think my room might be safer."

"If you want to play it safe . . ."

Blue gave the door a shove, but he caught it before it closed.

"On the other hand," he said. "I hate to be alone with a nightmare."

Blue smiled and reached for his hand. "Will you just get in here and shut the stupid door?"

He stepped inside and kicked the door shut. "All you had to do was ask."

HAVING THE COFFEE had been a bad idea, Blue thought sometime after 1:00 a.m. She was still awake, tired and restless and too keyed up to sleep. Tad lay on the bed, stretched out across most of the mattress, sleeping like a baby. If he was troubled by giant cocoa beans, he didn't show any signs of distress. She had lain beside him for quite a while, hoping for sleep and finding only disquieting thoughts. Finally she'd gotten up, slipped on his shirt and curled up in the uncomfortable chair by the window.

It was quiet, both inside the hotel and outside. In the patch of dark sky visible through the window, Blue could see a couple of dozen stars. Down below on the street a neon sign flashed on and off, too far away to read, but sending its message into the night just the same. It was amazing how crystalline and clear one's thoughts could be in the early hours of the day, when emotions were still and the rest of the world was sleeping.

Tad had been right. She was thinking about Rob's offer. She hadn't meant to, but there it was, cropping up in front of her thoughts, beckoning her with memories of accounts she'd handled, successes she'd had. She'd been good at that job, better than most, and she had hated losing it. She'd hated losing it very much.

There had been a time when she would have accepted an apology from Rob and headed back to California with no qualms and no regrets. Other than her wounded vanity, she had no reason not to. Some people would, of course, believe that she had broken up his marriage and now had come back to reap the spoils, but she knew it wasn't true and eventually everyone else would, too.

And she'd once again be in a position to achieve her goals, fulfill her ambitions in the career she'd always planned. There wouldn't be many opportunities like this. Even if she eventually managed to get a toehold in another marketing firm, it could take years to work her way up to a vice presidency. And Rob had said she could step right into the position, virtually name her own price.

He was in a bind, of course. She had no illusions that he would make her the offer for any other reason. He had more pride than she. Maybe he even thought he could bring her back and have the affair he'd been accused of having. It would be just like Rob to think that an apology and a generous offer would bring her around to his way of thinking.

But whether she took the job or not there would be no affair. She wasn't interested. She had lost the admiration and respect she'd once felt for Rob. If she went back, she would do so for her own advantage and to prove to anyone who was paying attention that she didn't need to sleep with a man to further her career. She had too much self-respect.

But that wasn't the problem, was it?

Blue sighed and turned to look at the man in her bed. She had a great deal of respect for Tad. And admiration. And so many other emotions she couldn't name them all. This must be love, this aching feeling that was never quite satisfied. With Tad she was always either laughing or arguing, happy or completely exasperated. There was no in-between, no middle ground. He'd made her smile again, made her laugh, taught her to savor the moment, shown her how to fly a kite. He'd teased her and pleased her and made absolutely no promises. He'd kissed her and made love to her for the fun of it. And now, here she was, weighing what she'd always known she wanted against the chance that he might love her, too, and the even greater chance that somehow they might have a future together.

The odds were against them. She was older, and although the age difference really didn't matter to her, it might matter to him. Josh was right. Tad should have children, another son, a daughter or two. He would be a wonderful father, and Blue couldn't deny him that. But she felt that she was past the age to be a patient, energetic mother. Tad had said that was nonsense, so maybe there was a middle ground, a compromise they could reach on the question of having children. But what if there wasn't?

And their philosophies were different. He liked spontaneity. She liked structure. He spent Monday afternoons at the zoo. She spent regular hours at the office. She wanted to plan for the future. He wanted to live for the moment. She wanted a career. He wanted to have fun.

He sighed in his sleep, murmured some soft whisper and drifted back to contented slumber. With a bittersweet smile she watched him and loved him, wishing she could believe there could be a happy ending to their story—knowing it wasn't to be. The risk was too great, the possibility for failure too high.

It was better to end it now on a good note, a we-had-a-great-time-didn't-we note. She could walk away now. She'd get involved in work, and she'd forget about the way he smiled and the way he laughed and the crazy things he did. And the crazy things she did when she was with him.

She'd go back to feeling confident about who she was and what she wanted and how to go about getting it. She could do that . . . if she walked away now. Before she fell any deeper into love and spoiled what they had.

So that was her decision. Tomorrow morning she'd tell Tad she'd changed her mind and had decided to accept the job with McKinley Enterprises.

She'd tell him she'd had second thoughts about throwing away the opportunity. She'd point out how foolish it would be not to accept an apology and a big salary *and* the title of vice president. She'd tell him it was the chance of a lifetime, the chance she'd been waiting for.

What she wouldn't tell him was that her decision was a compromise, another one of those choices that ruled out a different choice she might have made. She would say she'd miss him. She would ask him to take good care of Little Zeke. And Josh. And Uncle Horse and Aunt Grizelle. And Ellie. And . . .

A tear slipped down her cheek, and she wiped it away with her fingertip, surprised by her sadness. She had no business crying. She'd made a decision. The best possible decision for herself. And undoubtedly the best one for Tad, too. She'd have the career she wanted. He'd marry some young woman and have beautiful children. Maybe he'd ask her to be their godmother. Maybe she'd agree.

And when those children were old enough, she'd show them her Sky Dancer kite and tell them about the day it flew higher than any kite had ever flown before.

Another tear escaped, but this time she didn't lift a finger to stop it.

Chapter Fifteen

"I think that's everything," Tad said, closing the flaps on a cardboard box and looking around the nearly empty apartment. "Did you check the bathroom? Your hairbrush was still in there the last time I walked through."

Blue didn't answer. Instead she sank onto the nearest box and put her chin in her hands. The walls were bare, the cupboards, too. Her clothes were out of the closet, her moss-green towels were packed. In ten frantic days, she'd managed to turn her life inside out, all under the pretense of getting her life back in order.

It had been a week and a half since she'd told Tad that she was accepting the position with McKinley Enterprises. He'd congratulated her, wished her a wonderful life and asked her if she was ready to order breakfast. Not by a blink of an eye had he indicated how he felt about her decision. As far as she could tell, he was genuinely happy for her, glad that she was getting the chance to do what she'd said she wanted to do.

Uncle Horse had reacted much the same way, except that he had said he'd miss her and hoped she'd visit from time to time. Aunt Grizelle had smiled sadly at the news and had seconded Uncle Horse's suggestion of frequent visits. Ellie had exacted Blue's promise that she would come for the wedding...whenever the final date was set. Jim Bill was continuing to be "difficult" and Ellie hadn't quite made up her mind what she intended to do about him. Marry him, yes. Go to school? Well, she was thinking about that.

"Don't worry, Blue." Tad pulled up a box marked "pots and pans" and sat next to her. "You'll find an apartment in California almost as good as this one. Not as cozy, maybe, and there probably won't be a rose garden, but it'll seem like home to you in no time."

"I've already found one," she said and thought she probably should insert some enthusiasm into her voice. "When I flew out there last week, I leased an apartment. It's the same one I lived in before. Well, not the exact apartment, but the same building, same layout."

"You'll hardly even realize you were gone, then. It'll be like these last six months were just a dream."

Yeah. A dream. She was on her way back to her old life as if nothing had changed, as if she were the same person she'd been before. "I'm getting a new car," she said, still with a noticeable lack of excitement. "Comes with being a vice president. Part of the whole package."

"You're kidding. A car? A new one? I'm going to have to talk to Uncle Horse about that. I should have a company car, don't you think? Especially now that I'll be the one and the only vice president at Grizelle Gadget and Toy Company."

"Uncle Horse might let you drive his model train, but that's probably as close to a company car as you're going to get."

"Now, now. Don't be smug. Some day, years from now, you'll run into me at a trade show and I'll be sporting some pretty snazzy wheels."

"And you'll challenge me to a race in *my* wheelchair."

He folded his hands and rested his elbows on his knees. "For a woman who's about to merge into the fast lane, your spirits aren't riding particularly high. Is your turn signal stuck?"

Blue veiled a sigh and offered him a half smile. "Changing lanes is hard work and everything has happened so fast. I don't feel as if I've had a minute to catch my breath."

"I thought you wanted it that way."

She did. It was easier than having time to think about what she was doing—all the possibilities she was leaving behind. "Oh, don't pay any attention to me. I'm tired, that's all."

"No time for that. Your bon voyage party is only a couple of hours away. Ellie will expect you to be bright-eyed and bushy tailed for your last hurrah."

The sigh couldn't be disguised this time. Last hurrah, indeed. Last straw was more like it. Blue hadn't wanted a party. She wasn't sure she had the moxie to get through one. And what if she had to dance with Tad? What would she do then?

She'd survive, because she hadn't come this far to lose her courage now. She was doing the right thing. At least, she kept telling herself she was.

"I hope Josh is in a better frame of mind tonight," she said. "He hasn't said anything to me since I told him I was leaving. I can't tell if he's mad or sad or just doesn't know what to say."

"The news hit him pretty hard," Tad agreed. "I think he'd pretty well decided that you and I would be the perfect adoptive parents. Now he's going to have to figure out some other way to fulfill his fantasy."

Blue wanted to say she was sorry, but that was silly. No one else was sorry. "Do you think he'd like to come to the airport with us after the party? I know he'd get a kick out of seeing the McKinley private jet. It's kind of impressive."

Tad stood abruptly and walked to the kitchen. "I'm sure it is, but I don't know if Josh will want to be there to see you leave. That might make him uncomfortable."

"Oh. Well, perhaps it would be better not to ask him to come along. In fact, you don't have to drive me out to the airport. I'm sure I can get a cab."

"I think after all we've been through together, Blue, that I should be in on the final goodbye. It just seems fitting."

Was there a trace of edginess in his voice? she wondered. Was he hiding his true feelings? Was there a chance that he didn't want her to go? "Tad, I—" What could she ask? How could she say anything without creating a whole new set of problems? "I want to thank you for…well, for everything. I know I wasn't always easy to get along with in the beginning, but you…made me laugh. And I appreciate that."

He turned and waved his hand in dismissal. "Think nothing of it. You have a nice laugh, well worth any effort I put out in coaxing it from you. Just don't forget how to use it, once you get back to your old routine."

"I won't." She would, though. There had never been much time in her old routine for fun and games and laughter. "And I'll make time to fly the Sky Dancer, too."

Their eyes met across the room, and he was the first to look away. "I'm going to put these boxes in the van," he said. "Why don't you take a last look around and make sure you haven't forgotten anything? Your hairbrush, for instance?"

Reluctantly Blue stood, stretching a little and wishing she could step over the boxes and into his arms. There hadn't been any touching between them since that last night in New Mexico. And she ached all over with the need to be close to him. But, of course, she'd get past that feeling. She'd have to.

The phone in Tad's apartment rang just as he carried the first box out to the van. Her phone had already been disconnected. Her number was no longer in service. How easily the pieces of her life were being disassembled and relocated, she thought as she stepped over the packed cardboard boxes and made her way through the bathroom and into his side of the pool house. She reached the telephone on the fourth ring and picked up the receiver.

Two minutes later she was running through the house, her heart pounding in a frightened, staccato rhythm. "Tad," she called. "Tad!"

He glanced over his shoulder as he shoved one of the boxes into the open back of the van. Blue was coming toward him, half-running, her hair swinging frantically across her cheeks, her green eyes wide, her voice raised as she called to him. He turned immediately and met her halfway between the carport and the pool house. His hands lifted to her shoulders, his heart stopped in a cold panic. "What is it?" he asked. "What's wrong?"

"Joanne Knutson just called. Josh has run away."

"What? Where did he go?" Tad grimaced. "Why does she think he's run away? Why would he do that?"

"I don't know." Blue's answer was full of honest worry. "Joanne said he was supposed to come straight home from school so he could get his homework and chores done before Ellie's party tonight. When she checked with the school, she found out he hadn't been there at all today, and then when she looked in his room, she found a note."

"A note?" Tad felt a spurt of hope. "What did it say?"

"'Don't bother looking for me. I'm running away and I won't be back'." She gripped Tad's arms and the tension ran from her into him. "Joanne is really scared, Tad. So am I. Why would he do this? Why would he do this today of all da—?" Her voice broke and Tad could see dread blend with the fear in her eyes. "It's me. He ran away because I'm leaving. That's it. He's done this because of me."

"He ran away because he's a thirteen-year-old boy who's trying desperately to get a grip on his own identity." Tad released Blue and turned toward the carport, anxiety flooding him, questions crowding his thoughts. "Has Joanne reported this to the police? Is she sure he's not at one of his friends' houses?"

"She said she's called everywhere looking for him. She even called Franklin and asked him to look around to see if Josh is hiding there."

Tad stroked his jawline, wondering what to do, where to go, trying to think the way Josh might be thinking.

"He can't have gone too far," she said. "He's only thirteen. I mean, where would he go?"

"I don't know, Blue, but I'm going to look for him. I'll check the toy company first. Franklin has been known to overlook the obvious. And if I don't find him there, I'll—" Tad didn't finish the sentence. He just strode purposefully toward his car.

"I'm going with you," Blue said. "If he's upset because I'm moving, then I should be there when you find him."

Tad wasn't so sure. While it was undoubtedly true that Blue's impending move was the reason for Josh's actions, it was probably more of a catalyst than a cause. Josh had fantasized long and hard on his "family" and now he'd been forced to face reality. A tough job for a thirte-year-old.

Not all that easy for a twenty-seven-year-old, either. Tad had spent the past ten days telling himself he had to keep a smile on his face. He had no right to taint Blue's choice with messy goobyes. He'd told her not to consider him in her choices—he had no right to complain when she did as he'd asked. He wished her well. He hoped she'd have a long and successful life. He wanted her to be happy. And if he could have figured out a way to do it, he would have run away from reality and tried to hide with his fantasy, just as Josh was doing.

"Where do you think he is?" Blue asked.

Tad started the car and backed from the drive, spraying gravel as he did so. "I don't know, but wherever he is, we're going to find him."

"HE AIN'T HERE." Franklin hitched up his trousers and adjusted the holster at his hip. "I looked this building over from basement to roof, and the kid's not in it. I'd bet my badge he's hidin' out at some friend's house." The truth was Franklin didn't have a badge. He had a security patch. But that fact didn't seem to affect his insistence that Josh was not going to be found anywhere inside Grizelle Gadget and Toy Company building. "I'm tellin' ya, you're wasting time here."

Tad didn't think so. "You may be right, Franklin, but for my own peace of mind, I have to look."

"I'll check in the offices upstairs," Blue said with a look that told Tad she agreed with him.

"I'll start in the basement." Tad walked off in one direction, Blue in another.

Franklin sniffed loudly. "I'll go outside and look around *one more time,* but I'm tellin' ya, the kid ain't here."

Tad knew he'd have to make amends later to the security guard, but he couldn't take the chance that any place had been missed. Finding Josh was too important. And they would find him. It was probably a good guess that he wanted to be found. He was protesting Blue's decision in the only way he knew how...by running away and thereby calling attention to his unhappiness. Tad knew that once he was located, those adolescent feelings of helplessness and hopelessness would have to be dealt with. He only hoped he, himself, had enough wisdom to answer a bunch of whys and why nots he didn't understand himself. He hoped Josh wouldn't ask him how *he* felt. He hoped Blue wouldn't be there to hear the lies he would have to tell.

"Josh?" Tad called softly as he opened the basement door and started down the steps. "Josh?"

The basement was dark, with only a few windows to cast rectangles of light on the floor. It seemed best to leave it that way, so that Josh, if he were here, would come out into a dark room, rather than one flooded with artificial light. The silence was nearly complete, except for the low hum of the heating and cooling equipment at the far end of the basement.

"Josh?" Tad paused on the middle stair and gripped the metal handrail. He listened for a sound, any noise that might indicate he was not alone. Nothing. Just the sound of his own heavy sigh. "Josh," he said. "I think we need to talk. About Blue. About the fact that she's leaving us."

The words rang hollowly in the stillness like the melancholy drip of water from a faucet in an otherwise quiet house.

"I know you're unhappy," Tad continued. "I know you don't want her to go. And I'm right there with you, buddy. I don't want her to go, either. In fact, I hate to even think about it. I can hardly stand the thought that tomorrow she won't be here." His voice trembled and he swallowed the unsteadiness. "But it's not up to us, Josh. It's her life. Her choice. And you have to let her go. *I* have to let her go."

It was true, of course. He'd been telling himself the same thing all week long. Blue had a right to choose her own destiny. He had no right to say or do anything to change her mind. Just because he'd been foolish enough to construct a fantasy future around her was no reason to act like a fool when reality stepped in. She deserved his complete support, his unreserved blessing, his wholehearted understanding.

"I have to let her go," he repeated to the silence. "I don't understand her reasons, Josh, but I believe she's doing what she thinks is best. And that's all any one of us can do. We'll get through this, together. You and me, buddy. We have Uncle Horse and Aunt Grizelle, Ellie, Fred and Joanne, Franklin. You and I will be fine. And Blue's going to be fine, too. She's happy about this. And she'll come back to see us from time to time. Maybe you'll even get to fly out to California sometime to visit her."

The slight echo of his voice came back to his own ears, ringing with false enthusiasm. It *was* false. But hell, what was he supposed to do? Tell Josh that he hadn't been so miserable, so desperately lonely, in years? Tell the boy that everything he'd just said was a coverup for the unhappiness he felt?

But then, Josh wasn't here. The basement was empty and he was only talking to himself. "I love her," he said and then he repeated it in a firmer voice. "I love Miranda Blue Garrison. And I don't want her to go. Not now. Not ever."

There, he'd said it. He'd stated his honest, gut feeling to an empty room. With a heart empty of hope, he turned to leave . . . and heard the click and soft whir as Zeke's computer switched on.

"Tad?" It was Josh's voice, not boyishly high, but husky in the throes of puberty and distress. "I love her, too. Why does she have to go?"

There was a pause—a few heartbeats of relief—before Tad ran down the rest of the steps and across the floor to Zeke's station. He grabbed Josh's arms and pulled the boy into a hug that lasted almost a full minute. "You scared us all to death, Josh," he said over the knot of emotion in his throat. "If I wasn't so happy to see you, I'd be really mad."

"I didn't think anyone would miss me," the boy stammered. "I came here instead of going to school and I fixed up a pretty good hiding place while you guys were working upstairs. Franklin looked all through those boxes, but he never thought to look behind the computer desk."

"What were you planning to do?" Tad asked. "Didn't you know everyone would be worried and looking for you?"

"I didn't think anyone would notice I was gone. I figured if you could let Blue leave, you wouldn't care if I wasn't around either."

Tad hugged the boy harder and wondered how adults were ever supposed to understand the tangled logic of a teenager. "Of course I care. And Blue cares, too. She's here looking for you, too. She insisted on coming, dropping everything else to try and find you."

Josh muffled a teary sniffle against Tad's chest before he pulled back. "But she's still going to California, isn't she?"

"Come on now, kiddo. You didn't really expect a little stunt like running away to stop her, did you?"

"I thought she might miss her plane."

"The company she's going to work for has a private jet. It's waiting for her at the airport and it won't leave until she's ready. I'm sorry, Josh, but no matter what you do, Blue is going to go."

"*You* could do something."

Tad moved away, stepped over to Zeke and absently touched the computer keys. "What do you think I could do, Josh? Beg her not to go?"

"Yeah. I mean, how's she going to know you want her to stay if you don't tell her? How can you say it's her choice if you never asked her not to go?" Josh's chin set in a determined line. "Are you afraid she'll go, anyway?"

He was. Tad recognized the truth the moment he heard it. He was afraid. So afraid of losing that he couldn't risk winning. It was a strange and awful realization, and he didn't want to analyze it in front of a teenage boy. "Let's go, sport. You have some phone calls to make and some tall explaining to do."

After wiping his shirtsleeve across his mouth and nose, Josh straightened his shoulders. "Yeah," he said. "I guess I do. I'm sorry, Tad. I didn't mean to cause so much trouble."

"You don't have to apologize to me. If I'd thought for a minute that it would stop Blue from getting on that airplane tonight, I'd have run away, too."

Josh gave a small, unsteady laugh. "You're too big to run away. You could never find a place to hide here. Franklin would have spotted you right off."

Relieved that the boy was safe and sounded less upset, Tad wrapped an arm around his thin shoulders and guided him toward the stairs. "I'd hide at the zoo," he said. "I fit right in with the monkeys and the—"

His voice stopped, as well as his heart, when he glanced up and saw a shadowy figure sitting on the top step. She sat there in perfect silence, elbows propped on her knees, chin propped on her hands. "Blue?" The whisper froze in his throat.

"Blue?" There was no hesitation in Josh's voice and no hesitation in the bouncy walk that carried him up the stairs to her side. "Hi. I didn't know you were here."

"I headed upstairs to look for you, but efficient Franklin had locked the door. So..." Her glance slid to Tad's, then flicked back to the boy. "I came after Tad to see if he had his keys with him."

Josh's chin dropped a notch. "I guess you know I ran away. I'm really sorry if you were scared. I just wanted to make you miss your plane so you'd have to stay, but I guess my plan didn't work too good. Tad said you're flyin' on a private jet, anyway. Do you think I could see it before you go?"

"I don't know, Josh. You've caused quite a commotion this evening. Joanne and Fred may not even allow you to attend Ellie's party."

"They wouldn't do that. It's your goodbye party. I ran away, but I didn't get into any trouble or nothin'. I just wanted to keep you from leaving."

"You should have talked to me, Josh. It hurts my feelings to know that you couldn't just tell me you were upset because of my new job. Am I that hard to talk to?"

Tad stood where he'd stopped at the foot of the stairs—staring up at her, heart hammering in his chest, feeling the impact of each and every one of her words.

"Gee, Ms. Garrison, I didn't know." The boy's voice dropped its pitch of recovery and reverted to a sad, humbled tone. "I didn't think you cared about me. I didn't think anyone did."

"That's nonsense," Blue stated unequivocally. "Pure nonsense and, what's more, you know it. Now, go outside and find Franklin. Then call Joanne and Fred and anyone else you can think of who might possibly be worried about you."

Josh's shoulders drooped, but Tad could tell, even in the dusky light, that the boy felt a thousand times better now that he'd been found. As Josh stepped around Blue, he leaned down to hug her. "I wish you weren't going," he said simply and then raced up the remaining couple of steps and out the doorway.

Sticking his hands in his hip pockets, Tad leaned slightly against the railing. "I wish you weren't going, too."

"Do you really?" She kept her voice cool, but it was tight with tension.

Tad dug his hands a bit deeper into his pockets and bravely lifted his chin, as if his pulse wasn't running scared. "How long have you been sitting there?"

"Long enough to know you were going to let me leave without saying a word. I had no idea you were such a martyr."

"I had no idea you would care."

Her chin came up from the cradle of her hands. "Oh, come on, Tad. You're starting to sound like Josh. What was I supposed to do? Write you a memo?"

The fear left him then, conquered by a leap of hope. "Would that have saved me from a week of sleepless nights?"

"As if you couldn't tell that I haven't been sleeping all that much myself." She straightened, but didn't get up. "Honestly, Tad, why didn't you say something? How could you let me go through these past ten days thinking you were happy that I'd be gone and you could be vice president here all by yourself?"

"You made your decision, Blue. After what I said at the trade show, I didn't think I had any right to voice an opinion. I mean, it's not as if you *asked* me."

"You could have said *something*."

"I slept with you. I made love to you. Did you think I'd do that just—"

"—for the fun of it?" she finished for him. "Yes, Tad, that's exactly what I thought. That's what you said. You kissed me for the fun of it. You made love to me *for the fun of it.* How was I supposed to know it meant anything more than that to you? How was I supposed to know if *I* was someone special in your life or just another 'fun moment' before you moved on to the next 'moment'?"

"You're the one who's moving. Not me."

"I'm not going to take the blame for this. You and I are different, Tad. I decided to take this job because I couldn't see there was going to be a future for us, and I'm past the age where I can pretend that love makes everything okay. I'm not Ellie. I know the reality of our situation."

Tad eased his hands out of his pockets. "What is the *reality,* Blue? Isn't it that we're both just scared? Scared to say I love you? Scared to take a chance on an uncertain future? Just plain scared that we might lose our hearts, our dreams, our lives again?" He took one step closer and then another. "Love may not make everything okay, Blue, but I love you and I'm asking you to stay with me and give it a chance. Please—" he paused, swallowed hard and summoned his courage "—don't go."

The simple words dropped into her mind and burst into a thousand magic images and sensations. Her heartbeat moved to double-time and she stopped breathing entirely. *Don't go,* he'd said. *Don't go.* "You really think you love me?" she asked, because it seemed suddenly important to be sure. "You don't have any ulterior motive for wanting me to stay?"

"Of course I have an ulterior motive. I love you, Miranda Blue. I want to marry you. I want to have children with you. I want to live with you and work with you every day for the rest of my life. I want to go to sleep beside you and wake up to find you still there in the morning." He stopped and the slightest smile tipped his mouth. "If that isn't a whole barrel of ulterior motives, I don't know what is."

"Which doesn't exactly answer my question."

His gaze clung to hers, promising so much more than she had dared hope for. "Yes," he said. "I really think I love you."

"And what if I still want to take this job?"

"Then I guess I'll have no choice but to go with you. Maybe Uncle Horse will let me commute. Maybe he'll open a branch office. Maybe—" Tad moved a step closer and ran an impatient hand through his hair. "Hell, Blue, you don't really want to go back to McKinley, do you?"

She was probably crazy to consider passing up the opportunities she'd been offered in California, but Tad was here and he loved her . . . and she was just crazy enough to think that was worth it. She'd come to care for her job and the people here in Texas far more than anything she'd left behind at McKinley. She rose and took a deep breath. "I don't want to go back to McKinley," she said. "Are you going to make me a better offer?"

"I'll try." He closed the gap between them. "No new car, though. Wheels are not a part of this package."

"Having a new car isn't that important to me."

"No company jet, either, and you'll have to continue as a co-vice president."

"I don't mind about the jet, but the title . . . Half of a vice president. That is definitely a drawback." She smiled to let him know she was teasing and waited to hear his response.

"We can take turns, then. You be•vice president one week. I'll be vice president the next. I'm willing to go the extra mile and make the compromise, if that will make you happy. But just so you know where I stand, I draw the line at 'professional distance.'"

"Agreed," she said, lifting her arms and wrapping them around Tad's neck. "You make me happy, Tad. Crazy, but happy."

"Let's get married."

"Okay."

He drew back and frowned at her. "Okay? That's all you can say after a formal proposal? *Okay?*"

"How about, 'Kiss me, you fool'?"

"Whatever happened to a simple, 'Yes, O master of my heart'?"

She smiled and wondered how she'd ever gotten through thirty-three years of living without knowing how wonderful it felt to be in love—really, completely, crazy in love. "Yes," she said. "Now, will you kiss me?"

"You messed up your lines."

"Don't push your luck, Janitor Man. Kiss me."

"First I'm taking you to the nearest justice of the peace before you change your mind. Come on." He tried to take her hand, but she kept both of them firmly clasped at the back of his neck.

"You realize that you're probably going to be miserable if you marry me." She leaned forward and pressed her lips to the center of his chin. "My parents will want to know what you plan to be when you grow up. Uncle Horse and Aunt Grizelle will insist that we live in the pool house and have dinner with them every night. Josh will expect us to adopt him. Ellie may want us to adopt her, too. Marriage to me may be more than you bargained for."

Tad drew her into his arms. "I'll tell your parents I plan to make a fortune in mud pies and toy robots. They'll be happy you chose such a wise man as your husband. I'll explain to your aunt and uncle that we'll need more privacy. They'll put a fence around the pool house. If we want to adopt Josh, we'll have to get in line. Joanne and Fred have expressed an interest and Uncle Horse said he was considering adopting the boy, himself, since he and Aunt Grizelle have no children of their own. And as far as Ellie goes, we'll give her a party after the wedding, and in the meantime she can write us long, newsy letters from college."

"You've thought of everything."

"No." His voice went suddenly deep and serious. "I've thought of you and how much I love you and how I almost let you walk out of my life without saying a word because I was afraid. I told myself I wanted your happiness at any cost, but I almost ruined our one chance to be really happy together."

"As your co-vice president I have to assume half the responsibility for that. I was afraid, too. I was ready to walk away—ready to resume a life that had no room for laughter, no time to smell the roses, no time to hear *Romeo and Juliet* read aloud, no time to fly a kite or kiss a lover. I was ready because it seemed like the only thing to do... until I took that first step into the basement and heard you say you loved me and you didn't want me to go." She looked up at him and let herself drown in the emotions that filled his shining brown eyes. "I love you. I love this crazy idea factory. I want to stay here, with you and Zeke and Little Zeke and Talk-to-Me Rose and Uncle Horse and Aunt Grizelle and Josh and Ellie and all the others, for as far as I can see into the future."

Tad covered her lips with his finger. "Wait a minute. Back up. I could almost swear I heard you say you loved me. Are you trying to slip that little fact past me like you used to try to do with those memos you write? Or do you just normally bury a declaration like that in the middle of a conversation?"

"It just slipped out," she explained. "I don't seem to have any control over it."

"It better slip out pretty often from now on. I'm counting on you not to hold it back."

"Okay."

"Okay?"

She applied a firm pressure to the back of his neck. "Okay," she said. "I love you."

This time he allowed her to draw him closer to her lips. "Okay," he said. "I love you, too."

Then, finally, he kissed her.

Zeke rolled from his station, smoothly negotiating the distance to the stairwell. No voice command stirred his programmed memory, but some unusual sounds blipped across the screen of his built-in computer in an array of flashing lights. When still no command was forthcoming, he backed again into his station.

"Mission Accomplished," he whirred.

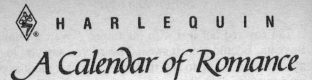

◆ H A R L E Q U I N

A Calendar of Romance

Be a part of American Romance's year-long celebration of love and the holidays of 1992. Experience all the passion of falling in love during the excitement of each month's holiday. Some of your favorite authors will help you celebrate those special times of the year, like the romance of Valentine's Day, the magic of St. Patrick's Day, the joy of Easter.

Celebrate the romance of Valentine's Day with

**#425 VALENTINE
HEARTS AND
FLOWERS
by Muriel Jensen**

Read all the books in *A Calendar of Romance*, coming to you one each month, all year, from Harlequin American Romance.   COR2

my VALENTINE 1992

Celebrate the most romantic day of the year with
MY VALENTINE 1992—a sexy new collection of four
romantic stories written by our famous Temptation
authors:

    GINA WILKINS
    KRISTINE ROLOFSON
    JOANN ROSS
    VICKI LEWIS THOMPSON

My Valentine 1992—an exquisite escape into a romantic
and sensuous world.

Don't miss these sexy stories, available in February at your favorite retail outlet. Or order your
copy now by sending your name, address, zip or postal code, along with a check or money
order for $4.99 (please do not send cash) plus 75¢ postage and handling ($1.00 in Canada),
payable to Harlequin Books to:

In the U.S.

    3010 Walden Avenue
    P.O. Box 1396
    Buffalo, NY 14269-1396

In Canada

P.O. Box 609
Fort Erie, Ontario
L2A 5X3

Please specify book title with your order.
Canadian residents add applicable federal and provincial taxes.

 Harlequin Books

VAL-92-R

Take 4 bestselling love stories FREE
Plus get a FREE surprise gift!